Opus Lupus and the Temple Gate

Lazlo Ferran

By the same Author

THE ICE BOAT

THE MAN WHO RECREATED HIMSELF

INFINITE BLUE HEAVEN

A KING AND A QUEEN

TOO BRIGHT THE SUN

SHORT STORIES

INCHOATE (VOLUME I)
EIGHTEEN, BLUE (VOLUME II)

Ordo Lupus and the Temple Gate

Lazlo Ferran

PRINTING HISTORY

Second Edition

Printed in 12 point Times New Roman

This is a work of fiction. Names, characters, places and incidents are products of the author's imagination or are used fictitiously and should not be construed as real. Any resemblance to actual events, locales, organisations or persons, living or dead, is entirely coincidental.

Cover images:

Front cover artwork by Ash Buttle

Back cover image of gargoyle face with snakes with permission from brechtbug
http://farm4.static.flickr.com/3497/3998031256_da93c32d7a_m.jpg

Acknowledgments

Thanks to Ash, Derek, Ellen, Gary, Janet and Lorna.

Author's note: This following tale was originally ghost written by myself, Lazlo Ferran, for an article in The Times newspaper and taken from tapes held secretly in a vault for years. The tapes were recorded during an interview with the anonymous man at the centre of the tale. The final chapter and epilogue are taken from various sources – for reasons that will become apparent later. Written out here in full for the first time, the situations and places in it are real, although I have tried to avoid using real names of people wherever possible. Codes at the beginning of each chapter, if deciphered, will reveal steps on the path, to the wisdom of Ordo Lupus.

Chapter One

htwjw si anmhtwj snhwppsuwnyw vmj vaspgjw wkgap hm htah vmj igyywii

"I feel so alone. Even though there's a whole city's congregation in the Cathedral, 158 feet below me, none of them know I am here or the battle that is about to take place above them. I crouch down behind the sarcophagus, right next to the builder's hoist, my hand near the knot that ties the rope to the massive oak roof-brace. And I wait. I am recording all this on the mini cassette recorder I have brought with me.

How did I get here?

Obviously the little wolf-angel statues had led me to this place and moment in time, and you could say that it started in childhood with the incident in Highgate Cemetery, but really, the hinge-point, or the point at which my life became unhinged, was the murder of Annie."

I felt as if we were under water. The air around us rippled and shifted like the surface of a clear sea, seen from underneath. Suddenly a dark slit seemed to open and something horrific came through it.

"Annie!" I screamed and threw her behind me, against the wall, crushing her there. A long, scaly arm whipped around me and took hold of her arm. It pulled her with a strength far greater than my own and though, in desperation, I pulled against it, the arm and the hideous black body that towered over me, topped with something like a giant snake's head, pulled Annie into the slit.

With one last scream of, "Daddy!" she was gone and the slit closed up. I ran at it, clawing at the air but there was nothing there.

"Please God, no!" I cried at the top of my lungs, the tears starting to fall. I did not understand at all what had happened, but the simple fact that Annie was gone was the only thing that mattered. I fell to my knees and wept for a few minutes, before the will to search and do something, gained strength inside me. I walked around sobbing, looking into every doorway, around every corner and eying every car suspiciously, before finally somebody saw the state I was in and spoke to me.

I couldn't speak for the sobbing and I started to hyperventilate, desperate for help, but unable to get my emotions under control.

Hearing my confused mix of French and English, the middle-aged man spoke in English. "Wait here Monsieur. I will get help! I will only be a minute." He ran to the end of the street and called out something in French. Several voices answered and he ran back. "Just a few minutes Monsieur." The normally pretty, tree-lined street of Nevers, looked like a scene from Thérèse Raquin. Murder had taken place and all was black and rotten.

The Gendarmes arrived and one of them recognised me from the earlier accident. I explained as best I could what had happened, at first believing that truth was best, but when their faces looked back at me with indulgent sympathy, I simply said that something or somebody had grabbed my daughter. A search was launched and before long I was in the police station with Rose holding my hand, the whole of Nevers ringing to the sound of sirens. Of course I was distraught, as was Rose, and at first she exerted enormous self-control to appear calm, but as each hour passed and nothing happened, she began to grow angry.

"You should have taken her on the main road. What were you thinking!"

Her angry words became a torrent and I felt an anger rising in me too. I had not told her what I had actually seen but finally I could take it no more. "It was a snake," I said quietly.

"What?"

I took a very deep breath before continuing. I felt a mad laugh forming in my mouth as I talked – as it dawned on me that my wife would not believe me. "I don't know if the Gendarmes told you but Annie was almost hit by a car earlier. I pulled her out of the way just in time. It was that 'evil presence' again. That is why I took the side street. Then suddenly the air around us seemed to distort and there was a kind of slit in it. Out of this something came, maybe five metres tall – like a snake with – with ermm wings. It had arms too and it reached for Annie and – and took her!" I burst into tears again as I finished.

To my surprise Rose put her arm around me. "Oh Darling." She seemed to believe me and the relief was a release for me. I clutched at her and sobbed into her soft and sweet-smelling pink cardigan.

A uniformed Gendarmes brought us each a cup of coffee and turned to leave us. We heard a chorus of loud voices starting up behind him and I stepped over to find out what was happening. The man who had given us the coffee stepped in front of me, blocking my path. "S'il vous plaît Monsieur. Asseyez-vous et attendez-nous."

"This is bad Rose. I know it!" I could see from the look of panic in her eyes that she agreed.

"Monsieur. It is very bad news. I am sorry." A well dressed officer in plain clothes was addressing us but we hardly heard his voice. He said something to the effect that a girl had been found viciously killed and they believed it was our daughter. They would need us to identify the body as soon as we could.

We held hands as we looked at the little body. Even her face had been mutilated but we recognised our little girl. Rose couldn't look but I had the unbearable urge to lift the sheet and look at the body. The Coroner's assistant grabbed my hand to stop me but I gave him such a challenging look he pulled his hand away. The sight was enough not only to make me weep for Annie's soul but for my own too. The indescribable horror of it all left us feeling numb, and over the next few weeks which stretched like forlorn eternities, we simply sat around the house staring into space, going through the most basic routines to get through the day. We never looked at each other. Edward had gone to stay with my mother in London, but even the burden of this guilt added to our sorrows. Mourning was so difficult because neither of us understood what had happened. However, it was only at THe end of those two heart-broken weeks that I discovered exactly what it was that Rose didn't understand.

The Gendarmes' report had made the case that Annie had been murdered by a perverted psychopath and although I had been helpful with my evidence, I'd had to avoid a description, by saying I had not seen the killers face, in order that they conduct any enquiry at all. We had even made the national newspapers and we often read them, not so much out of a wish to find any new evidence but because it seemed to keep Annie alive in some way. We hated each other for doing it though, and when we spoke it was usually hateful or at best polite.

I was surprised then when Rose looked up from another article one evening and said, "You did the right thing."

"What?"

"Keeping quiet about that wretched snake thing."

"Oh. Well they wouldn't have believed me."

"No. But I need to know now, darling. I cannot wait any longer. What *did* happen?"

"What do you mean?"

"I have listened to your story for too long now. You are sick and we both know it. I *have* protected you but now I need to know. You have to give me that much. I will keep quiet. Trust me."

"No! I mean – no I am not sick. That is really what I saw. You know, about my special, erm, talent!. I have a special sense for evil and you have *seen* this happening."

"Oh you and your 'special sight'! Just stop it! I don't want to hear about it any more. It's just luck or coincidence or whatever. It doesn't explain what happened to our little girl."

"You didn't see the body. You didn't see *Annie.* She looked like she had been squeezed by something!"

"It could have been anything. Who knows what a perverted psychopath might do to a body."

"You don't believe me."

"Whatever it is I need the truth." She screamed the word 'truth' with a vehemence I had never heard before in her, and with that she was weeping. I had nothing left I could add so I walked over to comfort her but she pushed me away.

We began to drift apart from this time on. Edward helped to bind us together but we were never close after this. The last time we visited England together was to visit my parents and my grandfather's grave. We had missed the funeral because my parents hadn't told us. I assumed at the time it had to be because they thought we had too many other things on our minds. Now I really wanted to see his grave.

Antonia's fiancé was a curious addition to the family for me, and we had to spend some time getting to know him, before finally visiting grandfather's grave.

My parents looked nervously at each other when I asked where he was buried.

"Yes. We could take you there but you will be disappointed son." There was that frailty about my father as he spoke to me.

"Oh, why? Did you keep the money for yourself and give him a cardboard box?" I said laughing.

"No." My father smiled weakly. "But it will not be as you expect. It's a lovely spot though."

I felt a little angry now and confused. I had liked the old man a lot and knowing there was a rift between him and my father, I began to suspect the worst.

"It's not what you're probably thinking son. There was a supplementary part to the Will – something we couldn't show you. Your grandfather requested just an urn and stone tablet."

"You mean you burned him? But he always said he never wanted to be cremated."

"Yes. That's right."

"But I don't understand. What are you trying to tell me?" My father was sometimes infuriatingly incapable of giving a straight answer, especially when he was uncomfortable with something.

"Best we take you there," he said. My Mother nodded and smiled. I think she would have hugged me had not Rose been there.

The tablet was small, flat and of polished black granite, and lay under the shade of a hazelnut tree on the edge of the old graveyard. It had my grandfather's name and then said simply. 'My spirit away to my family home, my body too. If you feel sad looking at me, then smile again for I look not at you.'

My anger left me immediately. I understood somehow, that my grandfather was not here, and I also understood that there was a secret, which I would learn eventually.

To satisfy Rose I attended sessions with a therapist for two years with no progress. Either I was not insane or else he could not find what was wrong with me. I never told him that I was sure I wasn't mad or even damaged. I began to look more closely at my grandfather's book and my own research so far into the occult powers in Southern Europe. At least the book offered me the glimmer of a possibility that I might understand what had happened to Annie.

It was the description of flying snakes at the end of the book which had caught my attention. I was desperate, and my memory of the creature's appearance could fit the description in the book. Understanding this became a passion for me, gradually overwhelming all other daily thoughts.

What I couldn't initially understand was the description in the book of all these 'snake like' things as Wargs. In my experience – in the works of J. R. R. Tolkien and many other classical works Wargs were described as moving on four legs and looking like very large dogs – in other words, wolf-like. I researched the etymology of the word 'Warg' and finally found an entry that offered an explanation.

"The Old English word 'wcarg'.

Mary Gerstein, in an article, has attempted to equate the Germanic word 'warg' with 'werwolf, but many experts now reject this. Warg and Wearg can be traced back to a root that may have meant 'strangler'."

As soon as I saw the word 'strangler', I thought of 'constrictor' and the family of snakes called 'constrictors'. Perhaps an eyewitness in Medieval Europe had described the serpents as constrictors or stranglers and the writer, not having seen what they were writing of, described them as Wargs. But then this didn't make sense either. The only thing that *did* make sense was that the writer knew the true meaning of the word warg and that the text was copied from a much older text, perhaps from as far back as the Dark Ages. The writer's name was Edgar de Boulon and I had tried many times to find out more about him with no success. I didn't even know if he knew my family or not although my grandfather had claimed he had.

The headline on page three of Le Monde newspaper instantly caught my eye. "Young woman's mangled body found in back street of Lyon". I read on. "The young woman, dressed in evening attire and now identified as Seline Godin was found on the night of Friday 11 July in the Rue Calas, a quiet street in Lyon. Police would like to speak to anybody in that vicinity around 11.40 pm. An intense police search is under way to catch the killer and although there is little evidence to go on the body is described as being crushed, 'as if by a giant fist'."

Spluttering into my coffee, I swung my legs off the table and reread the article slowly. When I finished, I picked up the telephone and dialed our home number.

"Darling. Have you seen the article in Le Monde today?"

"No. What article?"

"I am coming home. Wait there!"

I slammed the phone down, grabbed the car-keys, and paper, and drove home as fast as I could.

"God, you look a mess!" She leaned close to me. "And you stink. Look at this." She pulled at my shirt front. "You lost a button."

I showed her the newspaper.

"Um hm. Yes it is interesting. You know what I think?" she said after quickly scanning the article.

"What?"

"Well I hardly like to say, really?"

"Go on?"

"Well it *could* be the same murderer. Perhaps he is back." She looked nervously at me for my reaction. Obviously I knew she was thinking of a human murderer, but I didn't care. For now it was enough to have caught her interest.

The newspaper was dated Friday 14 July 1975 and Edward had become engaged to a nice girl in London some years ago. Rose – or the dragon, as I now called her, and I, had drifted apart and I had spent more and more time at the office, often staying late to read my occult books and getting very drunk, mainly on Ouzo, for which I had a taste. We were moving towards divorce and we both knew it. Since the day Annie had died, our marriage had been a train heading for the buffers. Nothing we could do or say seemed to make things any better. My one slim hope of redemption, and thus of saving the marriage had been somehow to prove that I really had seen that night what I had described to her, but the very pursuit of this truth seemed to her further proof of my madness.

I didn't stay, and back at the office, I rifled through piles of documents looking for just one particular one with a telephone number on it. In the years between the death of Annie and now, I had joined several occult societies. We had been through the 60s and it was much easier to show an interest in such things. One such society I had joined – the Venerable Order of St. John of Jerusalem, a revival of the Knights Hospitallers, had only in 1963 gained general acceptance as a serious society, and through their newsletter I had started up a correspondence with a Henry de Silva.

Henry lived in France – in Lyon in fact, but had been born in England and served in the Army in World War II. Shortly after his wife had died of cancer he had moved to Lyon to pursue his passion for genealogy. He believed his ancestors to have been Huguenots although I always thought his family name sounded more Spanish, which would make them unlikely Protestant refugees. However he was a genial fellow and his knowledge of Medieval France and the Occult was impressive. I was sure I could recall seeing his telephone number on one of his letters and I wanted to call him straight away. After turning half the office upside down I found it.

"Henry?"

"Yes?"

I explained who I was.

"Have you seen that article in Le Monde? About the girl who was found dead in Lyon? You must have heard of it?"

"Yes. Of course. How could I not. It's been all over the papers. Strange isn't it?"

"Strange? Well no. I didn't think so. Its sounds just like what happened to Annie!"

"Ah yes. I thought you would say that. You shouldn't get too excited dear boy but I admit, it has potential."

"Listen. Can we possibly get together some time? I really need your confidence and I have a lot of stuff to show you."

"Well certainly. I would love to have you."

"When is good for you?"

"Well anytime. My social calendar is hardly full you know."

"Tomorrow? Midday?"

"Um. Yes I think so. I will have to get my cleaner to brush the house down a bit."

He gave me directions and the following morning I stuffed all the books and documents I needed into my white Citroën DS and drove the 200 km down to Lyon.

I parked in the only space available, a few blocks down from a narrow four-story town house in the inner suburbs, painted in a pale shade of pink, with sky-blue awnings over the tall and narrow windows. I pulled on the antiquated bell-pull outside the paneled front door and a voice echoed in the narrow street from above. "Push the door when you hear the buzz! Come up to the second floor."

On the second floor landing Henry was waiting for me, leaning on a silver-topped walking stick and wearing a cream-coloured suit.

His pointed white beard jerked up and down as he welcomed me. "Come in! Come in dear boy."

He followed me in to his flat but I noticed he moved very slowly and seemed in some discomfort. He was even breathless before he lowered himself onto a Windsor back chair next to a lovely oak dining table against the wall by the window.

"Angina dear boy. Too much good-living in the Army."

I chuckled politely. "Where were you based?"

"India until the War. Then a spell in Burma."

He didn't look at me as he spoke. I knew the fighting in Burma had been some of the most intense in the War. I also knew typhoid and malaria were rife.

"So good to meet you at least dear boy. I hope you don't mind if I don't stand. Sherry? Or something else?" His brown eyes danced and glinted behind a delicate pair of gold-rimmed pince-nez glasses as he spoke.

There was a small silver platter with a cut-glass sherry decanter in the centre and three clean glasses upturned next to it.

"Sherry is fine."

He reached painfully over the table and poured a glass for me.

"Now what wonders have you brought me to look at?"

The first thing I showed him was the book by Edgar de Boulon. I had inserted white cards to mark pages of interest and he read slowly, affirming what he read with quiet 'um hms' while I slowly slipped the sherry. It felt very pleasant with a nice cool breeze whispering though the window in the early summer heat. I watched his face closely as he read the section about flying snakes and how they were supposed to constrict space. His eyes looked up at me just once for an instance. He finished reading and sat back in his chair. I knew him well enough from his letters to know that he formed opinions slowly, and gave them seldom, so I didn't expect an immediate response. He still seemed to be waiting.

"That last passage interests me the most. I erm.. Do you think I could possibly trouble you for another glass of sherry? Dutch courage!" I said grinning inanely at him.

"Of course dear boy. Help yourself!"

"Erm. You know I was with Annie when she was... murdered? Well I told The Gendarmes that I had not got a good look at the killer but actually I did. My wife thinks I am insane but what I saw most resembled a.. snake." I hadn't told Henry the details about what I had seen – about the snake, before. A bead of sweat started rolling down my forehead. I knew I could lose a friend now, or gain an ally, if he believed me. "Annie's body was squeezed... crushed as if by a giant fist or perhaps a large constrictor snake. " I immediately felt the absurdity of what I was saying and felt powerless to back up my description.

"Tell me more about what you saw!" I looked up and Henry was leaning towards me, eagerly waiting to hear more.

I smiled, grateful and relieved at last to find a willing ear. "Well it was huge! It towered over us but you know.. I couldn't see anything clearly. It was as if it were in a dream. Everything shimmered. In fact the air had seemed to be like water when it appeared."

"Yes. That would be so."

"What?"

"Don't mind me. We will discuss it later. Just tell me all you can about what you saw."

"Well Obviously once I could feel it take a hold of Annie I wasn't so interested in what it was. I just wanted to hold on to her but it was immensely strong. It was like pulling against a pick-up truck. There was no way I could stop it."

"But it was a snake you say? How did it take hold?"

“Yes sorry. Annie was behind me – against a wall but it seemed to have some kind of appendage – arms maybe. In fact in moments I felt it was more like a man than a snake. If it had eyes I could not look at them. It also seemed to be burning somehow, and I thought I could smell the stench of burning flesh. I am sure it must have made a sound like a scream or roar but I was shouting too and Annie was screaming so I cannot clearly remember that. I could not tell you about colours or even if it had wings. It was dark. That is about it really.”

“Yes.” Henry seemed to consider the information for a moment. “Yes I have heard of these – these Warg before. Actually I don’t think of them as Warg at all but it will do as a term for now. The book of your grandfather’s is very famous you know. In fact it is very rare and very valuable. I believe only five were ever printed. Actually the author is not Edgar de Boulon. That is just an alias for a Count, whose name escapes me right now, but what really interests *me* is this reference here. He turned the book to face me, open on another marked page and pointed to a book title mentioned in the text. “This is a book I have been seeking for years and I believe it is a book you really need to get hold of too. I have heard a single leaf of this book, of which only one copy is thought to have survived, is available on the black-market – for a very high price. I wonder if perhaps you might be interested in obtaining such a thing?”

I read the title – ‘De Secretis Scientia Occultis’. “Why is it of such great interest to us?”

“Well dear boy. What I have heard is that this particular leaf has some secret information about the snake-demons, as most of us in-the-know call them. Of course the whole book is probably of huge importance to us but I only know of the one leaf that is available for now. Who knows why? Perhaps it’s a copy. Perhaps the owner of the book needs to raise cash. Perhaps its a fake. There is only one way to know for sure and that is to get a look at it. Of course it’s way out of my price-range.”

“Well how much would you need?”

“Well I think the bidding will start at perhaps 8000 Guineas.”

“Whew! For just one page?”

“Well two actually unless it is an end-leaf or we are very unlucky. There should be something on both sides!” He laughed at his little joke.

”Hm. I could raise it possibly. My antiques business is very successful now. Let me think about it.”

"Well alright. But don't think too long. These things have a habit of vanishing just as quickly as they appear." The wit of this comment was not lost on me. "Now is there something else you want to tell me?"

"No. I don't think so."

"Are you sure? What about any special abilities of your own?"

I looked at him suddenly amazed. How did you know about that?"

"Ah ha! Well?"

"Well I am so used to my wife scoffing at everything lately I had begun to doubt it myself but you know during the War M.I 6 was very interested in my talents. In fact I think that is why they recruited me."

"Did they now?"

"It seems that I can sense the approach or presence of evil. Or at least bad spirits and usually I can avoid them myself although unfortunately that doeS noT extend to my friends of close family. I wish it did. It seems pointless being the only one protected sometimes."

"Now, now. Don't get bitter old boy."

"Sorry."

"Anyway that is what I thought you might say. You see I know a lot more about you than you think – or than I thought until today."

"I don't understand."

"No. I am not sure either and until I am I would prefer to make a few enquiries but I can tell you one thing."

"Yes."

"This death in Lyon is not the first of its type recently."

"No?"

"No. I noticed a previous one five days before in Avignon and another a few days before that in Montpellier. Are you seeing a pattern here?"

"Well apart from the fact that each is a little further North than the last, no."

"That is it. The murderer, whatever or whoever it is, must be traveling North. Each murder victim is described as being badly mangled in a similar way to Seline."

"Why is it travellng North then?"

"Well I don't know. Perhaps it is looking for something?"

"Um. Maybe."

After showing Henry the rest of my documents and a sample of the statues, including the large one of snake and wolf man fighting, he in turn showed me some manuscripts and maps that he had. They were fascinating and I took my time looking through them and taking notes.

By the time we had finished it was mid-afternoon and after a sandwich, I rose to leave.

"Henry. It has been a pleasure and very enlightening to meet you. I am going to seriously consider bidding for this book and I will call you tomorrow or the next day." Henry started to struggle to his feet. "Don't get up. I can see myself out."

"Such a pleasure dear boy. Such a very great pleasure for me. You are welcome any time."

As I left the room I noticed for perhaps the third time a very large crucifix on the wall above the ornate fireplace. I became conscious now of just how strange it was. Seemingly bolted together from two very misshapen cross pieces of some hard wood like oak, burned around the edges and carved loosely into some kind of relief design which I couldn't quite make out, because of the damage, it seemed a very odd thing to be hanging in Henry's lounge. My instinct was to ask about it, but my intuition was that it was too early to ask such intimate questions, so I left with just a call over my shoulder. "See you soon Henry. Take care!"

I opened the door to his flat and stepped out onto the landing. Facing the stairs, I wondered how on earth he managed them. I walked down the corridor on the landing towards the back of the building and saw one of those old lifts, in a wrought-iron cage stretching from top to bottom of the building. As I walked back to the car, I had a very uncomfortable feeling that I was being watched or followed. The hairs stood up on the back of my neck and for a moment I felt sick.

It didn't take me long to reach a decision on 'De Secretis Scientia Occultis'. I was seriously wealthy by now although most of the money was wrapped up in the antiques business but it was my business and there was no reason I should not start to enjoy what I had worked so hard to build up. Also, getting involved in the intriguing world of black-market deals for rare arcane books was too much to resist.

"Henry. I have the money and I want to bid for this page. What do we do now?"

"Excellent dear boy. How much?"

"I have 100000 Francs – just over 9000 Guineas but I don't want to bid above 8000 to start with."

"No. We will start at 7000 but I am sure it will end up more. Leave it with me!"

We drove towards Paris in my Citroën, and in the driving rain around Troyes, the radio reception became so bad I turned it off and listened to Henry talking, when he wasn't rustling the map.

"Typical French car, this Citroën – strange looking, but when all in said, it is well made. He tapped the dash with the head of his stick which he insisted on keeping between his legs as we drove."

As we took the curves in the road, Henry watched the headlights follow the track of the wheels to point out the road just to our left or right.

"Nice feature that." He chuckled to himself.

I was feeling cramp in my legs as we had driven all morning and into the early afternoon. We hadn't even stopped for food, Henry passing me egg and ham or cheese sandwiches as I drove.

Shortly after passing through a little village called Vatry, Henry called out, "Right at the next turning."

"Are you sure? We are in the middle of nowhere."

"Not nowhere dear boy, near to a beautiful rare manuscript!" His eyes shone as I glanced at him. The wipers were working overtime and I peered out into the watery gloom for the turning.

"There! I see it." We slowed and I turned the car onto a gravel track and stopped. "The instructions said to wait here, didn't they?"

"Um hm."

Just at that moment through a break in the clouds, the sun burst forth and the rain slowed revealing a beautiful rainbow arching across the gentle landscape before us. France had never looked more beautiful to me. We were in the Marne region of France, East of Paris and a major wine-growing region. Many of the fields we had passed had been vineyards but the fields here were green and fallow.

A figure in raincoat and galoshes appeared ahead of us and pointed behind him. I started the car and passed him, the car steadily crunching the loose stoned beneath its wheels.

"Wind down the window Henry."

"Do you want a lift?" I called to the man.

"No Sir. It is only one hundred metres." The man spoke in English but with a heavy German accent, I thought.

"This looks dodgy Henry. What do you think?"

"Hm. Not what I was expecting. This dealer has a good reputation though. I wouldn't worry too much. Probably just wants privacy."

Roughly one hundred yards on, I saw a sky-blue caravan beside the track and since there was no other possible meeting place I stopped the car here, and helped Henry out. The clouds were already scurrying away leaving blue sky in their place and colours and smells seemed even more vivid in the afterglow of the rain.

Parked next to the caravan was a beautiful silver Rolls Royce Silver Cloud. A splash of mud on its gleaming wing was an affront, like a smudge of lipstick on a fashionably decadent model in a photo shoot.

The door to the caravan swung open and a black-jacketed arm with black leather gloves, held it open while we climbed the three mini-steps to enter.

"Velcome Gentlemen! Sit down! Sit down!" This voice also sounded German but I couldn't yet make the shape of its owner as there were no lights on. I could make out a small, thin table supported by one spindly leg with a briefcase on it, and then, against the window behind it I started to make out the dealer. He had something like a trilby hat on and dark glasses and his pin-striped suit, although very expensive and probably Savile Row, struggled to contain any part of his massive frame, which I guessed to be all of twenty five stones. He also wore black kid-leather gloves and a white cane rested against the seat, to his right. He seemed to be blind.

"Champagne, Gentlemen?"

"That would be very nice," said Henry, lowering himself very carefully onto the stool indicated for him in front of the table. I too sat on mine, next to him. I thought, and I guessed Henry thought too, that we must look quite comical perched on such fragile stools at such a fragile table.

"André. Pour please?" said the large man.

The black-suited and gloved André, who must really have been a bodyguard, produced a silver tray from somewhere, with three filled flutes of Champagne Bollinger, nestled beside the opened bottle on it. It was delicious. André's piercing blue eyes looked bored but he was polite.

Suddenly the whole caravan started rocking from side to side gently and a might roar and whistle filled the air. A train rushed by somewhere nearby and I realised we must be right alongside a railway line.

"Now, Gentlemen. Let me show you something." A mantle of thick, silver hair flowed from under the hat of our host as he opened the case. I still could not clearly see his face. "Please use the gloves."

Two pairs of white archivist's gloves lay on top of the document and Henry and I both put on a pair. Henry then lifted up the single, brownish leaf with cursive latin script on it. He held it close to his glasses. To my surprise it had not be torn or even carefully cut from a book but unstitched, and it consisted of four, full leaves of a book, with the stitch holes clearly showing down the middle seam. I managed to conceal my delight and surprise, and noticed that Henry did the same.

"Oh yes. It's beautiful."

"You read Latin Sir?"

"Yes. But the buyer does not."

"Ah." I think he smiled at me, judging by the curling of his lips. "Please, if you can read it, do not talk to each other from now on about the content. Once you have approved it, Monsieur de Silva, your friend will propose a price."

I guessed he was nervous we were simply after the content and once we had deduced this we wouldn't want to buy. I kept quiet with difficulty until, I guessed, Henry must have read at least one paragraph. "Well? Henry. Is it what we are looking for?"

"Hm." He seemed miles away. "Oh yes. Yes dear boy. It is genuine as far as I can tell. The ink looks authentic and the vellum. It talks about what we are interested in."

"Alright," I said. "I am prepared to make you an offer. 7500 Guineas."

"Well that would be fine Mr er?" Neither of us answered him. "That would be fine if I didn't know how interested you are in this." He was relishing this and I knew he would want to go a lot higher. I decided to try a gambit of my own.

"Well if the man who wanted to buy this was also hoping to, one day, buy the whole document, then he would be a fool to offer over what he could afford for the first sheet."

The man laughed. "Touché!"

Henry smiled at me. He had noticed not only my ploy, but that I had already learned from him to use the word document, as a sign of respect, rather than 'book'. A book was an object, a document was a historical record, something much more vital.

"Point taken Sir. But I do believe you are prepared to offer a little more."

"8200."

"Um. A serious offer. But I would have to leave now if that was your limit. André. Would you?" He pointed to the document and André took it gently from Henry, placed it back in the case and closed it. Henry looked a little flustered.

"Really, I cannot go much higher. But 8400 I think is a very fair offer."

"André. Another glass of Champagne for us all." He sipped his and considered the offer. He took so long, I almost offered him more but managed to stop myself.

"Are you serious about the rest of the document Sir?"

"Yes. I would at least like to see it."

"How do you know I have it?"

"I don't. Do you?"

"I have access to it. A buyer who was to offer 8500 for a single leaf would secure a viewing, say within a week?"

Now I smiled. He was probably now exploring how much he could get for the whole document. I waited for a very long time, considering this.

"8500 it is then. And an appointment within one week?"

"Done, Sir."

I reached over to shake his hand but he pulled away. I knew then he wasn't blind.

I helped Henry as he rose stiffly from the seat with the aid of his stick, and we walked back to the car. The second bodyguard watched us while we started the car, turned around, and drove off.

We talked excitedly as we drove. Henry told me that the first paragraph had given him a possible explanation for the phases of strange deaths, from crushing, every sixty years.

"It says something about the heartbeat of God."

"Yes. Go on!"

"Well it says the victims of these demons called Warg are usually, but not always, crushed, and that they are summoned by the Devil." He looked at my face for a reaction.

"Well none of that is really surprising, all though it is a bit vague and par for the course for 13th Century superstition, don't you think?"

"Yes but the really *good* bit is this. It says – and I am not sure of this so I need to get home and check my Latin – it says that the serpents appear as if from water in the air! I feel sure that the next paragraph will reveal more. I caught a few words but that André fellow took it back from me before I could really see anything much."

We argued about what this might mean for a while, and after stopping for petrol, after perhaps two hours, I began to feel restless and impatient.

"I really need to know what it says. Let's stop now and read it. I can't wait." I pulled the car over at the next entrance to a field, and we stopped right in front of the old wooden gate. The sun was lowering in the West, although it was still early and a cloud, like a bloody gash, stretched across the sky just above the horizon. I opened the boot and passed the case to Henry, and then paced up and down in the early evening, as Henry read the pages of 'De Secretis Scientia Occultis'.

"It says here something about your lot – the Ordo Lupus. Yes. Notice that it distinguished between Wolf and Warg. Did you also notice how it said serpents earlier when talking about the water in the air.

"Yes."

"Yes. It also mentions something about a counter-brotherhood of some sort, and a Catholic priesthood who were violently opposed to both, believing them both heretical. There is something else about some kind of potent symbol or something but I cannot really make much of it."

"Tantalising but it doesn't really help us very much. I guess that is just what he wanted, the old scoundrel. Did you notice he wasn't even blind?"

"Oh yes. It's just a ruse, so that he can watch us better. I have seen other dealers do all sorts of strange things to get an edge. Didn't you feel me kick you under the table?

"Don't you think it's an awfully big coincidence that this one page just happens to have information about the Warg – the one thing I am most interested in? How did he know that?"

"Yes it is too much for a coincidence, but you haven't noticed the most significant thing about recent events at all, have you?"

"Haven't I? What's that?"

"Well its so obvious I am not surprised you haven't seen it."

He was being coy so I walked over to the drivers side door and stuck my head in. Henry looked at me sheepishly.

"Go on."

"Hmm hmm. Well I don't like to point this out to you really because I know how you are suffering inside. At least I think I know. I haven't lost a child myself – both of mine are grown up and married, but I lost many friends during the war and I am sure your suffering is worse." He chose his words carefully and I was touched.

"Henry. Just say it. Right now I badly need to understand things – understand just something. Anything to make sense of all this."

"Alright, dear boy. Well what struck me was that this serpent targeted your daughter at all. I mean, why you? You say you can sense evil and I believe you. From what you say, your grandfather had connections to this society, the Ordo Lupus, who seem to be opposed to these Warg. So why somebody close to you?"

"Yes. Yes, I never thought of that. I see what you mean. Perhaps that means something?" My heart lifted just a little, at the thought, for the first time since starting down this mysterious road to explain Annie's death. At the same time, a cold thrill ran down my spine. What was I dealing with here? Was a demon actually baiting *me*?

"Henry. You are a genius. Now let's get home and have some of that excellent sherry of yours." The countryside in the dimming light suddenly seemed threatening.

Henry, even with the aid of his Latin reference books, could deduce no more from the four pages of 'De Secretis Scientia Occultis', but he received an invitation for me to view the whole book seven days later.

Henry telephoned the evening before the meeting was to take place. "I have some bad news dear boy. The meeting has been cancelled. Mr Kalmus has sold to somebody else."

"Somebody else! Well who?"

"I don't know yet. I am trying to find out."

"Why the hell did they sell? I don't get it. Why offer it to us and then just sell." Shit!

"Hi, Henry. What have you found out?" I was answering an answer-phone message from Henry a few months later.

"Well I never did find out who the buyer actually was, but a friend has told me something very interesting. Apparently the Bibliothèque Nationale now has a copy. Now I know they didn't have a copy a few years ago but I don't know how recently they acquired it. They have kept very quiet about it and considering that most experts think at most there are three copies in existence, and possibly just the one, it is most unusual."

"So is it possible to see it?"

"Well yes apparently it is. It's held at the François-Mitterrand Library in Paris. You have to go there and see it."

* * *

Chapter Two

ymj rtwj dtz fyyjruy yt gwnsl twijw, ymj rtwi hmftx bnqq uwjitrnsfyj

"In the roof space above the Cathedral I wait. From the corner of my eye I just noticed something white protruding from one of my jacket pockets. Glancing at it, I realised it was the envelope with the divorce papers, which I had so hurriedly stuffed in my pocket on the day I left Nevers. I had completely forgotten that it was there. I pulled the crumpled envelope from the jacket pocket and leaned up against the cool stone of the sarcophagus to read it once more. It was the divorce papers, neatly typed and held together by a single staple – cold and seemingly indifferent but hidden within it were, encrypted, the final thoughts of me from my wife. I noticed a pink mark on the corner of a sheet. 'Nail polish', I thought to myself. But Rose never wore pink nail polish and neither did Cosette. Ayshea did, however. So that was what she meant when she said, 'I know something perhaps you didn't know.'

I read again the statement on a single sheet which Rose had added to the end of the rest of the papers. She said, 'I had never had any wish that it would come to this and no wish now to cause me any pain or even discomfort, but that it seemed to me that we could no longer find the common ground which a couple needed to stand upon, in order that we could exist as a couple.'

Throughout your unusual life you have experienced things in a way others could not have. I remember you telling me how you had felt scarred by the suicide attempt of the teacher at school – how you felt the tremendous weight of guilt that someone who had knowledge of a disaster before it happened but could do nothing to prevent it.' Yes. That had deeply affected me, I remembered."

I arrived at 8 am, outside 58 Rue de Richelieu, Paris, the location of the main Bibliothèque Nationale de France library, and found myself third in a queue in the bright sunlight. A middle-aged man in a suit, with a bang of slick dark hair over his forehead, was first, and a young, and rather gorgeous dark-haired beauty was second. I contemplated speaking to both, but then thought better of it. If either of them were researching the same book, alerting them, in any way, might make it even harder to obtain it. Standing in the queue, I was vaguely aware that I was attracted to the girl in front, but I was also irritated by this. I just wanted to get hold of the book and go home. Out of the corner of my eye, I noted that she was wearing one of those afghan coats with long fur trim and jeans with cowboy boots. Underneath the coat was a tight fitting, black jumper. She had a nice figure but I dismissed it. 'Way too young and silly', I said to myself. I thought she was about twenty-five.

When we were finally let in, I walked through the main library room, with its delicately scalloped roof, supported by thin spiral columns, and was surprised to find that the research room was a huge rotunda, much like the British Library in London. I asked one of the librarians in French how to go about requesting a book and was given a form to complete. Returning it, completed, I was given a ticket, with a table number, and told to wait there for the book. I waited, and waited, and after two hours I went back to the counter and asked, politely in French, if the book would take much longer to arrive. My question was met with the most imperious French disdain and a side-swiping "Please be patient Monsieur," in English. At 1 pm, finally, I saw a librarian walking towards me, but without a book that I could see. She leaned over and quietly said, close to my face, "Je suis monsieur désolé. Ce livre a été demandé par quelqu'un d'autre. Veuillez essayer encore un autre jour." Incredibly, I was handed back my form with a note. The book had been reserved!

In my impatience, waiting for the book, I had grabbed another book, a French translation of 'The Gardnerian Book of Shadows' by Gerald Gardner, to scan, hardly taking in any words at all. Although I had frequently glanced at the two ahead of me in the queue earlier, I wondered if perhaps I had missed something and that one of them, somehow, had priority over myself and even now, was reading it!

After a heated and pointless exchange in broken French with the librarian, during which she claimed ignorance of the book's whereabouts, hunching her shoulders apologetically, I prepared to leave, fuming. I grabbed my bag and stuffed my research paper and pens into it, and looked for my two competitors. I wasn't going to leave without making an effort to find the book.

The library was busy, and although I spotted the man with the dark hair quite quickly, it took longer to find the girl because she had taken off the coat. I walked purposefully toward the man, from the opposite side of the reading desk, so that he could see me approach. He didn't even glance at me so I stood on the opposite side of the desk and coughed once. He looked up, quite annoyed, and for a moment I felt embarrassed by my impertinence. In my most formal French, I explained my predicament, and with a heartfelt apology backed with a little annoyance of my own, I asked if he knew who might have borrowed the book for the last two days. With a look of quiet victory on his face, he raised the book from the desk so that I could see its title – something about Napoleon and the early years after the French Revolution. I apologized for bothering him and turned to find the girl. She was right over the other side of the large rotunda and while I approached I was grumbling to myself that the man had looked so smug.

I approached her from the front too, although a young man was sitting on the opposite side of the bench, but at the last moment I swerved to approach her from the side. It was an unconscious decision and not in order to avoid letting the man overhear. I wondered why I had done IT but then the girl was already looking up at me. For a moment I was astonished at her beauty and forgot to say anything at all.

"Oui?" she said.

I had noticed her long black hair before, but now she fixed me with two gorgeous eyes of cinnamon.

This time my politeness was genuine, as I explained my predicament. I also told her I had come from the South of France just to see the book, and as I proceeded with my plea, I looked deep into her eyes and tried to persuade her to help me.

She smiled, and, just like the man had done, she raised the book so that I could see its title. I was familiar with the book – 'Malleus Maleficarum' which was published in the 15th Century and basically a Catholic Priest's guide to torturing and putting to death witches. It was a very scholarly book and I immediately assumed she was some kind of historian.

"Pardonnez-moi," I said and walked back to the enquiries desk. I left my Nevers address, and explained that if I didn't come back tomorrow, could they please contact me when the book became available.

I decided to spend the afternoon sight seeing, but in the Louvre, I looked at many paintings and saw none. There was too much troubling me.

I went back the following morning to the library and still the book was not available even though I listened to the books ordered by the two people ahead of me in the queue. This time, though, the librarian, a much older woman looked kindly at me, and I decided to try one last tactic.

"Parlez-vous Anglais?"

"Yes Sir. Not too well these days but we can speak in English."

"This book has been reserved somehow for the last two days even though I spoke to the people who were ahead of me on both days and none had borrowed it. Today, I also know nobody in front of me borrowed it. Could you please find out where it is? Is that possible?"

As if flattered that I had called on her professional pride for help, she smiled at me. "Wait here Sir. I will see what I can find out."

After only a few minutes she returned holding a slip of paper, the 'fantôme' as they call it. This was the card that occupies the place of the book while it is being borrowed, and is the triplicate of the forms that are filled out.

"I cannot tell you who has borrowed this Monsieur, but I know this man. I have met him many times and he is a serious academic. Would you like me to speak WITH him?"

"Yes please. That would be very nice of you."

"What shall I say?"

"Well if I could borrow it for just one hour, I am sure that would be enough for me."

"Alright. I will try. Wait here."

Again she was gone a short while and returned with a hardly-constrained smile.

"The researcher said you can have it for two hours while he has lunch. In about fifteen minutes."

"Great. Could I just make a telephone call?"

"Of course. You can use this telephone but make it brief."

"Henry. It's me. I have the book but for only two hours. What should I copy? I had thought I would have more time to compare notes with you."

"Well dear boy. Just copy everything you can but if I was you, I would look for the missing page and start there."

"How will I find the missing page?"

"I don't know dear boy."

I put the telephone down and had an idea. I called over the librarian again.

"There is one page missing in this book. Could you ask the researcher to mark this place and in return, I can copy the missing page for him?"

Her eyebrows raised right up, but she went back through the door again. She returned, this time accompanied by a very serious looking gentleman, balding, with red hair, and glasses, in a tweed suit with a waistcoat.

He leaned over the desk, close to my ear and in very well-spoken English he asked, “You know about the missing page?”

“Not only do I know about it, but I have access to a copy.”

“Remarkable. The library, under my direction only recently acquired this book. Do you realise what that is worth?”

I lied. “Not exactly but I guess it is worth something.”

He pulled away and we both gave each other a long stare, each weighing the other.

“I see. Yes to me it definitely is. I am writing a book – a serious book about ‘De Secretis Scientia Occultis’, and I have competition, so it would be very useful for me to see it. What would you want in return?”

“A day with the book and an indication from you, which sections I need to copy, given my interests.”

“Which are?”

“Flying wolf-men and spirit-serpents – I think they are called Warg in this book.”

“He laughed quietly. Ah – the flying wolf-men. I agree to the terms Sir. The book will be here tomorrow, marked with the relevant sections, and to show my good will, I will be here in the morning too. You do not read latin, I take it?”

“If it would be easy, that would be very good of you.”

I left, jubilant, and decided not to tell Henry of my victory. I would surprise him with the copies later. I’d decided to splash out on a night of bar-hopping, and ended up at the Moulin Rouge. Drunk as a Lord, I had to get a taxi back to the hotel, and a night-porter helped me to my room. I woke late, with a hangover, but years of practice meant I was still at the library by ten. I spent all day photocopying the relevant sections, and after a few questions in the morning, copied some extra sections that the researcher had marked for me. I must have copied over one third of the book by the time I left, with the wad of paper in my bag, and several hundred francs lighter. I had agreed to fax my missing four pages to a number the researcher had given me, and I did so a few days later.

After visiting the family home, which no longer had any family in it – just Rose, to clean myself up, I went to the office for the night and on to Henry’s.

His housekeeper let me in and he seemed a little surprised to see me. For a little while he seemed uncomfortable, but as soon as I lay out the more interesting photocopied sheets before him on the dining table, he was as happy as a child with a new toy.

"This is fantastic. My dear boy. Oh! Look at this."

He had the housekeeper make a tray of sandwiches before she left, and we settled down for an afternoon of discovery.

Of course there was a lot to read and translate, and although Henry went as fast as he could, by the end of the afternoon we had only unearthed a few new details.

"Look here," Henry said. "It says that from the original Cathar monk who started the Ordo Lupus, have descended several families of Knights, some members of the Knights Templar too, and their descendants all 'have the sight'. I don't know what that means. They can 'see' the Warg perhaps? Like you? It says that only alternate generations have the sight though, and that they are all interred in coffers in a sacred place – the Crypt of the Ordo Lupus, logically enough. Doesn't say where that is though."

Later on I was peering over his shoulder, looking at an engraving when suddenly he grabbed my arm.

"Ah. Now this is interesting. Listen to this. 'It is said that the Serpents 'constrict' the fabric of the world making evil things happen to people and living off the souls of the dead, but every sixty years the fabric of space is rent and for a month the snakes have to survive by actually killing and taking on physical form'. Only the Lupus Angelus – or 'Wolf-angels' can kill the Serpents then."

"Wow! I like that. Wolf-angels. Do you think it means that these Lupus Angelus can only kill the Serpents or Warg during this period as well? I mean as well as being the only ones who can kill the Serpents at all?"

"I think..yes, I think it means that only the Lupus Angelus can kill the Serpents, but do you remember the special weapon or magical weapon? I think this is needed to do the killing."

Before I left, there was only one other passage which Henry translated which was of interest.

"Here you go dear boy. I have been working on this passage for quite a while. This is probably what you have been looking for. It says that there were two magical weapons brought out of Montségur by the two monks, and also that the place where the Crypt is, was built shortly after and a long way off. So the final siege of Montségur was in 1244 and you need to find somewhere built in the next 50 years or so, I would think.

"Me? Why just me? Aren't we in this together?"

"Yes dear boy, but think of me as the support team. I am too old to go traipsing around looking for secret crypts and coffers."

I left Henry's flat well after midnight and as I walked towards my car a strange feeling came over me again. I felt a presence like that on the night Annie was taken. I began to walk faster as a shiver literally ran down my spine. The air seemed colder around me, although it may have been my imagination playing tricks on me. As I reached the car and turned the key in the door, time seemed to slow, almost to a stop and I thought I would never make it into the car. After I finally managed to start the car, hands shaking and in a sweat, I drove off and the feeling receded. I couldn't help looking in the rear-view mirror, although I could see nothing in the street behind me.

I opened Le Monde, two days later, over a coffee in the afternoon, to another surprise. "Young man mysteriously murdered in Lyon during early evening of Tuesday. Is this again the 'crusher killer'?" The description of his injuries sounded just like Annie's. I had an old tatty road-map of France in a drawer and pinned it up on my office wall. Then I took some map pins and stuck them in where the murders had taken place, including Annie's, with dates taped to them. There was a definite pattern, at least in the recent killings, of movement northwards.

I was pondering this when Henry called. "Remember those markings on the bottom of some of your statues?"

"Um hm."

"Well there are marks ' on the bottom of the statue, aren't there?"

"Yes I believe so."

"Well I don't know if it is relevant, but there is mentioned a master craftsman – possibly a carpenter, called Piere Drang Clenn sometimes written Piere Drang-Clenn or even Piere Drangclenn."

Hm. Piere Drang Clenn. Piere Drang Clenn. I have never heard that name before. Is Clenn a place or something?"

"Possibly but spellings and names themselves were very fluid in those days. I wouldn't put much significance on it."

"It doesn't match 'SK' though.

"Ah. That is the initials? Then no."

"Is there anything about the roman numerals mean or B'vs or BV."

"Patience dear boy, patiencE."

"Henry, have you heard of the recent killing in Lyon, just like all the others?"

"I certainly have, and in a street not too far from here. Gave me the willies I can tell you. For a few nights I thought he was coming for me."

"He?" I asked, my chuckle strangled in my throat by the memory of Annie.

"The Devil. Old Nick."

"Oh. Don't worry Henry. Your flesh is too grizzly, like coq au vin."

"Take care dear boy."

"Yes Henry. If you find anything else out let me know."

Cosette, my secretary tapped on the door and stepped into my office.

"Hello Cosette. How are you?" There was a frown on her face, which stopped my conversation in its tracks.

"The Gendarmes are here to speak with you Monsieur."

"Downstairs?"

"Oui Monsieur."

"Shit. Tell them I will be down in two minutes."

I looked in the mirror, above the sink in the corner of the room, at my disorderly face, and quickly applied some shaving cream. Within three minutes I had shaved, washed my face, brushed my hair and put on a clean-ish shirt, and was descending the stairs calmly to speak to the Gendarmes.

I reached out a hand after introducing myself but it wasn't taken.

"Monsieur, I 'av to ask youer to accompany me to the Gendarmerie." He spoke in very heavily accented English so he clearly knew I was English already.

"Now?"

"Oui."

"What for, er if you don't mind me asking?" The French police are far more like the military than the English police and it wasn't good to be rude to them, or even curt. I vaguely hoped it was something about Annie. Perhaps they had caught her killer.

"I cannot tell youer 'ere."

As we reached their car, one of the two officers accompanying him put a hand firmly on my shoulder, ostensibly to guide me through the door, but it felt threatening.

Sitting at the interview table in a sparse room of the Gendarmerie, I noticed how little it had changed in the years since I last visited. I expected a folder to be laid before me, possibly showing some grim photographs or at least some officious documents, but the same officer who had spoken in my office sat opposite, with just a pencil and a simple form on one sheet of paper. He looked very sad, as if he was about to tell me something really morbid. He had taken off his hat and his bald head shone in the stark light of a single clear bulb, while his furry white eyebrows jumped up and down over his long face, as he talked.

"Your name, please?"

"I told him and he carefully wrote it in the space at the head of the form, in heavy, but clear script. He continued to fill in the form with my details while I grew more uncomfortable. About half way down the page, a large single box began which continued all the way to the bottom of the page. When he reached this, he paused and then asked, "Where were you on Tuesday night?" That was the night of the murder in Lyon.

"Wait a minute. Am I suspected of something?"

"Not officially, non. We simperly are asking some facts for now, Monsieur. I would be grateful if you could answer."

Since I had nothing to hide, I told him I had been in Lyon at Henry's flat.

"Now could you tell me pleeze, from about six in the afternoon, all the events ova your life until you came back to Nevers."

I soon found out that the long box on the form continued on for the whole length of the reverse side of the form and that there were as many sheets as they wanted, with the long box on both sides, to take all my details. I told them as much as I could remember and then the officer, who I later learned was Loring Parcaud, placed his hands together, on the table, almost as if in prayer, and fixed his doleful eyes on me.

"I am not satisfiered wiv your story Monsieur. Are you aware, that there have been murders, not only on Tuesday but also on these dates." He proceeded to list the dates of the spate of murders. "I would like to know where you were also, on those nightser."

Now I knew I was a suspect and I felt panic rising inside me. I could not remember where I had been on those nights. I searched for a way out of this dilemna.

"I would need to call the office. My secretary would have a record of appointments for me and some of these may be on those dates."

"His eyebrows rose to their zenith and he gestured for another officer, guarding the door, to bring the one black bakelite telephone in the room, to the desk in front of me. With the palm of his large hand, Parcaud gestured gracefully that I should use the telephone.

I called the Office and Cosette answered. She went through my business diary for the dates of the murders but there were no appointments at all on those dates. I really was at a loss to think what to do or say next. The officer by the door shifted uneasily on his feet and Parcaud stared at me for a very long time. Then he unclasped his hands and started rolling the pencil between his thumbs and forefingers.

"What I want you to do Monsieur is go home and look for any receipts or travel tickets you can find. Oui? Talk to all your friends – those you 'ave visited and find evidence for where you ave been on those particular days."

I was so relieved that he wasn't going to arrest me, I could have kissed him. I smiled at him but he stared icily back at me. "Thank you," I said involuntarily, and immediately regretted it.

"One of my officers will driver you 'ome. Pleeze do not leave the area for the next few deys, as we will want to asker you more questions."

"Where do you wish to go Monsieur?" asked the driver in the front of the car. I was tempted to say to the family home North of the town, where I presumed Rose would be settling down to watch television, but I couldn't face her.

"To my office please." I gave him directions.

I was so relieved to be released that evening, I just made myself a cup of tea and went to sleep on the sofa. It was only the next day that I first felt indignant at my arrest, and then later a burning anger set in. I realised that The Gendarmes must actually suspect me of killing my own daughter! The thought made my throat burn and I wanted to cough. I did as Parcaud had suggested and started to look for evidence of my whereabouts on those days. The problem was that so many days passed routinely, with my drinking and reading medieval literature stuck in my office, that they blurred into one, and even Cosette didn't see or hear me on some days. Many afternoons were spent in the company of just a bottle of ouzo, and on many such an afternoons the ouzo floated my mind back through the events that had led from Highgate Cemetary to empty afternoons in Nevers.

That day in Highgate, North London, not long before the Second World War, started normally enough. We *all* have a problem to solve when we are young and growing up: how to find a model of the world which allows us to succeed. Often it changes many times. Often it's inherited from our parents and never changes from birth – simply crystallises and hardens gradually. I was a bright child – everybody said so. My mother said I had a mind like quicksilver – I broke all the rules and I stumbled on my philosophy in a graveyard in North London when I was ten.

If you had known me then you would have said I was a charming boy – witty and polite with a nice smile and happy to play with almost anybody. This image however, might have hidden the thoughtfulness in my character. My parents were both intelligent – even part of the intelligentsia you might say, and I had been encouraged to think. I would weigh up the risks of a situation in a flash and then act. To all the other kids – many of whom I would have counted as friends, I would appear a 'man of action' but they didn't notice I was also observing them, building up a picture of the world and my picture was about to get sharper.

I was bored in front of the house and not able to find any of my usual friends to play with. I wandered aimlessly under the hot sun – away from our neighbourhood into unfamiliar streets until I saw a sign of dread – Highgate Cemetery.

For just a child's moment, I hesitated, then pushed open the heavy, creaking wrought-iron gate and disappeared into the city of stones within. I wandered wide-eyed through the many jagged lanes of tombs, some towering black marble with gold letters and some low to the ground and dressed in ivy. As the sun lowered behind the trees circling the stones, I found myself staring up at a huge tomb, ringed by a broken black rail-fence and declaring with magisterial elegance the mighty importance of the dead inside. Were dead people like the sleeping – as some of my school-friends said? I wanted to know and put my hands on the cool rails to step through the gap and into the magic space. I pulled my head out and walked around the rectangle, laughing at myself. Of course I couldn't go in. There might be ghosts and even if I wasn't eaten alive, or even worse, it was a bad thing to do. I picked up a blade of grass, placed it long-ways between my palms and blew a long raucous crow-note on it.

I ought to go home.

Just then a drop of water splashed coolly on my hand.

Rain.

A few more drops followed and I looked longingly at the hole in the grate of the big tomb. Almost like an emotion I was finally overcome and darted inside the fence and crawled through the hole to the dank but dusty space inside, my heart thumping.

I sat down on old rustling leaves, waiting for my eyes to adjust. After a while I could see dimly that there really was nothing inside the space at all except me – and some stones, like those outside, stacked against the walls. The biggest was opposite the small opening and I brushed off the dust and cobwebs to read it but couldn't. I heard voices outside and felt curiously excited at the thought that I was hidden from them, and just for a moment I thought of myself as a spirit, living in the graveyard. I twisted around on my knees to explore further, heard, rather than felt, a thud and then no more.

My next conscious thought was that is was very dark and I was very cold. The back of my head was sore and some of my hair was stuck to my head. A cold, clammy hand seemed to grip my heart as I felt for the way out. Try as I might I could not find it and I had to make myself sit still and think. I remembered the hole had been close to the ground and that there had been heavy stones leaning against the walls. Now one of them seemed to have fallen over the hole – lying now at a slight angle from the ground.

Panic overcame me and I cried.

Mum will kill me.

I started calling for help, louder and louder.

I went through alternate moods of cold despair and hope when I thought I heard voices.

Is that a whisper?

What is that?

"Who is that?" I cried.

He – for it was a he – sounded like my father but was whispering like a bear.

I will be lost forever because the gates will be locked and my soul will be eaten by ghosts.

But at midnight – as the moon crept overhead, I really did hear a female and male voice lost in some secret, private ritual outside. I tried to cry out and at first nothing came – then I heard my small voice cry, "Help!"

"Okay boy. Wait here," said the man.

That's a silly thing to say since the whole problem is that I can't leave.

"Don't worry. He will be back soon and everything will be okay," said the woman's voice.

Finally the heavy stone was levered aside, and after crawling out, I was lifted into the air by a huge fireman.

"Well my boy. You won't do that again in a hurry will you?" He ruffled my hair.

Home again, my mother engulfed me as she wept.

"Do you know how worried we were? Where were you?" My father just ruffled my hair. He was always the sanguine one.

What this taught me was there was a kind of insanity about the way the world worked. Boredom, the drop of rain, the tomb and the sheer impossibility of the stone that somehow managed to fall, for the first time in perhaps hundreds of years – I was left with a feeling of having being outwitted. It all seemed the work of an insane genius. Evil possibly, but an insane genius.

The immediate effect of accepting this new view of the world – this insanity, was an almost total loss of anger. Indeed I found myself quite at peace when faced with ludicrous events and sometimes could even laugh whereas before I would get frustrated and angry. I found myself observing my friends more at schools which lead to a certain distance, but the calmness I began to feel inside made it worthwhile. As the summer clouds rolled by over London I became more of a thinker and storer of experiences. War was approaching though you would hardly know it – the Empire seemed still to cover half the world and my father still brought home gifts in the evening – a balsa wood model plane or a wind-up toy train which whistled when I pushed it across the Wilton wilderness in the lounge.

My father was an engineer, something to do with radio, and his reward was our lovely house between elevated Highgate and leafy Crouch End. My mother was one of those women men seek out, a blaze of light and beauty and quick wit with the reputation to match.

When they were going 'up to town' to some posh London Nightclub to dance to the Ray Noble band, she would put on her finest beads and furs with a hat from among those she stored in the small room, and then he would look adoringly at her an you could sense a rhythm building in them – a need to dance.

Antonia, the eldest sister, but younger than I, was a devil. Nadia, the youngest and blonde but going darker, was the mouse – the one who sucked her thumb and skulked around my mother's slacks when anything too noisy was going on. She was three years my junior and Antonia one. The Italian-sounding names were an invention of my mother from a holiday she'd had to Naples, early in her marriage.

My relationship with this 'insanity' continued to grow and I could often see it approaching like a dark cloud. Some would say it is my own demon and I have certainly considered this at great length as I have grown older. It would happen like this: I drop my only coin and seeing it roll away, I chase after it but I slip, kicking the coin, which drops through the grill of the only drain for half a mile. This mean I don't have the fare home which means that I have to walk and then get knocked over by a car.

The next big incident involving this malevolence happened at school.

The first fifteen minute break arrived and we were all ushered out into the cool spring air. I had jabbed Ionwyn in the ribs as I had run past him in the corridor, and Miss Silver had told me off. I cursed her briefly under my breath, before grinning and saying "Sorry miss."

Later on, and uncharacteristically, I might say, I was caught out as the ring-leader of a prank Paul and I carried out at the expense of Spiffy. Paul was just given a ticking-off while I had to spend all afternoon picking up litter.

It felt strange to be in the playground when everybody else was inside but it was sunny and I didn't mind it after a while. Just before 4 pm, I was walking across a piece of land we called the triangle between two blocks and the path was surrounded at that time of year by puddles and mud. I felt compelled to step off the path to the right into the mud. It was such a powerful feeling – as if my life suddenly depended on it, that I didn't hesitate. As I trudged across the mud, I had the sudden urge to turn around, and thought I noticed something move, through the window of a room, on the corner of the block opposite. That room was hardly ever used, being a storage room.

Teachers having an affair.

I couldn't help moving closer to the building. I could see something moving from side to side – swaying, as if it was a coat hung from the ceiling. Not knowing what I was looking at, and nervous at being caught, I edged closer, to one side of the window, until I was only about ten feet away. I peered in and jumped in horror. It *was* a human, hanging by the neck from a rope.

Suicide.

"Bloody Hell," I heard myself say as I ran around to the entrance of the building only to find a large group of my mates coming out. I pushed past them, ignoring their calls and ran straight to the room with the hanging. I wrenched the door handle down but the door was locked. I banged on it. "Stop!" I cried. I was shouting at the top of my lungs and suddenly I heard a teacher's voice behind me.

"Hey. What are you doing boy?"

"Sir. Sir. Come quick. Somebody is hanging in there. I saw it from the playground!"

He and some other teachers followed me as I ran back to the room and had to push through a crowd of pupils gathering at the end of the corridor. I felt a dread as I approached the room.

Just before I was pushed aside I noticed the shoes on the suspended body – pretty patent leather shoes and I knew who these shoes belonged to. Miss Silver was a pretty brunette and a favourite of the boys. She had always been kind to me and I hoped against hope that she would be alright. I was left outside with everyone else. I walked up to the most senior boy and he looked enquiringly at me.

"It's one of the teachers – a woman. She has hung herself I think. I saw it from the playground."

I saw two magpies and thought of the song – 'One for sorrow, two for joy'. I was walking near Queens Woods – on the green, in early summer.

Joy. That's good.

I had been feeling down all day, and I was trying to cheer myself up. Miss Silver had never come back to the school and the memory left a stain in me. I took more and more to wondering alone, and I felt I was growing apart from people – even Antonia, Nadia and Paul. I had tried broaching the subject of 'the darkness' with both my parents but faltered at the first post. I felt very alone. I was reminded of what my mother had said one day in the kitchen.

I asked, "Don't you ever think that one day people might be able to travel to see distant places just by thinking about it."

She had replied, "You are always chasing rainbows".

I wasn't chasing rainbows but perhaps she had spotted my struggle. Of course it wasn't my only worry.

I always worried about my eyes. When I was seven I had run around a corner at school and surprised Theo, who was a big guy, and he had instinctively stuck out his fist and hit me in the eye – turning my blue eye, brown. The condition is called Heterochromia, I was told. My vision also suffered and I often had bouts of blurriness in that eye – my left. At one time doctors told me I needed glasses, and I thought I might lose sight in that eye completely. Blindness was what I often dreamed about now – waking up sweating with a vague fears I often could not put my finger on, but would later realise were about sight. I sometimes pressed my fingers hard into my eyes, holding them there for a few seconds, before releasing, and watching the kaleidoscope of colours shooting through my vision. I did it because I believed one day I might lose my sight completely and I wanted to experience it intensely while I could. Lately I had begun to feel an even darker, waking-fear. I sometimes felt that the other eye – my good eye, was getting blurry too, and I feared I might go completely blind.

"Irrational," I told myself.

Nevertheless the fear was there. Beethoven was my favourite composer – I empathised with his fear of going deaf, and his eventual horror at actually going completely deaf. I was also a little short which bothered me. My mother told me I had not eaten properly for nearly a year after the accident and this was why I had not grown properly. I ate as much as I could now to try and make up. From my poor eyesight and slight shortness came a deep insecurity although I often wondered later in life if the insecurity wouldn't have developed from any kind of negative experience when I was young and whether in fact it was there anyway from the beginning. It was affective when I was facing physical challenges and pre-eminent with girls. I loved Natalie Houghton from afar but I never did get the courage to talk to her.

At the start of summer in June or July I think, on a warm Saturday morning we set out for Hertfordshire to visit my grandfather.

Grandma had died many years ago, before I was born and I was slightly scared of Grandfather Hugo, although he was always smiling and quite nonthreatening really, sitting in an ancient wheel chair with his long white beard, dangling in the many cups of tea we made for him. He was usually looked after by John, my father's brother, who lived nearby, and when we arrived he was already sitting in the sunny back garden, facing North, away from the house and the street of houses behind him. Antonia and Nadia fussed around him, Nadia climbing up onto the blanket covering his knobbly knees.

"Hello, my little Lord," he said to me, calling me the name he reserved for when my deeds had been particularly good.

"Hello." I said smiling. I didn't like formalities. As my mother and John continually wheeled him in and out of the house through the french windows, bumping his glasses off his nose each time he mounted the little step, we passed a pleasant afternoon exploring the house and garden, and drinking ginger beer with our mouths full of salmon sandwiches.

I always liked his library of books and shortly before we were to leave, my father left me alone with him while all the others put on their coats.

"Your father has told me about your little adventure at school."

"Oh sure. It was nothing really. Anybody would have done it."

He smiled at my self-deprecation and my informality – something he secretly approved of I knew.

"What do you want to do when you grow up, my little Lord? Hmm?"

"Oh well you know. It's hard to know really." I was walking around the room, running my fingers absently over the glass cases of books lower down and peering up and the gold-lettered titles on rows of books, nearly to the ceiling.

"Well, what are you good at?"

"Sport and art and science. I am good at lots of things."

This unexpected confidence and honesty beguiled him and he laughed quietly.

"Yes you really are one of us, aren't you? Although I think most probably you are more talented that your father and myself."

"Oh I doubt it Grandfather." He had been a writer – a journalist at the turn of the century, publishing a few obscure books on gardening and the history of Hertfordshire, before later becoming a local newspaper editor and ending his days writing a weekly column about Hertfordshire, its history, and gardens.

"Oh I think so. I truly think so. It runs in the family you know, having a multitude of talents. Did you know we are from Southern Europe – the Balkans in fact?"

We visited him rarely and although I suspected he had a great deal of knowledge, this was the first time he had talked to me directly about anything so interesting. I faced him. "Really? Wow! Father never told me that. Where exactly?"

"Ah well that is the biggest question. That is for you to find out I think. There is a family tree I have drawn up somewhere. I will find it for you. In the mean time I want to give you this." He leaned forward, and lifted an old brown-coloured book off of the table in front of him. "Here. Take it," he said thrusting it towards me.

I was a little nervous but gladly cradled the heavy old book in my hands. I turned it so that I could read the spine. 'A History of the

Supernatural and Mythical Beasts and Customs of Central and Southern Europe' by Edgar de Boulon.

"I knew him you know – Edgar. Yes, I even contributed some of the passages myself. There is more to our family than you know yet, my little Lord. Yes. Read this if you are interested, as I am sure you are, or will be soon. Have you heard of the Knights Templar?"

"Ummm." I wanted to say I had but I hadn't. "No."

"Well. They know secrets and they will help you but do not become a slave to them. And do not hesitate to ask me if you have any questions. Write them down for when you visit me next time. Now I think you had better go. They will be waiting for you."

"Goodbye Grandfather." I held out my hand and he took it and shook it before placing his other hand on top of mine.

"Goodbye my son."

I had a strong feeling secrets were about to be revealed to me as I climbed into the car, clutching the old book.

* * *

Chapter Three

1 2, 3 5, 5 8, 4 6, 1 3, 3 5, 3 3 , 3 5, 2 4, 7 8, 3 6, 4 9

"From my reverie about my childhood, I look up at the sloping walls of the roof-space above the Cathedral. I listen intently for any sign of the Serpent but still I can hear nothing other than the distant sound of the organ below. I return to Rose's statement. It went on, 'I remember too how much you said the Bombing attack during the war also affected you. I also know that you have a greater capacity for getting to the truth than anybody else I have ever met." This made me smile and think about my spell in Intelligence.

Three years after the visit to my grandfather, Nazi Germany invaded Czechoslovakia. It was 1938 and I was already in the Air Cadets, then just created as the Air Defense Cadet Corps. Hendon Aerodrome asked for, and took, two cadets each from four of the local schools and ours was one of them. Of the five boys who volunteered, Paul and I, both good at sport and academically, had been put forward and excitedly attended preliminary parades, two evenings per week in an old hut in a cold corner of a local football ground. Paul was, in all ways a natural, but my eyes would have stopped me, were it not for the favours called in by my Headmaster. After a few months of drilling, aero-modeling, map reading and long hikes that left us exhausted but physically fitter each weeks, we were given our UNIFORMS – army dress but with the badge of the Air Defense. We were led at first by Squadron Leader Hennesy, a real Squadron Leader and one with a big moustache, although we later realised that he was retired from the RAF. He drilled us relentlessly into the night – static drill, basic drill – quick and slow, banner drill, band drill and other drills. Occasionally we would compete with other units at football or athletics – mostly during the week long camps at Easter and during the summer school holidays, and Paul and I met many friends who we would later go into combat with. My favourite exercise was probably what they called 'marksmanship' but we called 'shooting' in loud voices. We only had one old Lee-Enfield No.8 .22 rifle, which used to jam occasionally, inducing a healthy wariness in us, but the awed look on the other kid's faces in school WHEN YOU told them your average was up to seven on the range, was priceless. The best thing of all of course was flying but we had to wait a long time for that. Every few weeks we would meet at Hendon Aerodrome, and in our quiet corner of the airfield was a ragged old Tiger Moth which we were allowed to clean and fuss over. Occasionally when Hennesy wasn't around we would sit in it, of course and imagine what it would be like to get above the North London clouds.

As the spring of '39 crept in, we finally had our chance to fly. One Saturday, in the bone-penetrating damp air of Hendon, I left the ground far below me as Squadron Leader Hennesy took me for my first circuit. I had been the fourth in line as we leaned against the hut in our thickest coats, passing around a roll-up one of the boys had brought, and acting as if it really was nothing – both the CIGARETTE and the flying. I found myself humming 'Onward Christian Soldiers' to myself, a habit under stress which irritated me, and I instantly changed it into the 'High-Ho' song from 'Snow White and the Seven Dwarfs'.

The flight only lasted a few minutes and I don't think I felt the cold blast of air as I peered out over grey London with my hands lightly resting on the joy-stick, feeling Hennesy's movements in the cockpit behind me. I wanted so much to take control, but like the first time my father let me drive the Rover for a few yards in a country lane, I was nervous of the power of the beast. I think I remember having a grin that seemed to go right around my face the whole time I was in the air. I climbed out of the cockpit, back on the ground and my friends all patted me on the back.

"Your face!" said Paul, clutching his belly, laughing. "Its just white and red and your eyes are white goggles with tears just..." He couldn't finish the sentence.

"Wow! Paul, you wait. You will love it! I mean it's not fast – like a Hurricane, or 109 but its just like well I dunno. Ha! Ha!"

I woke up sweaty and heard an unfamiliar whining sound, like a moaning demon. The siren – which I soon realised was what it was, was followed shortly by a crump sound in the distance followed by a few more. I guessed what it was, and padded over to thE curtains to peer outside at the night sky. It was the first air-raid of my war and the pit of my stomach, so recently filled with never-ending feelings for Natalie, was suddenly filled with fear. There were a few flashes on the horizon and a few moments of vibration each time a bomb exploded, interspersed with the hornets drone of German bombers. I heard Nadia, quietly crying in the next room, and I was about to go to her when I heard my mother's voice gently comforting her.

Probably Heinkels.

I was caught in a fascination, not wanted to go back to bed, wanting, in a horrified way, to see something more, but soon it was all over and I went back to bed, and eventually, back to sleep.

It was not long before I TOO, was delivering bombs over the territory of the enemy. Flying low over the grey waves, we spied the Dutch coast ahead, and I raised the stick to bring the Blenheim over the pretty buildings on the sea front. The two Bristol Mercury engines roared at full revs and the voice of our navigator, Ferret, crackled thinly in my earphones.

"New heading skip. 270 degrees – expect flak in two minutes."

At that moment I had that feeling – of a malevolent presence and I knew an evil fortune was with us. Suddenly I felt complete calm come upon me, as if my centre had become a clear pool of water under the dappling sun. I was alert to what was going on around me but somehow I was separate from it.

It had been planned as a bold, day-time raid on docks, and we were to approach the docklands from inland after swing around from the South. If we surprised the Germans, their guns would be pointing the other way and we would get a good run at the warehouses along the quay-side.

The attack was a disaster. With fighters above us, we were forced to stay low and the Anti-Aircraft guns decimated the squadron, shooting down the Squadron Leader, leaving me, as SECOND-in-command, to save the rest of us. I turned back inland AFTER bombing, an intuitive move to outwit the enemy guns, and it seemed to be working UNTIL I found myself staring at quiet bit of airspace ahead of us, and thinking that something wasn't right.

"AA box!" I screamed into the mike. Breaking left! Tommy, call the others now!"

I gunned the engines and dipped the left wing, simultaneously looking over my left shoulder for any other planes that might be there. Recently we had heard of a new danger over Germany – the Anti-Aircraft Box. The idea was to train all one's guns on a small imaginary box in the sky, at a point where planes might fly, and wait for them to enter. Since the guns had already been calibrated it was then simple to launch a devastating rain of shells into that small box, bringing anything down that flew in it. As we reached about ninety degrees the first of the following planes entered the box and we heard the shelling begin.

"Too late for most I think skipper," called the gunner's mournful voice in my ear.

I jinked the plane right again to bring it around facing the route to the coast again and saw three of four planes explode.

"Four down skipper and me fockin leg hurts. I think I am hit."

"Okay, hold on Tommy. I can see cloud ahead. I will get us out of here."

"I know you will boyo."

There were just two planes following us, S-Sugar with onE other, and we had a bloody small chance of escaping now. There were at least twenty fighters above us, just waiting for us to get clear of the coastal guns. Our only chance was a patch of thunderclouds maybe five miles out which we had passed under on the way in at 200ft, avoiding the radar. Thankfully they were still there. We came under heavy fire from Me 109s, which shattered the windscreen in front of me, just before we reached the cloud. Ferret broke it with a Very pistol. The air at 200 mph was at least warm but blew everything loose around the cabin. The Blenheim shuddered as it struggled for height. I found myself humming 'Onward Christian Solders' which quickly became 'Hi Ho!'

The starboard engine coughed, as if answering me. I looked at it reproachfully, daring it to cough again. It didn't for several minutes but then coughed again, and then again. I was starting to feel angry now. Everything had gone against us, most of my friend had probably died, at the end, after surviving all this, the engine was going to die and we would die with it. The engine continued to cough for what seemed like an age and then finally I saw black smoke streaming out of the manifold. As we lost height and dropped out of the clouds I looked for fighters but they had all gone home.

Ferret appeared beside me and shouted in my ear, "Great Yarmouth five minutes skip. Think we can make the coast?"

We chucked everything out that we could to lighten the plane and I gunned the starboard engine to clear the cliffs at the coast but there was a large bang from the white-hot engine-cowling soon after and I had to stop it. Seeing the spires of Norwich ahead, I turned slightly North to take us around it and over Great Plumstead. We would never clear Norwich and if it had been any other county than flat Norfolk we wouldn't even have reached this far.

I brought us in to Horsham St. Faith gently and the Blenheim settled comfortably onto the long runway and we finally pulled up near the DISPERSAL area, smoke billowing out of the white hot engine and the plane surrounded by red fire-tenders and ambulances. I turned the engine off and we wearily climbed down and fell on to the grass. Willing hands carried us to the ambulances and as the doors closed I could see men using an axe on Tommy's gun position to get him out.

Neither Ferret nor I were too badly hurt and after patching up and a cup of coffee and a cigarette, something I only smoked in the direst moments, we were both taken for debriefing.

I gave a full account, only mentioning that I had had hunches about the AA Box and the explosion later. When asked what had happened to S-Sugar I said, "I don't know. Maybe he got hit by a fighter."

My story was taken down politely and then I was released to the mess where I had bacon and eggs. Before finishing, I managed to get some news about Tommy. After finding out he was going to be alright – out of action for a few months but alright, I went to my dorm. I was so tired I fell asleep immediately. The bed was welcoming and I fell immediately into the deepest sleep.

At BREAKFAST one of the reserve pilots came up to me. "You're wanted in Debriefing. What the fuck happened out THERE? You are the only bloody plane that came back. Everybody's talking – the whole bloody RAF. Nobody can ever remember anything like it."

I felt slightly angry at the question. "It was a bloody blood-bath. Thats what. It was a stupid plan from the start and then it just went wrong. And more wrong." I kept it short. I didn't want to say anything really. I didn't want to speak to anybody.

I went to the Debrief Room again. It was highly unusual to be debriefed twice.

H. W. Wolstencroft was sitting on the edge of the desk, relaxed and smiling, holding out a cup of black coffee, as I liked it, in a white enameled mug. I felt ill at ease.

"At ease. Sit down. This is just going to be an informal chat. We just want to clear up a few details. As you may know, everybody is talking about this one – quite a prank you pulled there. We are thrilled of course that you came back alright but your story doesn't agree with that of Flight Sergeant Ferris – or Sergeant Anton, although he could only give a brief statement given the state of his health right now. Now can you please start at the point where you say you suspected there was an AA Box. Where have you heard of such a thing?"

"Well, – err, I think I read about it in some flight magazine Sir. And we chaps talk about these sort of things – you know?" I didn't tell him about the tea I'd had with Paul a few weeks before. Paul had risen to the rank of Squadron Leader and then had a run in with a 109 and been wounded. He had some kind of post with Air Intelligence and we had chatted about AA boxes over tea in London.

"Not really. Boxes are not new, it's true. But as far as I know there have been very few cases during this war. What made you think there was one there?"

"It just seemed so quiet over the harbour. Too quiet."

"But Ferris said you thought the guns would have stood down anyway?"

My mind was working fast now as I didn't really want to go as far as to talk about my personal beliefs in this company, thinking they would be considered superstitions or worse. "Yes Sir."

"That was a question."

"Yes Sir. I don't know Sir. It was just a hunch I guess. I really cannot say."

He gave me a long cold stare looking right into my eyes from his perch with his sombre, Ministry brown eyes. We always suspected Wolstencroft – Wolsey as we called him – actually worked for the Secret Service in some capacity. He often seemed to have a sixth sense about things – as if he had some secret informants.

"Hmmm. Alright – moving on to the incident over the sea. Now you cannot tell me *that* was a hunch too?"

"Yes Sir. It was."

"Even though it meant nearly crashing into another plane? *And* there was absolutely no warning – couldn't have been?"

"Yes Sir."

"Yes Sir? You mean yes sir, you agree or yes sir, you have heard my question?"

"No Sir. I mean I am not that facetious Sir. I am saying that *is* what happened Sir. I know it's difficult to believe but I don't know what else to say."

"So I am to believe that you have had two very improbable hunches in one day which meant your survival when the whole of the rest of the squadron have been lost, possibly killed?"

"Err.. Yes Sir."

"Umm. Have you had these hunches before?"

I wondered for a moment whether to deny the truth but there was a steady look in his eyes. "Yes Sir. A few times – actually quite a few times."

"And has it saved your life?"

"I thought hard. "Maybe once. When we were training at Hendon Sir in the Cadets Corp. We were to take turns piloting an old Tiger Moth and I let somebody go ahead of me. He was really keen to go and I dunno.." I looked at my feet at this point – I felt a little ashamed. "I just felt a little apprehensive about it."

"Go on."

"So he went up first and the Moth collided with a Hurricane coming in to land. The Hurricane was okay but the Moth just fell out of the sky and hit a hanger. They were both killed."

Again he gave me one of his penetrating stares. "How did you feel about this?"

"At first I felt guilty about it. But I have tried hard to remember how I actually felt on the line and I know I did not consciously send somebody to do something I was not prepared to do."

"Okay. Let's leave it there. I WILL write up a report. You are free to go. One thing though. Don't talk to anybody else about this."

"No Sir." I saluted and left.

Two weeks later I was summoned to the Station Commander's Office and told I was being transferred to a night fighter squadron – flying Beaufighters. I was relieved. There had been a lot of talk about the Dutch mission and I often felt as if I was viewed with some suspicion by many on the station.

My time on night fighters was short. I guess I was drafted in because of my science qualifications. Airborne Radar in 1942 was in its early stages and there were many technical difficulties to sort out. On only the third mission my vision became blurred so that I could hardly see the instruments, let alone the exhausts of the German bombers I was supposed to be looking FOR, peering out into the moonless night. Then during a dawn landing my eye blurred at the crucial moment and we hit the ground REALLY hard, making my Radar Operator swear in the back. HOWEVER I had already been spending a lot of time on the station learning about the new black magic called Radar and my fascination combined with my experience with photography lead me to apply for a posting in Intelligence. After a brief spell at Boscombe Down, I was transferred to Harrogate.

I arrived at Harrogate by train, a little disappointed. I had hoped I would be assigned to Station X – Bletchley Park, but I was soon to learn that Air Intelligence was in fact the air component of M.I.6. I now learned why I had been stationed here. I was immediately put into the photo lab where my qualifications and experience in photography could be used. I fitted in very easily and found staff there very affable but perhaps my knack of avoiding malevolent forces had attracted attention in higher quarters. Was I the observer, developing the photographs to the highest quality possible, or was I being observed?

* * *

Chapter Four

- (13885,12613,12251,13200,13916,5099,2275,14055,13730,11755,4888,6421)

"I know it can't be long now before the Serpent puts in an appearance. Time is running out for it – its allotted month on Earth ends today so it has to show. I desperately need to find the Sword – this silver ornamental Sword that was the only weapon that could kill the Serpent, but still I have no idea where it is. If I cannot find the Sword my position is hopeless. I put these thoughts aside as I read on. She talks more about Annie and the effects of the tragedy on our marriage. 'No. What has drawn us steadily apart my darling is your refusal to include me in your deepest thoughts. I feel like a woman who has lost her place in the castle of your mind. It's very hard for me to go on. Yet I am hesitant to feel like this – not quite confident that I hold the ground that I once thought I did (not high, but maybe as high as yours). You were there and you saw what happened. I only have reports and briefings and rumours to keep me company. But I am a Mother first and my pain is too great to be healed by 'theories' and 'plans of attack'.' I looked away from Rose's statement for a moment. My memory of Annie's death is a never-healing wound, aggravated by the fact that I was the single witness, and still further by the disbelief of others. I went on reading. 'However, I know this is not your way, and that you need to find the truth in your own way. From the antiques shop in Sofia where you first picked up a wolf statue, to your pursuit of the truth about Annie, nobody could say you are not the most tenacious seeker of truth. In short, I wish you every success for the future my love, and I hope that one day you will find love again and perhaps remember what we had. Then you may forgive me. I know your first conclusion, given the passionate man that you are, will be that I simply do not believe in you any more. It is true that the whole drawn-out affair with Annie has been a severe drain on our emotional resources and I do not hold the same views as you, as to the 'how' and 'why' of her murder. It is also true that some have accused you of being the traitor, in some vague way that they usually cannot specify. I still know this about you however – that you loved Annie deeply and would never harm her.' I put down the statement.

I remember the antiques shop in Sofia had been where I met Rose and the farmhouse where we had spent our first night together."

I stayed with Air Intelligence until just after the Normandy landings in June 1944, and rose to the rank of Squadron Leader – a rank that amused me with its irrelevance. My day-to-day work continued with photography, although after coming up with a new developing process I moved on to interpreting photo information.

Shortly after D-Day I was visited by a man from 54 Broadway, London. He had a long mackintosh on, unusual for that time of year, and arrived after dark.

"I won't beat around the bush. We are looking for volunteers to do a little op for us in France. Similar work to what you are doing now. Not dangerous I don't think – well at least not front-line work but we need somebody with a bit of initiative and apparently you are just such a chap?" There was only the slightest question in the way he inflected the sentence. The job in France led later to another one in Bulgaria.

Bulgaria had started the war as a neutral country but had soon joined Germany and in fact invaded parts of Northern Greece on behalf of the Germans. A large resistance movement had opposed this and Britain had supplied them with money and arms. British and US agents had been in the country for years liaising with the resistance and generally trying to persuade the Government to side with Britain. On 8 September, a few weeks before I arrived there had been an unexpected development. The Government announced Bulgaria was joining the Russians. The British had apparently feared this and had lobbied hard against it but had failed. I was now going to be part of a team to try and reverse this decision. I was dropped in by parachute from an RAF Halifax with another agent who called himself Mr Blue. Our job initially, was to listen to radio traffic from local resistance groups and the NKVD – forerunner of the KGB, and pass on any useful information on to M.I.6. Later we would be given more active assignments. Sofia was where I met Rose.

Leaving the main market in Sofia capital of Bulgaria, I window-shopped down a side street and an old bell clanged as I pushed open the door to a dingy antiques shop. I had given in to the shop because it had an air of neglect; perhaps collectors might have missed something ancient – something hiding in the shadows. Circling the centre table with its piles of leather-bound, finger-browned volumes, I resisted the urge to run my fingers across their sensual surfaces, remembering how I had been allowed to do this for a moment at my grandfather's that time. I lifted the cover of one very large book and then lowered it in disappointment.

"I'll have that wrapped," I heard a clipped strong feminine voice say to the shopkeeper in perfect Bulgarian. The shopkeeper replied quietly in more colloquial Bulgarian – words I didn't quite pick up.

"It's for my niece. For when she gets older," she said.

I was drinking in the whole atmosphere of the shop – sound, light, dust on my fingers, which was such a relief from the daily grind of intelligence.

She knocked my elbow as she passed on her way to the door, and I glanced in surprise – saw her scowl at me, but I couldn't think why. I shook my head slowly and muttered, 'Rude'.

"It's fake you know," she said to me in crisp English, just as my glance returned to the books.

"Oh? How do you know?"

Turning away from me she muttered something under her breath before wrenching the door open and striding off towards the market in her raincoat and scarf – red shoes clippetting on the paving.

I glanced at the sallow, deflated old man behind the till, for reinforcement, but the antiquarian's glance had already returned to a book at the end of his nose.

"Hey. What is this?" I said to myself, a few moments after my eyes first rested on the bronze sculpture, hanging by as piece of string on the side of a bookcase. I could easily have missed it, had I not had the word 'wolf' glowing neon in his mind during my search. It was some kind of satyr, with hind legs of a goat, chest and arms of a man but a woolly mane and eyes and snout of what looked like – a wolf! I hefted it – a dealer's trick to distinguish bronze from lead or copper, and it felt good. I ran my index finger down its neck to feel its rough metal-fur mane. It was only about six inches high so would get through customs without any difficulty.

I paid for the little statue, and left. I didn't think I would see the woman again but I did, one night a week later.

It was late – I was late, and I was walking quickly through the shiny streets back to our little office, taking a shortcut. I had dipped into a an old cinema, to see a film I had never heard of, meaning to leave before 10 pm but I had fallen asleep. I heard the sharp clatter of high heels moving quickly towards me from the street ahead. As she came right up to me, I tried to work out who she was. She fell right into my arms, crying.

I was shocked for just the tiniest instant but then my instincts cut in and I enveloped her in his arms, and quickly moved towards the shelter of a shop doorway. It was the girl with the red shoes.

"What's wrong?" I asked her in Bulgarian.

She shook her head. "I cannot tell you."

I was wondering how she found me? Was it coincidence? Is she a Russian agent. I was wary but her hands felt warm and warm women's hands are honest hands, I thought, noticing a curious bronze-coloured ring in the shape of a coiled-snake on her finger. I instinctively raised her chin with my fingers to look into her eyes to see what I could read there.

She looked terrified.

I heard men's voices shouting out. I knew she was in trouble. I moved further into the doorway hoping the dark of the night would hide us both as the men passed.

"Who are they and what do they want you for?"

Her eyes were liquid pools of passion and pain and I could resist them no longer. I leaned into her and I kissed her soft ruby lips. Yes, I really badly wanted to do that.

Softly, so softly with her lips, she held my kiss for a few seconds, then pulled away, slapped my face and ran away into the night.

Oh no! Not again! Damn. This woman will kill me.

She had a really hard shell but I remembered something in the kiss. Something so soft and innocent and lovely, I already missed it even though I could never have imagined its existence a moment before. Her full name was Rose Nikolaeva Paneva and Iater found out that she was the sole-survivor of a resistance group called the Jazz Club Gang and used the codename Dora. It turned out that M.I.6 very much to get Dora and her baggage back to London. I was to accompany her – when I had located her. This proved to be a very difficult and dangerous task, but after a chance surveillance photograph allowed me to identify her by that unusual snake ring, a meeting was set up using a go-between and I finally managed to win Dora's trust. We were not out of the woods yet, however as the documents we needed were hidden in a cave in the mountains. A gunfight ensued during which I shot my first man, and a car chase, which ended in an overnight stay at a farmhouse owned by her friend who I knew only as 'Bear'. It was in that farmhouse that the chemistry of wartime comradeship turned into the chemistry of love for Rose and I. After a narrow escape from more of the NKVD we finally made it back to Sofia with the documents. I was sure somebody had put in a good word for me, and we were on the next flight out on a Lysander.

By the time Rose was fully debriefed, war in Europe was over and she was not inclined to do any more spy-work so she started her civilian life. I remained in London, acting as a liaison officer for her but I was looking for a change of career. Rose and I continued to see each other and our romance blossomed. In September 1945, we were married and moved to a little house in Wales. It reminded Rose of the mountains around Sofia and it was as far away from the war and spies as we could get. I commuted up to London each week and stayed with Paul who was now a Civil Servant in the Foreign Office. I dropped subtle hints that I was interested in joining too, and he pulled some strings. I attended an interview at Whitehall and soon enough I was pushing a pen for the Government.

Meanwhile, things were not going so well in Wales. Rose was happy enough pottering out in the considerable garden, planting flowers and joining in local community projects, but soon she grew bored. It was my first experience of what women wanted being something completely different to what they said they wanted. Now she wanted somewhere closer to London and so, with the help of my parents, and some cash I had saved, we moved to a small 2-up, 2-down just outside Reading – close enough to get to London in two hours.

Just before we left Wales, I was standing in the lounge one day, with a cup of tea, looking out of the window at the beautiful garden under the bright July sun, when I noticed the little bronze figurine from Bulgaria standing on the sill. I had put it there when we unpacked and it hadn't been moved or touched since. I picked it up and hefted it in my hand. I turned it over to look at the base. There were some crude characters scratched into the bronze, or into the mould that created it – it was hard to say. I had noticed it in Sofia but never had time to ask anybody what it meant.

"B'vs IV sk" The 'sk' was in very small script.

I wished now that Rose and I had had time to visit the place in the North she had mentioned, where there were many such statues.

I went in search of Rose. "Rose, are you sure you have seen more like this in Bulgaria? The workmanship seems more French than Bulgarian"

"Umm Hmm. Definitely. They are made in Bulgaria I think. They are considered a sort-of charm in the mountains. Wolves can be a big problem there but many years ago – I mean in medieval times, some worshipped a minor god who took the form of a wolf-man."

"Hmm. That's really interesting. My grandfather once told me a tale that the earliest known of our family had run away from Prague to

France because he and his young wife had been attacked by a flying wolf and she had been killed and eaten. My father thinks it is a total fabrication and told me to pay no attention to these tales. There was a distance like a gulf between my father and grandfather – an acknowledged gulf as if something had happened many years ago and neither made any attempt to bridge the gulf."

"Were you close to your grandpa?"

"Well, not really close but he fascinated me and I felt a lot of affection for him. We all did, except my father."

Rose held out her hand and I placed the little statue in it. She turned it over and read the markings. "Yes, it does seem French. How strange – but who knows."

"Maybe you could take me to that place Rose? How would you like to take a holiday there? Your last name is mine now so nobody would spot you at customs and you could keep sunglasses on all the time or die your hair."

"Oh could we? You know I didn't want to say but I ree-ally miss it! Oh I am not worried about being spotted, I think it would be quite exciting."

So it was, a month later that I found myself in a bazaar in a little mountain town called Gomi Lom, not far from the Romanian and Yugoslavian border and within the same mountain range that extended up into Romania.

"Oh look at this!" said Rose, tugging at the sleeve of my jacket. It was only a locally woven rug and I was keen to find anything to do with wolves. I had the little statue with me in my pocket and not knowing what I was looking for, I looked for something like this. We had hired a car and parked it on the edge of the town and now we were jostling with the locals who were after food and clothes.

"Where are the wolves?" I asked playfully.

"Oh, you are so impatient. we will get to them soon. Just be patient." She pulled me into a shop to buy locally made bread, and catching the look in my eyes of patience almost expired, she led me to an arched alcove in the town wall. Behind an ancient and rickety table sat an old woman with current eyes in face like an old loaf. She eyed us suspiciously, especially Rose, until Rose asked her something in Bulgarian. The woman smiled at me then and pointed to the back of the alcove. There on a crate, at knee height, were just what I had been looking for. Four little statues stood there, similar to the one I had – two of them identical in fact, and on the floor beside the crate, something much larger. I knew it would be too expensive but I had to look at it. It was about two feet high and was a confidently carved statue of a wolf-satyr, battling a snake, just as large, entwined around it. What was unusual to somebody who was already familiar with the wolf-men statues was that the snake had tiny horns, The old woman cackled something behind me and warily I glanced at her. She seemed to be indicating I should lift it which I then did, with some difficulty as it weighed about fifty pounds. I turned it over in my hands to see the base and I could just glimpse something similar to my little statue. I couldn't hold it up long enough to look.

"Write down what it says. There is a pencil an notebook in my jacket pocket," I said to Rose.

"I can't do that. It would be an insult to her. If we are not going to buy it then we shouldn't let her know. I will memorise it and then write it down outside the shop."

"Alright. Got it?"

"Yes."

I put it down and guided Rose out of the shop, smiling at the proprietor who watched us with suspicion.

"Right. Where next?"

We searched through many shops and stalls that day but never found anything nearly so interesting as the tall statue, so when we had exhausted all other opportunities, we went back there. The old women cackled as we entered the alcove. She said something to Rose.

"What did she say?"

"She told me it's original. Not like the others. She said there is no other like it."

"Hm. I bet." However, as I looked more closely I began to believe her. The smaller statues which were identical to my own, each had a patina that one associates with fairly new bronze statues. Also the edges were still sharp and there was not the discoloration you get with very old bronzes. It was just possible it was an original. My own statue had always given me a good feeling when I handled it, as if it were giving off some good energy. I always felt as if the person who made did so with good intentions – something that what Rose had told me about locals worshipping such a god, seemed to confirm. The energy I felt from the large statue was of a different order of magnitude entirely.

"Ask her where she got it, dear." The woman shrugged and said something to Rose.

"She says they come from all over. There is never one single source. She says many believe that once they were kept in the castles all around these mountains, and in Romania, and that when the castles were captured during wars in Medieval times, the looters sold these things onto the market and they have been here ever since.

I ran my hands over the big statue again. I wanted it but I wasn't sure if it was original, and worth anything. The old woman could see my indecision.

She said "It's real," in Bulgarian that I could just understand, now I was getting used to her dialect, spoken as it was by someone with hardly any teeth. "Some of those statues are fake but that one is original. Two hundred dollars"

I whistled. "Two hundred. No way. Seventy."

She cackled and slapped her knee. "One hundred and fifty," she said.

"Ninety," I said.

"I must go to cook. Take it one hundred and forty or leave," she said, and started to take things from display on the front of her table.

"One hundred," I said, but I it was a half-hearted offer and she knew it. I knew now I would have to pay her more than I wanted.

She indicated I should go away with her hand, palm towards me. "Leave the shop," she said, and the look in her eye was of one who was determined to hold her ground.

I was unsettled by this so I quickly offered one hundred and forty.

"Yes," she said, and held out her hand. I had to search my pockets to find the amount. It was almost all I had.

Back in the car, Rose showed me her note of the markings on the bottom of the statue. This one had slightly different markings on the bottom. It had the usual 'B'vs' but then it had the roman numeral 'V' and 'ep' instead of 'IV' and 'sk'.

The rest of the holiday passed almost without incident. Rose met her remaining brother, who had been in hiding until the end of the War. Then in a bazaar near Sofia, where I would have least expected to find anything of interest, I saw another little wolf-satyr statue. At first I smiled to myself as they were ten-a-penny, but then I saw that there was something different about this one. I picked it up and it felt different – worn, with the sharp edges removed. Also it had a very mottled pattern on its surface, typical of really old bronzes. This one also had the 'B'vs', the roman numeral 'V' and 'ep', just like the large statue which confirmed for me that it was different to the rest. Perhaps both this and the large statue were made by a master craftsman and the others by a copier or apprentice.

"God! It must be original!"

"Not another one! You and your wolf-men. Can't you leave it. We have enough stuff," said Rose.

"No, this is different. Until now I only half believed the story that they were originally talismans. Now I believe it."

I bought it and added it to the increasing collection I was bringing back to England. Friends would later offer me good money for some of the antiques and we went back the following year to start what became, over time, a small antiques business. Shortly after the second trip, I heard, on the grapevine, that a post would be available in Sofia for a British Diplomat, and after talking it through with Rose, I applied. It wasn't long before I received a letter of acceptance. My experience during the War must have been in my favour, but it would not surprise me if Paul again hadn't spoken up for me. He smiled when I asked him.

"They just asked me for a reference."

We had a few months before we were to leave, and not wanting to take our feet completely off of the property ladder, Rose and I took a holiday in Burgundy to look for a small cottage there. After the War, the French railways had remained completely destroyed until now. Recently the Orient Express had began running regular services again and passing through Sofia, it went on to Lausanne and then into France at Lyon, before reaching Paris. Not far south from Lyon was the town of Nevers. It seemed fairly sleepy which suited us, but still had good amenities and communications. Property was cheap there too, and we soon found a small cottage which needed some work, about five miles north of the town. We received the keys from the irascible previous owner, and sat in the dusty lounge on sheet-draped furniture for only about ten minutes, before leaving. An old black, white and brown cat sat licking its paw on a wall around the front garden and glanced at us blankly as we drove by. I thought I could detect some Gallic inscrutability in its green eyes but Rose just said "Ahh."

The job of Envoy, as my title now was, was at first fairly mundane. We had a nice flat in one of the more salubrious suburbs of Sofia, and I spend much of the day reading and responding to diplomatic correspondence. I knew that I would have to endure a few years of this before progressing onto more interesting work, so I just decided to get on with it. In the mean time, since the salary I earned was so substantial, paid as I was in pounds, against the local currency, I had no trouble at all accumulating a great deal of antique artifacts, and where they turned out not to further my own study, I boxed them up and shipped them back to my parents' house in Highgate. Selling these would be a 'nice little earner' for me and would offer some security against the vagaries of diplomatic life. A rude word here or insensitive remark were sometimes all that was necessary to end a career.

The house in Nevers turned out to be a very good idea. If we left Sofia late on Friday we could take a sleeper and then have all weekend in the French countryside before catching the train back on Sunday night and waking up just in time for work on Monday. We could also meet friends in Paris if we stayed longer, and sometimes family came from England or we would go there. We also started camping in the beautiful region around Nevers. Camping really caught on as a craze around this time and we bought a full-sized tent which would accommodate deck chairs and a double mattress as well as a stove. It was made of canvass and there was a trailer available for it, which we bought, to tow behind an old Citroën I had also bought. At first we struck out in any direction, reveling in the freedom that camping brought, but we soon homed in on the Forêt de Folin, a forest, about 40 miles East of Nevers, in gentle rolling hills. It was almost unspoiled, with hardly a house to be found in a day's walk.

I read my grandfather's book during one of these camping trips and discovered many interesting and strange things. Early on in the book there was a description of a secret temple to the Ordo Lupus – which translates as 'Brotherhood of the Wolf', or perhaps not so secret, as there was a newspaper-clipping taped into the book describing the Aachen Temple, which is entered by the Wolf Door, named after the legendary wolf who apparently tricked the Devil out of possession of the temple. The Temple was built by Charlemagne and contains his bones. The book went on to describe flying Wolf Men in Bulgaria. None of this helped me understand the markings on the bases of the statues I had collected. The latter parts of the book talked in more detail about history of this supposed secret society, the Ordo Lupus. One, most interesting part of the book, described how the Ordo Lupus had been a breakaway sect from The Knight's Templar and that even earlier than this, one of the two monks who had escaped from Montségur Castle during the persecution of the Cathars in the 13th Century with a mysterious treasure, had been the founder of the Ordo Lupus.

There was also a description – in an unrevealed location, of a secret chamber in the roof of a Cathedral, which contained the stone coffers of many former members of the Brotherhood, and also mention of female seductresses – servants of both the evil snakes and the good Wolf-Men. Finally there was a description which was the most fascinating of all – of flying Snakes which were invisible and 'constricted' the fabric of the world making evil things happen to people, and living off the souls of the dead. The images were almost Biblical – difficult, and at first I didn't take it too seriously.

It was in the winter of this year, 1947, that Rose and I realised there was something wrong with our marriage. At first the sly family references to children were taken in good spirit by us, but then when questions started appearing in letters, I started to feel uncomfortable. Eventually Rose and began to feel pressure in our love-making, which had always been glorious and I still thought she was the most beautiful woman I had ever seen. We talked about it, and I regret to say, in those uninformed times, when she volunteered to see a doctor alone about it, I simply agreed. The doctor in London said there was absolutely nothing wrong with her and that we should go on trying. We did, but by the following summer we were both feeling the strain.

We took a break in Burgundy and packed for a one-week camping trip to Forêt de Folin. We were starting to avoid talking to each other and during the journey to the forest, window down, wind tussling her brown curls, Rose stared out of the window and smoked – something she had recently taken up. I wanted to say something and spent hours trying to think what to say.

After we had found a nice spot under some trees, not far from a stream and small waterfall, we set up the tent and then I poured us both a tumbler of sherry. We sat back in the deck chairs and watched the sunset with the glasses in our hands. As usual there was a silence between us, but it was peaceful, encroached as it was by birdsong.

"It feels like we have been married a lifetime," joked Rose. We both laughed but it was like watching a stone fall into an abyss.

I stood up quickly. "I'll get the chocolate."

Rose caught my hand. "Wait." I looked at her and she smiled up at me and in her eye I saw that glint of female desire and longing.

I pulled away from her as gently as I could. I didn't want to say I wasn't in the mood and I didn't need to. Inside I felt self-loathing though. I knew I had finally reached a point where I feared making love. I feared the pressure of needing to get her to conceive, of creating a new life. It was becoming not just a performance, but a battle, and increasingly we were on opposite sides. I was so close to hating her, I had to push the thought from deep inside me. I had seen many other marriages go that way, for other reason,s and now I just wanted to delay the inevitable.

"I'm going for a walk," I said as lightly as I could, but my voice sounded heavy, aggressive and dark.

"God! It doesn't matter!" she screamed after me, her suddenly hoarse cry excoriating the air.

I walked and walked, kicking weeds and undergrowth as I went, for what seemed hours, when in truth it must only have been twenty minutes. Dusk was fast throwing its night-blanket over the beauty of the forest, but it was still light enough to make out details, as I reached a rocky outcrop just above a place where two streams entwined. The mad tumble of fluorescing foam calmed me for a moment, and I stopped still. Suddenly I noticed a slight movement from the corner of my eye – something that wasn't a branch moving in the slight breeze. Remembering where I was, I was cautious and glanced, rather than looked at the place of motion. On a rock, its back highlighted by the purplish light on the horizon, was a wolf, looking directly at me. I cold chill ran down my spine and I stood stock-still. It seemed without fear, and its yellow-orange eyes were staring mercilessly through me.

We stood still looking at each other for the longest breath. We both seemed to be waiting for something, listening for something, I couldn't tell any more if I was breathing or not and then I saw the wolf exhale, its nose flaring slightly. As if it had caught a sound in the distance it glanced away and in one smooth movement was gone.

I didn't move for several minutes at least. I was overwhelmed by the moment – the privilege of being so close to something so wild. I turned back for our little camp and as I walked, I realised I felt completely calm and at ease with myself. I reached he camp and Rose was getting ready for bed. She didn't speak, as I started to undress. I didn't speak either and this prompted a question from her.

"You were gone a long time?"

"A strange thing happened. I saw a wolf."

"Really?" She seemed as amazed as I was.

"Yes, But you know – I really saw it. I mean we looked right at each other. It was strange."

"Tell me about it," she said and I saw her reach towards my forearm but then pull back, too nervous to touch me. I felt a stab of remorse, and, taking a deep breath, I pulled her towards me. I had intended simply to hold her and tell her about the experience but then I kissed her and then kissed her again, more deeply. Her lips yielded and her body seemed to melt at my touch.

I started to pull at the blouse she had just been undoing when I entered the tent, but I wasn't bothering with the buttons. I couldn't wait to see her naked body.

"Oh yes, Darling."

As I quickly undressed her and kissed her all over, I felt that she was giving herself to me more completely than ever before. We moved like birds on the breeze as they take flight for some distant dark and secret land.

She said, "I want you so much."

I felt an indescribable wave rise inside me which I was sure I could not ride and yet I opened my eyes and looked at her and knew with her it would be alright. I knew that she was with me and I shuddered slightly as I looked to her to see where to go – what to do. "Are you with me?" I said.

We reached the final crest of the final wave together and I collapsed on top of her, exhausted but very happy. She held on to me and we lay like that for a while, breathing hard.

I wanted to say, "What was that?" but I knew she had felt the same thing and words seemed unnecessary. It had been an incredible experience and I felt as if something special had happened.

It was about four weeks later, back in Sofia that I found Rose sitting neatly on the sofa when I came home from work. Normally she would still be bustling about or at the very least, reading a magazine. She was looking straight at me.

"Hi darling. Everything alright?"

"I am pregnant."

I gave her a long, penetrating stare, before realising she was telling the truth.

"But that's wonderful!" I shouted, hauling her to her feet, lifting her up and swinging her about as I kissed her furiously.

"Bloody great! Bloody fantastic! At last."

I rushed out and bought the biggest bottle of fake Dom Pérignon Champagne I could find and we invited all our friends round to break the news.

After another thirty-six weeks Annabel was born, and two years later Edward.

Eventually I retired from the Civil Service to take up the antiques trade full time. We spent about half our time in Nevers and half in London, and we were wealthy and relatively happy, as the kids grew up.

So what of my encounters with evil? Sometimes it was mild, as if I had a demon running about, turning on all my taps, but sometimes it was a much more focused genius, a vile intellectual presence, as it was on the worst day of my life.

This most terrible day dawned ordinarily enough. I was walking Annabel to school in Nevers. My antiques business had really taken off by this time – I had an office in London, another in Paris and a large one in Sofia, with a small office and one secretary in Nevers, where I organised it all. Usually I would drop Annie off on my way to work, leaving her only about half a mile to walk through town. She was fifteen and quite capable of the walk on her own. However on this day she had exams and had been fretting about them the night before, so I said I would walk her to school when I kissed her goodnight. She smiled up at me, saying 'Thank you Daddy'.

I parked the car on the outskirts of town and we started off, reaching one of the main streets within a few minutes. I looked at Annie at my side and marvelled at her long, dark, curly hair. I often thought she looked like a gypsy, no less when her dark brown eyes looked questioningly at me. Even now, at fifteen, there seemed a lively skip in her gait as she walked. When she was a small child she had always been running – running to see what was behind something or round a corner.

I was feeling a growing sense of unease and I took hold of her soft hand. This feeling of unease is difficult to explain if you haven't felt or recognised it. It feels as if one is stepping closer and closer to an abyss. One feels one's confidence, 'sense of rightness' and safety all being stripped away from you. It was once best described by a soldier who survived the Normandy Invasion as being like 'balancing on the head of a pin'. Disaster was close at hand and the day could go either way. As we neared a busy intersection of four roads, I suddenly pulled Annie away from the corner and pressed her against the wall.

"Daddy! What are you doing? Is this another one..."

There was an almighty crash and the sound of scraping, breaking metal as a car left the road and careened towards us. I hardly had time to shout "Annie!" before it hit the corner of the wall, just where she had been standing moments before.

"Daddy," she whispered, and clutched me tightly. Annie had seen these moments of foresight before so she wasn't surprised, but this was the closest she had come to being killed.

Fortunately the driver was not injured and after a stream of profanities he stepped from the car and asked our forgiveness. We stood by until the Gendarmes arrived and cordoned off the area and ushered the crowd away.

My hand was shaking and beads of sweat were dripping from my brow as we went on towards the school. I said quietly under my breath, “Annie. We must be very careful.” She nodded silently.

We turned into a quiet street where there was no traffic and cut a corner off our journey. The sense of an ‘evil presence’ was overpowering me and I felt rather than saw things moving in and out of my vision. I felt nauseous.

I stopped and looked around me.

This can’t be right.

That was when the air split and the Serpent stepped out from eternity to take Annie from me.

* * *

Chapter Five

3236, 6194, 126, 2049, 277, 250, 251

"The note from Rose goes on. 'You are closer now to your friend Henry than you are to me. That is all I have to say really.

On a practical note, I want to keep the house in Nevers – you rarely come there any more anyway and Edward still feels that it is his home.'

She was always resentful of the relationship I had built up with Henry. For me, the aftermath of Annie's death was a need to investigate, myself, what had actually happened and get to the truth. I had never revealed the truth of what I thought had happened to the Gendarmes, simply because they wouldn't believe me. I had, however told Rose."

Thursday, 3rd of August – seven days ago, started like many other days. An eye opened, forced to do so by the spike of light that pierced the grey airlessness of the office, through a commercial blind, at the top left of the window. I nearly fell off the sofa before realising, once again, that I was on the sofa, and not a bed. I finally struggled to the small fridge which had a kettle on a tray on top of it. There was a dirty mug beside the kettle with a tea-caked spoon inside the mug. I pressed the red button and leaned against the sofa until the cloud of hot vapour filled the room. It has to be said this is probably my favourite time of day as nothing has usually gone wrong yet. With milk from the fridge, I finished making the tea and sat back down on the sofa to enjoy the tranquility of half-wakedness. Then it was time to get ready. I clumsily tore open the packaging of the new electric razor I had bought, and put the two big batteries in it. Then I walked into the small room with a toilet and shower, which passed as a bathroom, and placed the shaver on the topmost of two shelves above, and to the left, of the toilet, and under the tiny frosted-window near the ceiling. I found a pair of grey flannel trousers that were almost clean, and swapped my only belt from the previous day's trousers onto this pair, but as I did so the pin on the buckle became somehow bent in the wrong direction and broke off! Cursing, I suddenly stopped and listened. I had heard a loud bang from the bathroom. I was sure of it. I walked into the room and looked around. I could see nothing amiss. Shrugging my shoulders, I walked out and considered what to do about the belt. I didn't have time now to buy a new one, but I had plenty of money and I could buy one later. So I took a ball of string from a stationary drawer in the main reception room downstairs, and cut off a length to use as a temporary replacement. I would wear a long pullover to cover it. As I cut the string with a blunt pair of scissors they nicked my finger slightly but the cut was not too bad. Sucking my finger I looked proudly at my trousers, held around my waist now by fine white string. I boiled the kettle again, but this time took the cup off of a thermos flask and poured the hot water into it, with the two last tea bags.

I walked back into the bathroom to shave. Where was the razor? It was nowhere to be seen! I swore and went back out into my main office and searched for it, but I couldn't find it. I went back into the bathroom and, placing my hands on my hips, I tried to recall events a few minutes earlier. With some clarity, I remembered putting the razor on the top shelf. I eyed the toilet suspiciously. The toilet seat was down, which was a bad sign. I rarely closed the seat before going to bed. Saying a little prayer under my breath I walked over and lifted the lid. A cream razor-shaped rectangle shimmered below the surface of the water. I would have laughed if it hadn't been so awkward. The razor must have somehow slipped off the shelf, which was very smooth, and bounced sideways off the shelf below, into the toilet, making the lid close in the process. None of this was unusual and I simply lifted the razor out of the water, and placed it to dry on a tea-towel on the fridge. It was probably ruined but only time would tell. The annoying thing was that I needed to take a razor with me.

So my demon is in a lighthearted mood today.

I had packed most of what I needed in my old black leather bag the night before – maps, spare clothes and a raincoat, an envelope with most of the 9000 guineas, a few books, a notepad with important telephone numbers on, and pens. To the inventory now, I added the sandwiches from the fridge, which I had bought in the boulangerie the day before, the thermos of tea and various cakes and croissants from the pâtisserie. I looked around the room and added the original little bronze flying wolf statue, which I had kept in the office since Rose and I had started drifting apart. Finally I was ready, and stood to take one last look around the room before leaving.

The telephone rang and I jumped. I forgot to mention the name of my company as I answered.

"Hello?"

"Hello. Are you the man who was in the Richelieu Library last week?"

I thought for a moment. "Yes, I was."

"My name is Georgina. I was the dark haired girl in the afghan coat."

"Really?" I sat up in my chair. I should have asked immediately how she'd found my number but I was too flattered. "What can I do for you?"

"Well its nothing really. I just saw your face in Le Monde and I believe you are innocent and there is something I want to talk to you about."

My mind was doing back-flips. "In the paper? Me?" Are you sure?"

"Oui!" She laughed. "Have a look at today's edition."

"I don't have it here. What does it say?"

She read the whole article to me. Basically, paraphrasing, it amounted to 'suspect called in for questioning on Crusher Killer murders'. It mentioned my name and Nevers and said that the Gendarmes believed I had been in each of the locations of the murders at the right times. "There is even a grainy photograph of you." She described it and I recognised it as one which was taken a few years ago at a business lunch with the Mayor of Nevers.

"Oh no!" I said out loud. "How could they do this?" It felt like they were putting pressure on me – a known police tactic when they believed someone was the culprit but couldn't prove it.

"Don't worry. I know you didn't do it."

"Do you? You are one of the few people who does," I said sarcastically.

"I think I may be able to help you."

"Really? How did you get my number?"

"Oh you would be surprised what a girl can do with a little wiggle and wink at an old librarian."

I thought for a moment and then remembered that I had left my contact details behind the counter in the research room of the library.

"I am just going out actually and I may be gone for a few days."

"No problem. Let me give you my number at home." She told me the number and for a moment I was not going to write it down, but then while she was talking I memorized it, and reached over, stretching the receiver cable to take a pen from the bag, and wrote it on the notepad.

"In Paris?" I asked.

"Um hm."

"I have to go. What is your name again?"

She laughed. "Georgina." Now I was equating the name with her face, I didn't think it would be hard to remember.

"Okay Georgina. I have your number. I will call you."

"Bye then!" She had put the receiver down. I threw the pen and notepad back in the bag, zipped it up, pulled a jacket on and grabbed the car keys. On impulse, I grabbed the wet shaver too, and threw it in the bag before leaving. On my way through the reception I noticed a white envelope in the pile of mail on the floor, by the door, with my Rose's handwriting on it. I picked it up and stuffed it in my jacket pocket. It was dawn and Nevers was still deserted as I started the Citroën and drove north.

I needed to get away for a few days. My plan was to pick up the camping gear from our house and then drive to our favourite camping area, via Lyon, where I wanted to pick up the photocopy sheets with translated passages from Henry. As I left Nevers I looked in my mirrors and noticed that a little red DAF, behind me when I left the office, was still behind me. I took a right-turn which I knew would bring me back to my route via a left turn later on, but when I was back on course, the DAF was still behind me. "Police," I said out loud.

I pulled up on the driveway of our house and rang the bell but Rose didn't answer. Surprised, I used my key to unlock the door and went inside to make a cup of strong coffee. The house looked exceptionally tidy and Rose was not there. Looking out of the landing window, I could see the little DAF through the trees, parked at the end of the drive, on the main road. The driver was not in the car. I would have to lose him.

I backed the car up to the trailer and set about checking all the gear under the tonneau cover, on the trailer. I left the tonneau loose, and then locked the car. I stood around for about a minute, to make sure I had been noticed, and then set off cross country for a little walk. I was sure I could loose the tail, and he wouldn't be able to resist following. Sure enough from the corner of my eye, after I had walked for a few hundred metres, I could see a flash of green and white moving erratically some way behind me. I walked into a heavily wooded area, and started down a track which wound on for several miles. Knowing how it changed direction at fairly steady intervals, I increased my pace until I was just in view of the tail, at the end of each section. This would surely lull him into a false sense of security. When I was almost at the end of the wooded section, I turned left into the trees and made my way to another, smaller track, which led at an oblique angle back towards the house. The main track led into more woods about two hundred metres further on over the other side of a field. The tail would have a dilemna to deal with when he reached this spot. Could I have reached the woods on the other side or did I turn left or right? He would have to make a decision and then he would have to search. Within twenty minutes I was back at the house and quickly moved the tent, containers and generator into the back of the car. I tied down the tonneau cover and drove North. I never saw the red DAF again. After traveling North for ten miles I turned East and later South towards Lyon. I turned up an isolated track and unhitched the trailer. I could travel much faster without it, and further than they would estimate if the Gendarmes were to set up road blocks. I transfered the tent, and a few other things into the back of the car. As I drove towards Lyon, and Henry, I turned something over in my mind – something that had really started to bother me. Annie's was the only death by the Warg that I knew of, which didn't fall into the pattern of the sixty year cycles. What did it mean? Were there other deaths which hadn't been recorded, or was Annie in some way special? And then another thought started to nag at the very edge of my brain. Was I special? Was Annie just, in fact, a victim in some larger struggle, an innocent bystander? I mulled this morosely for some time and then let it drop.

One other thing that I had filed away for thought in a quiet moment like this, was who told the Gendarmes that I was in Lyon the night of the most recent murder? I puzzled this out in my mind but I could find no answer that made sense. I reached Henry's flat in the middle of the afternoon. I parked some way off from the flat in another street.

"Henry. You will never guess what has happened to me."

"The Gendarmes have been here dear boy!"

"What? When?"

"Yesterday afternoon, about three."

"Hm. About the same time I was taken in for questioning."

"You were?"

"Yeah. They didn't have any evidence but they took a long time to release me, and have been following me ever since."

"They followed you here?" Henry was trying to sound calm but the timbre of his voice rose slightly at the end of his question.

"No. I lost them. I want to go away though, for a few days. Somewhere they won't find me. They suspect me of the murders Henry. I don't know why. I don't know how they even knew I was here on the night of the last murder. I think – no, I am sure they believe I killed Annie. Which makes me really angry!"

"Yes. My dear boy. We have to do something!"

"What did they ask you? Did they ask you about me?"

"Yes, they asked about you. But mainly they wanted to know what we were doing together that night and exactly what time you left – which actually I told them I couldn't remember."

"But what I don't understand is how they even came to suspect me in the first place!"

"I don't know dear boy." Henry wasn't meeting my gaze as he said this. For a moment I thought even Henry was starting to suspect me.

"Anyway I can't stay long. I just wanted to pick up everything you have translated. I won't tell you where I am going."

"Its all over there." He pointed to the writing table in the corner of the room and I picked up the heavy pile of sheets.

"See you later Henry."

"Take care dear boy."

I drove north on the main road towards Beaune, but before I reached it, at about lunchtime, I turned left towards Autun, and drove to the place where Rose and I had camped when I had seen the wolf. Leaning on my side after finishing some sandwiches, I heard the rustling of the thick envelope in my jacket pocket. I took it out and opened it. My heart sank. It was divorce papers. It didn't come as a complete surprise of course – I had seen Rose's Volkswagen parked outside a solicitors in Nevers several times so I suspected we were close to this point. Had we become so distant, so strange to each other that she felt a letter was enough to end our marriage? I read it. It was mostly the usual sort of thing, and at the end, next to a gap for mine, there was Rose's signature in neat blue script. She never used black ink. She disliked black and never wore it if she could avoid it, because there had been 'too much death' in her family. This little detail about our life together tore at my heart, and my lips trembled. Attached, was a sheet with a statement by Rose, but I didn't want to read it.

"Rose!" I called out loud. The forest answered me with the gentle sound of trees swishing in the cool summer breeze and after a long while, I felt better. The thought entered my mind that perhaps Rose couldn't bear the thought of confronting me herself. I wanted to find out what had happened to Annie more than ever. After the loss of Annie, losing Rose's respect was the hardest thing to bear. I still wanted that back.

When it was almost dark, I walked to the rock where I had seen the wolf, and I stood there, listening and watching until my feet hurt and it was completely dark. In my disappointment, walking back to camp, I realised that I hadn't gone there just to think, but to find something I had lost.

Lying on the sleeping bag, that night, watching the branch shapes play across the canvas in the moonlight, I wondered again why Annie had been chosen, and in fact whether I was mad, taking seriously these Serpents. Another thing that puzzled me, was why the police questioned Henry and I. His flat wasn't so close to the crime scene that he would have been routinely questioned by the Gendarmes. It was just possible that he told them about me. It seemed so unlikely though. Henry had been a good friend so far. I must have fallen asleep with these uncomfortable thoughts going around my head because I awoke with a stiff back and the sound of a pheasant, rattling, outside.

There was nothing here, and I had experienced my moment of solitude. Now I needed to decide what to do. I went for a walk to think things through. I hadn't gone far before I came across an old man walking his collie. He stooped on a long stick, with both hands, as I gestured to him to stop for a moment, and eyed me curiously beneath hairy brows.

"Have you seen any wolves here lately?" I asked him.

"They sometimes come this far north from the Pyrenees – during harsh winters, and stay for a while but I haven't seen any for years."

As the sun reached its highest point in the sky, an idea, and then a plan formed in my mind. If felt that I was in somebody else's game. I didn't know the rules and I didn't know the aim of the game, but it seemed to me that there was something I could use to help myself, if I accepted the game. Somewhere, hidden in some crypt was some kind of weapon such as a sword perhaps, and possibly in that crypt I might find the answer to the another question – what had happened to my grandfather's body. If indeed he was a member of this secret society called the Ordo Lupus, then perhaps I should become one too. Perhaps he meant to initiate me and never had the chance. In any case my life seemed irrevocably entwined with their fate now. I needed to find somebody in this Brotherhood, but the only thing I had to go on was the clues about the whereabouts of this crypt. I would try to find this Secret Crypt and hope that this would lead me to someone, or at least something, that could help me. The place to start looking was Paris so I would go there. Pleased with myself for at last forming a plan, I whistled, as I walked back to the camp.

I had to pull up my trousers several times as I walked. Henry would normally have been shocked at my appearance but I guess he'd had too much on his mind. I packed the tent and other equipment into the car and drove west, intending to turn onto the main road heading north for Beaune and from there, on to Paris. I stopped at a trucker's café where I hoped I would not be recognised, and, after a lunch of burgers, eggs and chips, I tried to call Rose at our home. After ten rings, I hung up, and called Cosette in the office.

"Cosette?"

"Ah. Hello Monsieur." She always mixed her English and French quite delightfully.

"Cosette. Can you do me a favour? I cannot get hold of Rose and I am going away – possibly for a few weeks. Please can you keep trying our home number until you can tell her, but if you can't get hold of her within three days, send her a letter."

"Um hm. Okay. Ah! Monsieur? Can I tell her where you ah going?"

"I would rather not Rose. I want some privacy."

"Ah. I see. I am very sorry what has happened to you Monsieur. The Gendarmes – the way they treat you is very unfair."

"Thank you Cosette."

"There is a letter has come for you."

"Ah yes? Could you open it please and tell me what it says?"

"Yeser." I heard the sound of paper being torn. "Hm mm. It is from Mr Barton-Brown."

"Ah. The researcher. What does he say?"

"He says thank you for the fax. He found it very interesting. Da da da dah. Then he says that he has found something you maybe do not know about. De de de dah. Let's see. Yes, he says that he wanted to prove it wasn't false document so he had it testeder. Um hm. With ultra-violet light they could see hidden marks on the paperrer – one on the bottom of each page. He says the characters were 'U' 'S' 'U' 'S' and that this made him check the other pages in the book. Nearly all pages have these characterers which spell words in Latin. He hasn't finished the other chapters but here is the Latin verse for all the pages in the Chapter which yourer pages came from."

"Yes. Go on Cosette!"

She started to read the latin words to me, but I had to stop her and borrow a pen and a napkin from the nearest customer of the café, as I couldn't possibly remember it all. After many mistakes and repetitions, and many centimes later, I had the full verse.

"Merci beaucoup, Cosette. You are a star!"

"Au revoir, Monsieur. Take very great care."

I stuffed the napkin in my pocket and left the café. My plan, once I reached Paris, was to translate the verse Cosette had read to me, and see where that lead. I also thought I would contact Georgina. Perhaps she could help me.

Georgina. Tall slim and black-haired with eyes of cinnamon.

Later that night, in a cheap hotel room , decked out with pale pink and white, vertically striped wall-paper, and reproduction baroque furniture, I took out the napkin and laid it on the bed. I read the Latin and wondered at it.

Unus super parietis,
Per securis, conicio oppugno in vallum,
Is quisnam semotus vexillum.
Iterum vexillum eram perspicuus,
Nostrum vir remuneror Le Pilon.

I was frustrated that Barton-Brown had chosen not to translate the text for me – he knew I could not read Latin, but then again perhaps he felt this was just too easy. In any case I could telephone Henry in the morning and get it translated over the telephone. I stared hard at the text but I could not understand any of it, so eventually I went to bed.

I called Henry but he didn't answer. I tried again half an hour later and still he didn't answer. So I went for a walk. It started drizzling lightly as I walked – the sort of drizzle that brings no relief from summer heat, and I reached the river Seine, and turned to walk northwards along its Eastern bank, watching the water dappling in the rain.

I decided I would call Henry one last time at 11 am and if he wasn't there, I would call Georgina. I told myself I needed to make some progress somewhere, and that this was the only reason I would call her. I felt so restless, as 11 am approached, that I couldn't stand still, and kept asking passers-by the time. I made the call at 10.59 am and still there was no answer. I took out the folded sheet of paper with Georgina's number on and dilled it. There was a long pause, in which I had time to reflect that although I told myself over and over again my interest in Georgina was strictly professional, my thumping heart told another story. I almost put the phone down, hesitated, and then heard a velvety voice at the other end.

"Oui?"

It was only a week ago, and I remember I found myself smiling, and cradling the receiver like a lover as I spoke softly into the mouthpiece.

"Georgina?"

"Ah. Hello. I recognize your voice. It's my favourite murderer!" She giggled like a little girl with delight at her joke. Her accent was slight, and her pronunciation of English was impeccable.

"Yes" I laughed too. It was the first time for ages that somebody had disbelieved the idea of me as a murderer, to the extent that they could joke about it. I was warmed by her trust in me. "You said you had some information for me?"

"Oh. Yes."

I realised that I had used this information to sidestep the more formal procedure of asking her to meet me somewhere. I must have sounded awfully callous, and I immediately regretted it. "Sorry. That was very impolite of me. It's just that I am very nervous talking to beautiful women on the telephone."

"Beautiful, strange women too," she corrected.

"Yes. Would you like to meet for a drink somewhere? Tonight?"

"Ha! Ha! Yes, that is the more confident approach that I am used to. Wait." She seemed to be thinking for a moment. "Yes. I could meet you tonight but it would have to be late. Around ten o'clock – perhaps ten thirty. You won't mind if I am a little late will you?" She added the question almost as an afterthought, her tone solicitous.

"I will cope. Where would you like to meet?"

"Ah yes. You don't know Paris very well? How about the Café Cardin de Paris, on the Boulevard Saint-Germain, near the Muse Eugene Delacroix. Do you know it?"

"No. But I will find it. I will be there."

"Okay. I will see you later."

"Yes.

"Good bye."

"Yes. Bye." I found myself listening to the end-of-call tone, its steady hum somehow reassuring.

Towards the end of the afternoon, after a balmy few hours drifting along the Seine, looking at paintings, and flicking through the dusty pages of secondhand books, I suddenly glanced at my string belt and realised I didn't have anything decent to wear that night. Most of the men's boutiques on the long Boulevard de Sébastopol stayed open late so luckily I didn't have to rush, and after some indulgent or disapproving looks from the assistants, I was kitted-out in a nice blue suit with a white shirt and black, polished shoes in an expensive-looking boutique. I had even bought cufflinks and as I walked into the Café Jardin de Paris fifteen minutes early, shaved – using a disposable razor, and doused in cologne, I thought I was ready for even this sultry beauty. At eleven I began to have doubts. After a while, the noisy heat inside had become uncomfortable so I had moved to a vacant table outside, and now I sat watching passers-by suspiciously or the occasional flashing light of an airliner in the darkness above.

"Hi!" The soft but clear voice was right next to my ear and I turned just as Georgina passed me to sit in the seat opposite. "Really, I must apologize completely for my late arrival. I was at the opera with a friend – a man, and I could not get away politely before now."

"At the opera? But you didn't tell me. You shouldn't have left just for me. Whatever will your companion think?"

She blows air through her lips dismissively and rather endearingly.

"He a friend of my boss and really I felt obliged to go on this date. We met at work and that's where it should stay as far as I am concerned."

"I am not sure he will agree."

"Ah well he may have wanted to make love to me, it is true, but I think in this case he was more interested in being seen with a pretty young woman than actually doing anything." She was already breaking a crust of brown bread as she spoke. "I am starving. Have you ordered?"

"No. I was waiting for you of course."

"Ah a gentleman – or at least someone who is prepared to pretend – and even that is rare enough these days."

I raised my arm and a waiter brought the menu and then left us. I was flattered by her candidness discussing her relationships and I felt confident enough to let my eyes range quickly over her, while she scanned the menu. She had a long and very dark blue – possibly purple, evening dress on, with a silver tiara around her hair, which was carefully piled into a bun. This revealed two lovely ears with silver peal-drop earrings of extraordinary size – probably fake, I guessed. Her long white gloves were folded on her black velvet purse on the table and occasionally she played with her left earring, rolling it between finger and thumb. She was an unusual picture of both sophistication and youthful rebellion which showed in her movements which seemed deliberately inelegant. Her cleavage showed a swooping valley of promising pale flesh, where my eyes lingered for just a moment too long.

"You look very elegant tonight." She paused. "Your eyes are the most beautiful pair of blue and brown eyes I have ever seen." she said without looking up from the menu.

I may have turned a pale shade of red at that moment although she wouldn't have been able to see.

"What are you drinking?" she asked

"Ouzo."

"How quaint. An artist's drink. May I order some wine?"

"Please do." Without even asking for the wine menu, she ordered an expensive bottle or red, one I had heard of.

She rolled the glass around in her hand, and grinned, as if the wine were chocolate.

It really was very good – full-bodied and slightly spicy, with an oak aroma. She looked for my approval. "Yes."

"Ah ha ha. You English men are so – erm restrained. When I saw you in the library and then you spoke to me I thought at last here is an informal English man, but no – you are formal like all the rest." I must have looked slightly hurt because she added, "Sorry. I am slightly drunk and I sometimes get a little bit rude when I am drunk."

The waiter returned and we ordered two rounds of fresh mackerel with oyster dressing, followed by profiteroles.

Georgina cleared her throat and sat up straight. "I have heard you have a certain talent."

"Oh?" I nearly choked on the mackerel. She peered at me from under those exquisite black eyelashes with a look halfway between playful glee and intellectual curiosity.

"Well?"

For a moment there seemed to be an impasse, but I relented.

"Well I don't know how you could have possibly heard anything. Perhaps you haven't?"

"Just guessing? No. I have my sources." She slowly licked the oyster sauce from the spoon with her ruby red lips and I imagined myself kissing them.

During the War, I often found I could get out of trouble or even avoid it. I don't know how. I just seem to have a sixth sense. You can believe it or.."

"I do believe it. But only since the War?"

"Okay. Since I was a boy." Stupidly I looked around me before continuing. "Normally I don't admit that to anybody." We both laughed momentarily at the melodrama of my glances.

"But I am not just anybody."

I looked into her eyes, and she held my gaze. I almost thought her pupils opened up and I fell in to them.

"Come on Mr English Mystery Man. We must go. Eat up quickly and pay the bill."

"Go? Where are we going?"

"I want to walk along the river with you, and talk."

As I waited for the waiter to bring the change, my hand lay on the table and she put her hand on mine, touching my wedding ring with her index finger. "Where is she?"

I laughed. "Actually I don't know. She could be back in our house near Nevers or she could be in London."

"You are not close then anymore?"

"No. I guess you would say not."

"Most French men would have taken off the ring before meeting me."

I had thought about it but when I casually tried to remove it, it would not come off and I decided not to try any harder.

We left the café, me carrying a bottle of champagne, and Georgina the remnants of the red wine. We headed towards the south bank of the Seine. She occasionally leaned against me as we walked along the bank, the drink taking its toll on her balance.

"So you were a student of history and now you work in an advertising agency for a boss who tries to look up your skirt all the time?"

"Ha! Yes you are very close. Only thing wrong with your guess is that I work for a publisher and I don't wear skirts to work. But my boss tried to look down my dress instead. Oh Theo, you are such a devil" She raised the bottle in a toast to her boss and then downed a long swig or wine.

We reached a wrought-iron bench, typically French and typically elegant. We sat down and she leaned against me, as if she were my daughter. I put an arm protectively around her shoulders.

"Umm. I am a little cold actually. Its surprising how cold it gets at night, even in August." She drank more wine. "Oh. Nearly gone." After a pause while we both watched the steady rippling movement of the Seine, she asked, "What is your wife's name."

"Rose."

"Rose, Such a lovely name. Is she *very* beautiful?"

"She is – of course. But not in the way you are."

"Am I? Beautiful?" She turned her face towards me and I longed to kiss it but I couldn't. She looked away. I squeezed her shoulder just ever so lightly, involuntarily"

"It's okay," she said. She lifted the bottle of wine to her lips for a moment. "Oh. All gone."

"Shall I open the champagne?"

"No! not yet. Let's walk."

We stood up, but she kicked off her shoes and picked them up. It was only then that I noticed how expensive they were – some kind of silver-lamé strapless shoes with high heels. They must have cost a fortune. She skipped on ahead of me. Come on slow – how do you say? Camionette?" She laughed, a high laugh like laughing water.

"Coach. Slow-coach! I am old."

"Oh you are not that old..." In mid-sentence she stopped as she was looking back at me. She seemed to be looking at something over my shoulder and a worried frown came over her face. Then she held her hand out and I walked up to her, taking it and falling in beside her. I glanced back.

"What's wrong?"

"Come on. Don't look back." We walked quickly for some distance until we came to a junction on the path and we turned left between two old buildings. "Run," she whispered, and we did. When we reached the main street which ran parallel to the river, she turned right, crossed the road, all in bare feet and her footsteps hardly made a sound on the tarmac as she ran. As we crossed the road I thought for a moment that I heard footsteps echoing in the passage behind us. We reached the other side of the road and a little further on were some barrows, covered by tarpaulins – probably part of a market during the day. She turned between them and then through a narrow passageway and down some steps onto another street, at lower level, and we ran back in the direction of the café we had eaten in earlier. I was getting out of breath when she pulled me into an entrance lobby and stopped. We waited for perhaps ten minutes without speaking.

"It's okay now. I think he's gone."

"Who's gone? What is going on?"

"We were being followed."

"Yes. I guessed that. But by who?"

"Pastor Michel"

"Who the Hell is he?"

"Yes. You might well ask," she said smiling. "Luckily I know this area. Otherwise maybe we would not have lost him. They know where my flat is now but not my sister's. Let's go there."

I had become so intoxicated with her company I had completely forgotten to ask what information she had. Now I just seemed to be going along for the ride.

After what seemed an eternity of passages and long narrow roads we reached a modern, steel-framed door to a block of flats, with an entrance phone and camera.

"Hi tec!" I said.

In her sister's flat, which was ultra-modern, and expensively furnished with black leather and white walls, she took the champagne and poured two flutes.

"On there. On the table!" she called out as I sprawled, out of breath on the long leather sofa.

On the glass coffee table in front of me was opened a brown leather-bound scrap book. On the opened page was a blurry photograph of a group of Catholic priests standing in rows, as if having a year photo taken. I hadn't seen Georgina open the scrap book when we came in but she might have.

"Who are these?"

"These gentlemen are your enemy. Move over. Here!"

I took the champagne but put the glass down. Georgina settled next to me, her hip just touching mine as she sank into the plush, giving leather.

"They are a fundamentalist Catholic group – sect, if you will, of priests out to stop the Ordo Lupus."

I sucked in my breath at the mention of the brotherhood – she must have heard me. "You *know* about the Ordo Lupus.?"

"Yes. My father was an expert. I think he was a member but he died too young for me to know for sure."

"Oh I am sorry. Did he talk to you about it a lot?"

"Actually, no. Never. But he left a lot of books and papers. This is one of them. Pastor Michel is one of those but I could not tell you which because the picture is too bad. It was taken many years ago. He has been following me for few months now. He may have followed you – or one of his friends might have."

I recalled the time I left Henry's and felt that something was following me. That had definitely felt supernatural though.

"What more can you tell me?"

"I can tell you that you are in very great danger. From studying your case – what I have read in the papers, I think I have come to understand some things better which I have been trying to work out for years." She stood up and went into the kitchenette. "Are you hungry? There is come chocolate here."

"Not really hungry but I never say no to chocolate. I don't really like to ask but did your father die in tragic circumstances?"

"Tragic and violent – yes. That is all I will say for now."

She sat down next to me but this time pulled her legs up under her and leaned against me. She put a plate of expensive confectionery on my knee and I politely took one. It was delicious. I felt that she wanted me to put my arm around her but I couldn't do it. I had never been unfaithful to Rose and I just didn't feel comfortable in this situation with a strange woman.

"You said I was in great danger?" I said.

"Yes. So am I."

"You said you had something to tell me – some information you could give me?"

"All in good time. How is the champagne?"

Up until this moment, I hadn't drunk any but I was feeling guilty now so I quickly drained the flute, which prompted Georgina to refill it. She reached behind her and loosed her hair which fell in great black drapes around her delicate and beautiful face. I could feel the velvet-soft touch of her hair on my shoulder and it excited me.

"Wait. I want to put on some music. Is Ravel alright with you?"

"Yes. Sure. I love Ravel." She went to a modern hi-fi unit on a glass shelf and chose a cassette. After a few moments the gentle idyllic sound of the opening sequence of 'Daphnis and Chloe' started to fill the room, and I let my head rest back on the sofa with my eyes closed to listen. I felt Georgina sit back on the sofa and rest gently against me but I didn't open my eyes just yet.

After what must have been a few minutes I heard Georgina speak. "I have been scared the last few weeks."

"Really?" I said putting my arm instinctively around her shoulder as I opened my eyes. She leaned into me and I could see above the curve or her neckline, deep into her cleavage – almost the entire shape of her breast. It surprised me and I felt a pleasant hardness between my legs. She seemed to be looking directly at it and this excited me more, as if it were an assignation.

"The *Good* Pastor and his cronies have been hunting me all over Paris." One night they smashed the window of my car and stole some documents I was studying."

"Are you serious? If they are religious men, how could they do such a thing?"

"Religious! Yes, their kind of religion. Intolerant and extreme. They will kill anything that they feel violates the Catholic Church's beliefs."

"Kill?"

"Yes. Kill. I do not exaggerate. Do not underestimate them."

"But one thing I don't understand. Pastors are usually found in the Protestant Church."

"No. If you go far back enough in time, Pastors were prominent in the Catholic Church too, and in the fundamental strands of the Church there are still fundamentalist Orders, usually of monks, but sometimes priests who *defend* the faith.

"You know a lot about these people."

"I know a lot more and I will tell you, but I need protecting."

"And I want to protect you." It seemed as if somebody else were speaking using my mouth. I hadn't intended saying that, but I was rushing along now on a fast river of passion. Talking of the things that affected us both, while seeing the curve of her beautiful breast had removed the barriers I had felt were between us, and now I wanted her. I stroked the nape of her neck with the back of my index finger and she lifted her face to look into my eyes.

"Am I really beautiful?"

"Oh yes." We hung there in space for a moment, her lips moist and eyes wide with eager longing and submissive desire, and then I leaned forward slightly and kissed her. Her warm mouth opened as I tasted the sweetness of her lipstick and then explored the inside of her lips with my tongue.

"Ah!" she sighed. The music was building now, painting a sound picture of mounting waves in the sea around the enchanted island, and as the satyric flute ran up and down the register, I gently pushed her dress down to reveal a naked shoulder. She pulled her arm through the opening and then the other while I continued kissing her, and then the dark blue dress fell to her waist. She was really stunning – lovely full breasts and a slim waist with just the faintest downy line between her navel and the top of the folds of her dress, just above her legs.

"You are so beautiful."

"Oh. Show me." I started to stand – to take her to the door which I thought led to the bedroom, but she stopped me. "No, here."

She was already undoing the buttons on my shirt and I helped her, pulling it off, and then unfastening my trousers. Before long I was naked and pulling her dress off her hips, and looking at her completely naked, as it fell to the floor. She climbed on top of me and, hard as I was, I just lay back while she took control, lowering herself onto it, allowing me to see the whole of her beauty, her face, her long black hair cascading around her lovely breasts and the soft 'V' just above my own hips. We rocked gently as I felt her youth taking the hand of my many long lonely years, and showing me the rhythm and dance she wanted to explore. Finally we came together, just as the music subsided at the end of the storm.

I wanted to say "Excellent choice of music," but I knew we would both laugh and the moment would be lost.

I wondered at what seemed like her experience, which had moved things along smoothly, and put it down to the youth of the day.

She lay on me, her sweating forehead resting under my chin, and I rubbed her shoulders affectionately.

"That was great," she said. "That felt really good. I don't want to move right now."

"Then don't."

We fell asleep like that, for a little while, her light body on top of mine, and then, when we became a little cold, we walked hand-in-hand to the bedroom, and climbed under the soft white sheets of a large bed. There we made love again before sleeping until the morning.

"Georgina. Can you read Latin?"

"Yes. Read and write it." Her voice was slightly muffled as her mouth was pressed against the pillow.

"Good. Come with me to my hotel. I have some something I need translated."

"Okay. I didn't have anything planned today."

By mid morning we were sitting on my hotel bed, with many of the latin sheets Barton-Brown had sent me, laid out around us. The napkin though, was the centre of attention. On it was written the Latin which Cosette had originally dictated to me in the café.

Unus super parietis,
Per securis, conicio oppugno in vallum,
is quisnam semotus vexillum.
Iterum vexillum eram perspicuus,
Nostrum vir remuneror Le Pilon.

Under this, after only a short while, Georgina had written her translation.

Alone upon the wall,
With axe, throws assailant in the moat,

he who removed the flag.
Again the flag was bright,
Our hero's reward Le Pilon.

Georgina had laughed when she translated the final line. "Hm. It's quite sexy. The last part – I don't know if it is a joke or not but it certainly sounds like one. 'Le Pilon' is a typical medieval pseudonym for a man's cock. Where did you find this?"

"It was encoded in pages from the book I was trying to borrow in the library that day – 'De Secretis Scientia Occultis'. Each letter of the poem was at the bottom of each of the pages, written in lemon juice I believe, or something similar.

"Wow! Okay, so you want to know what it is about?"

"Yes. Do you know?"

"Well. A man is defending some kind of building, standing on a wall with an axe and throws down a guy who stole the flag. The flag is raised up again – possibly in the sunlight, that part is not too clear, and then the hero gets his reward, which I can best translate as 'The Rammer'. I would say it is pretty unusual to have homosexual overtones like this even in an occult book of that time."

"Hm. Its not much to go on. Could The Rammer be some kind of magic weapon – a battering ram for instance?"

"Could be. Honestly I really cannot tell you anything more than that." After a pause while we both thought, and she added, "Do you know which country the book was published in? Looking at the latin here it seems idiomatically French to me. It would be a help if we knew for sure. Then we could search in the library for Le Pilon and see what we find."

"Yes. I believe it is French. I tried to buy the book a few weeks ago and my source told me it was French."

"You tried to buy *this* book a few weeks ago?"

"Yes. This *very* book."

"That is very strange. I don't understand how it could be bought by the library so quickly and quietly and then be on loan so soon."

"No. Me neither."

"And how much did you offer?"

"8500 Guineas."

She whistled. "Come on. Let's have breakfast and go to the library. There is no time to lose."

I was eating waffles with jam and cream in the small hotel restaurant, with Georgina reading a copy of Le Monde and sipping coffee next to me, when she sharply slapped my hand. "Look at this." I looked. She was pointing at a small photograph on page two. "Isn't that the man you were talking to in the library?"

"Let's see." I pulled the paper towards me so I could peer more closely at the photo. I read the caption to be sure. "It's Barton-Brown! Oh my God! He's been killed!" I read the first few sentences of the caption out load. "English History professor found dead in hotel room from what appears to be strangulation. The Gendarmes are seeking any body who was in the area and may have seen anything suspicious to contact them. Anonymity is assured. The hotel has been sealed and staff are being held for questioning." Further down an article gave details of the hotel's location, just a few blocks from the library.

The hairs were standing up on the back of my neck as I read the article. The unnamed danger I had felt following me for the last few weeks suddenly seemed a lot closer. Now, the truth of what Georgina had said about my predicament the previous night really hit home.

"Does it sound like the other murders?" Georgina spoke, breaking the spell I had been under for a few moments.

"Sorry baby. No it doesn't sound like those. They were crushed." A pain gripped my chest, thinking of Annie and I must have grimaced, because Georgina squeezed my wrist affectionately. "We will never get that information now. The Gendarmes will be all over that library."

"Do you think this has anything to do with the book?"

"I don't know. Maybe. But in any case I am linked with the book, so yet again I am going to be in the sights of the Gendarmes."

"Why is it so important to find the meaning of this poem?"

"It's all I have to go on. The poem was encoded in the chapter on the Ordo Lupus and I believe it's a clue – something important." I decided to take a risk. "I believe there is some kind of secret weapon or knowledge that could help fight or defend against the thinG that does those murders. I don't know what that is but I think the poem is a clue to its whereabouts. I think I have to find it before these things or this thing, finds it."

"Ah yes. I have heard of this magic object. Do you really believe it exists."

"I don't know Georgina. I really don't. Sometimes the whole thing sounds crazy to me. But I was standing right there when Annie was dragged away. Whatever took her was bigger and stronger than anything else I have ever experienced. It wasn't human." I knew my voice was getting louder as my emotions were getting the better of me.

I felt a mixture of anger and frustration, and my voice sounded sharper than I intended.

"Sorry. Well it's too dangerous for you to go but I can go. I am a regular so they won't suspect me. And if I go now perhaps I will be there before the Gendarmes realise that is where they should be looking."

"Alright. I will walk with you some of the way. I need to go for a walk but I'll come back here and wait for you. I am worried now that the staff will give me away. Don't tell anybody about me. Okay?"

"Of course not!"

We left together and took the back streets towards the Richelieu Library. We both had dressed down to become less conspicuous and Georgina wore a simple cardigan over a white blouse and a black knee-length skirt. Her jet-black hair shimmered when she stepped from shadows into the harsh direct sunlight.

"Your hair almost looks blue-black."

"My mother was Italian."

"Ah."

"You know Georgina, you still haven't really told me who these priests are – like Pastor Michel. Do they have a name and do you think they could have murdered Barton-Brown?"

"I am not really sure. They are very shady. In my father's notes, he refers to a Council of Bishops and he wrote that he believed Pastor Michel and many hundreds of others defer to them."

"Defer? You mean he didn't say they report to the Council?"

"No he was very clear about that. I suspect it is to avoid any documentary evidence against their actions."

"Hm. Does the council have a name"

"Well my father refers to them as the 'Concilium Putus Visum'."

"What does that mean?"

"Roughly it translates as the Council of Pure Vision or possible Pure Light. I just call them the Jackals."

I laughed. "The CPV"

She laughed too. "Yes. The CPV."

We reached an intersection and Georgina stopped. "The library is just over the street. See you later." She leaned forward and kissed me. Then she snapped on a pair of tortoise-shell rimmed glasses, which she took from her handbag. I smiled. "I don't need them," she said. "They deter young hopefuls."

* * *

Chapter Six

435, 536, 1782, 1836, 1976, 2823, 4840

"It must be nearly noon now. I am still leaning against the sarcophagus in the Secret Chapel. My nervousness is increasing and it's all I can do to hold steady the wad of paper that is the divorce papers, in my shaking hands. I force myself to concentrate on the final part of Rose's note to me. 'On a practical note, I want to keep the house in Nevers – you rarely come there any more anyway and Edward still feels that it is his home. I also need some kind of allowance – you are a relatively wealthy man now and I did give up my career aspirations to bring up the children. I won't impose on you more than that though. I only need some stability while I find my feet again. Anything else, such as photos or furniture or any other possessions please don't hesitate to contact me – for the moment through the solicitors, but perhaps later we will be able to talk on the phone. Rose.' I turn the sheet over but the other side was blank. I had received the divorce papers on the same day I had left Nevers for Paris. I still didn't know then the location of the Cathedral where the Secret Crypt was hidden but I was close."

Back in the hotel, I couldn't settle. All sorts of questions were crowding my mind. I tried to read one of the books I had brought –

'A Guide to Interpreting Medieval Literature' by C. D. Bosely, but every time I reached the bottom of a page, I would have to read it again because I hadn't taken anything in. I put it down and stared out of the slightly-dirty window. Some heavy clouds were forming over Paris and it looked like it might rain. It would be welcome, because the only air-conditioning in the room – an old fan, was struggling to keep me cool. I gave some attention to some of the questions in my head. Georgina was a mystery to me. As I had walked back to the hotel I had glanced down at my old trousers, admittedly now held up with a proper belt, bulging around my middle-age paunch and wondered why she was interested in me. But then again I had learned in life not to question too much when things go right, and God knows most things were not going right at the moment. She had originally said she had some information for me, and yet I was still unsure if she had given me this information. Every time I had tried to make certain she had, she seemed to side-track me with another tidbit of information. What worried me the most was the death of Barton-Brown. Did this mean, since I knew some secrets from the 'De Secretis Scientia Occultis', that I was also a target for the killer or killers? Finally, were the CPV behind the killing? I needed more information and I didn't know where to get it. I was also uncomfortably aware of time passing, although I didn't know why. In desperation I took out 'A History of the Supernatural and Mythical Beasts and Customs of Central and Southern Europe' by Edgar de Boulon, the book my grandfather gave me, and searched for any signs of secret writing or marks anywhere in the book. My grandfather seemed to know what he was doing, and I thought maybe he had left a clue for me. I held the pages over a powerful light bulb, and up to the sunlight, but I could find nothing.

Georgina returned at about six, out of breath and looking very flustered. She flung her handbag on the bed. "I was followed nearly all the way home by the jackals *and* the Gendarmes! I lost them I think, but only a few blocks from here. It's not safe here anymore. We need to go to my sister's. Tonight!"

"Okay. Calm down. We will go. Did you find anything?"

"Not on your poem no. Nothing on Le Pilon. But there is a book – an English book – an Encyclopedia of French Medieval History held at the Bibliothèque de l'Arsenal. Its a very comprehensive book I am told. There might be something in the index. I will go tomorrow," she said, sitting on the edge of the bed.

"Tomorrow is Sunday baby."

"Oh sheet!"

"Don't worry." I put my hands on her shoulders and gently massaged them.

She took my hand and looked up at me. "I'm sorry." I leaned down and kissed her soft red lips. She pulled away.

"There are some things I need to tell you. Time is getting short. I was not sure at first but now I have found out that in fact your friend Mr Barton-Brown was garroted and not really strangled. Garroting is a favourite method of killing by the Jackals. I think it was them.

"Oh now you tell me!"

"Well I wasn't sure. They usually do the garroting with rosaries."

"And the other things?"

"They will have to wait until we reach my sister's flat. Come on, we must pack."

While I finished stuffing everything that I could in my bag, and piling the new clothes on top, Georgina called room-service and ordered a taxi. We walked to the taxi separately, the distance between the hotel doors and the taxi being only a few feet, so it was unlikely anybody would have time to react if they were watching. As we sped through the glittering, bustling streets of Paris, Georgina's hand lay on my knee, but she didn't say a word. She had the taxi driver drop us a few blocks from the flat, and then we criss-crossed from one street to another, in a circling approach to the flat. Finally we were inside and Georgina let out a big sigh. It was a few moments before she flicked on the lights.

Once I had unpacked and she had fixed us some coffee, she seemed to calm right down. It was as if the polished glass and leather of the modern apartment really suited her temperament. Rather than sit beside me, she pulled a polished steel chair out from under a small table, turned it towards me and sat on it, cross-legged, with the coffee cup resting on her knee.

"There is something that has been bothering me all day and I have to talk to you about it. Really, this is the thing I wanted to tell you in the first place, but you haven't been completely open with me, so I held back."

I was a little surprised. "Haven't I? Go on."

"I think I know what you saw when your daughter was taken."

"You know about that?"

"Yes. I know quite a lot more about you than you think. I made it my business to find out."

"Of course I was flattered and didn't want to ask why, in case it was some reason other than that she was fascinated by me."

"What you saw or probably sensed, since it is not properly visible, was some kind of giant serpent, possibly with wings."

I was shocked. Georgina seemed to know for certain the one thing I had been trying for years to prove. I looked at her quite differently, and she smiled back. "You should have told me," she said.

"Do you.. Do you know what they are?"

"The snakes? Yes I do. Or at least I can tell you what my father wrote. She disappeared into the bedroom for a moment where there was a bookcase, and returned with a small black notebook. She found a page and started reading. "I found a passage in a very old manuscript which I believe reveals the origins of the evil Serpents. Paraphrasing, it basically says that there are these winged snakes who are demons and they are fighting winged wolves who are actually also fallen angels, but who are trying to get back to heaven by killing the snakes. God gave them the form of wolves so they would be different from the snakes. There are also some kind of magic weapons, but so far I have not been able to find out what they are or where they are."

"Um. I knew some of that but some of that is new. Thanks baby for telling me."

"Wait. There is a note scrawled after this which says that the snakes only appear for periods of one lunar month at a time."

"Yes I knew that, although I didn't know it had to be a lunar month. That's roughly twenty-eight days isn't it?"

"Twenty-nine and a half actually."

"Oh. Okay."

"I have been thinking. When was the first murder recently, like that of your daughter?"

"Annie. Her name was Annie. Erm. I am not sure if I can remember. The newspaper article was on the 14 July, and I think the murder was three days before – so that would be the 11 July."

"I thought it would be something like that. Let me work it out. That means the end of the lunar month – the time when the snakes will disappear for another sixty years, is Wednesday. That's not much time if you want to find it."

"Yes. Yes, I see what you mean although to be honest I hadn't been trying to find the serpent, just the weapon."

Georgina commenced cleaning the flat, which hadn't been done since we left the previous day. She seemed a bit self-absorbed, and I guessed it might be something I had said, but I was too absorbed myself, trying to fit the new information with what I already knew, and work out what it all meant. I found myself sketching timelines on a rough outline of France which I had drawn on a piece of paper.

"I am just going out for some groceries. Do you need anything?"

"Some Ouzo, or cans of beer, would be nice."

"You and your Ouzo. I will see what I can find. What do want to eat tonight? Is spaghetti bolognaise alright? I am a rubbish cook but I can make an okay bolognaise. My mum taught me."

"That's fine." I heard the door open. "Take care."

"I will."

I continued to think about the serpents and started to pace the room while I was thinking. I wandered into the bedroom, glancing at the books on the shelf to see if any of them could be helpful. I saw the little black notebook which Georgina had replaced, and the brown leather scrap book but I left them alone. My curiosity about their contents was almost overwhelming but I didn't want to violate Georgina's trust by snooping. I saw a copy of the 'Malleus Maleficarum', translated by Montague Summers. What caught my eye was that she had been reading this book in the library when I first met her, but that had been a different copy. I pulled it off of the shelf by its spine and flicked through it. It was well thumbed – more so than the other books, which bothered me. There were several other occult books next to it, but nothing that could be of use to me right now. I made myself another coffee, not being able to find tea-bags, and swore at myself for not suggesting tea when Georgina had asked if I had wanted anything.

The spaghetti bolognaise was passable. It could have done with less bay-leaves and more garlic but I didn't criticise Georgina's effort. There was a bold red wine to accompany it and she had lit some candles. It was very romantic and I touched her hand as it lay on the table in front of me. She pulled it back.

"That ring. It obviously has some great sentimental value for you." I was pointing to a bronze or copper ring in the form of a tight coil on the second finger of her left hand. On the evening I had met her at the Café, most of her jewellery had been dress-jewellery but this had stood out as something more personal.

"Oh. That? Yes it is personal. It was a long time ago." Her eyes avoided mine. I knew then that I had done something, or said something wrong. I thought I knew what it was.

"You are still upset that I didn't tell you all I knew about the serpents."

"Well. It shows you don't trust me!"

"No. It's not that exactly, although I had only just met you. I am just so used to people thinking I am nuts when I tell them – actually I have only told two people, my wife and a friend called Henry, and neither believed me.

"Oh! You should have trusted me. That's all!"

"Well I do. How could I not after what we have been through? Sorry if I was a little insensitive earlier. I was just so absorbed, I mean involved in the information you had given me." I had learned that 'sorry' was always a good word to use when you were out of favour with a woman, especially if you hadn't done anything wrong."

"I am just so scared! That's all" She laid her hand on top of mine. I took it and kissed it. She looked into my eyes and I could see more than vulnerability there.

"Let me wash up." I started carrying dishes to the sink, but she took hold of my arm. I looked at her and put down the dishes and held her waist to kiss her.

"Do you really trust me?" she asked. "Sometimes I think you just think of me as a scared little girl."

"No. You are more to me than that."

"Really?" Her sudden neediness was driving me wild with desire. I felt myself harden and pushed her against the table. She pulled herself up to sit on it. She had a long black summer-dress on, and I pulled it up past her waist to reveal white panties. I wanted to tear off all her clothes. "Go on, then," she said. "Its only a cheap dress."

I reached inside the low neck- line of the dress and ripped it apart, revealing a lacy white bra, which I quickly ripped from her full breasts, which hung loose as she panted, leaning forward to ease herself, one leg at a time out of her panties. I was fully hard now and undid my belt and button, letting my trousers fall to my knees and she pulled down my underpants, taking my hardness in her hands. "Go on then," she said.

We made love long and hard on the table top, me on top, her panting like a panther in season, both of us sweating to the conclusion of our spiritual joining.

"Does that feel good to you baby?" she said stroking my face afterwards, as I lay on top of her. I was exhausted.

We both showered and when I came out Georgina was standing by the phone, smiling at me. She seemed incredibly tense though, as she paced up and down for the next hour, picking up books and turning on and off the television.

"Wait!" I said when the news came on. I watched it for anything about the Barton-Brown murder but there was nothing.

"Let's go out!" Georgina said. "Its too early to go to bed and I don't want to stay in, this evening."

"But I thought you were scared of the jackals?"

"They don't usually operate much at night. They are scared of demons."

"Hm. Okay. Where shall we go?"

"How about the Eiffel Tower? It is open late tonight and the view at night is so pretty."

"Yes. Alright. That would be nice."

"Bring a coat," she said, grabbing the afghan coat I had first seen her in. "It might be cool up there."

In the taxi we ordered, Georgina seemed to get even more tense as we drove to the Tower. "What's wrong?" I asked squeezing her shoulder.

"Oh. I guess things are getting to me. Don't worry about me."

At night the stairs on the Tower are closed off as a safety precaution, so we waited in the queue for the lift. As we clattered up for what seemed like miles, I was reminded of the old lifts of large shops in London, which had dark metal cages, when I was a boy.

As we went higher, my stomach started to turn at the dizzy sight of the ground, far below. Georgina laughed at me. Once, I glanced at her and she seemed focused on the face of a man on the far side of the lift. I thought to ask if she knew him, but then she looked at me and smiled.

"Are you ever afraid of the dark?" she asked later, with her hands clasped on the railing of the viewing platform, at the top of the Tower. Her hair, black as the night around us, gently wafted in the breeze.

I looked out over the sparkling myriad of little lights below us, and considered her question. "If you mean did I want the lights on in my bedroom when I was a boy, then the answer is no. But during the war, over enemy territory, I was afraid of the darkness around us. It seemed malignant – solid, like a gaping wound in the fabric of sanity."

"You have never talked about the War before. You were a pilot?"

"Pilot in the RAF, yes. It sounds very romantic I guess but I was only a bomber pilot."

"And that's where you really discovered your secret talent?" I looked to see if she was teasing me. She had a grim smile on her face but it was genuine."

"There was a raid. It was a very bad raid. Most of the squadron were killed and mine was the only aircraft to get back. My – intuition or call it what you like – saved us."

She nodded. "I am not afraid of the dark. I love the dark! Partly because that is when the Jackals sleep. Even when I was little – I remember once on holiday my father grabbing my arm roughly, and whispering harshly for me to follow him. We were near a beach and it hurt my arm as we ran to escape from someone. When I turned once, I saw a man chasing us, but I couldn't see anything about his features or anything.

"Is it too difficult for you to say anything about how he died?" I asked.

There was a long pause which I did not want to interrupt. "My Dad died in 1972. I was away at boarding school – in England, when I heard about it. I remember the Matron calling me to her office and she gave me a cup of tea. This was something they never did with the girls. I knew something bad had happened. She told me, my father had died.

She was really very nice about it but it was hard for me. My mother collected me the next day and took me to Paris. I don't remember the funeral very well except, smiling faces and black everywhere. My mother was never really interested in his papers – his hobby as she called it, but I had grown up sitting on his lap, in his study, asking lots of questions – and sometimes getting answers. Maman packed all his papers up after the funeral, and put them in a suitcase. I didn't want it at first, but later I nagged my mother about the suitcase in the attic, and she said I could have it when I was eighteen – although really I think she wanted to burn it. I think she connected it with his death."

That seemed to be all she was going to say, so I put my arm around her, and we walked around the circuit of the observation deck several times. I noticed she was still stiff with tension, and she glanced towards the new arrivals from the lift, when we passed. Then, suddenly she shook herself loose. "I will be back in a moment," she said.

"Sure," I said to her receding back, surprised.

I wondered back to the place where we'd stood when we had been talking. I waited for perhaps ten minutes before starting to worry about her. After hesitating several times I went to look for her. Coming around one of the corners of the platform, I saw Georgina facing away from me, and towards a man it appeared she had been talking to. He was as white as a sheet and was looking from her face, to mine, and then to something in her hand.

"Georgina?" I called.

"Stay away! Wait for me back there."

"What's going on?"

"Listen. I don't need your help!" she said turning to me, but as she did I saw the man dart around the corner, away from us and then I saw the gun in Georgina's hand.

"Now look what you have done!" she shouted. She seemed incensed for a moment, almost forgetting who I was, but then in a level voice she said. "He is one of the Jackals. He tried to kill me. Follow him. Make sure at least he leaves the Tower. You can do that at least, can't you?"

I was confused by her anger, and the gun, but did what she asked. I was acutely aware that I too might be a target for the 'Concilium Putus Visum'. I peered around the corner and could see the same dark-haired man, dressed in a blue bomber jacket, waiting in the short queue for the lift. I quickly pulled my head back, and waited until I heard the lift-doors clank shut. I went and stood inline for the next lift, and when it came I took it down to the second floor. I took the lift down, and checked each deck in turn before returning to the top deck. Georgina was standing there at the railings clutching her handbag, which I assumed, now held the gun.

"Where the hell did you get that gun? Did you know he would be here?" I was quite angry with her. Then I saw that her face was white and so were her hands, gripping the railing. To my complete horror I saw that somebody, presumably Georgina, had cut a hole in the safety fence with wire-cutters – big enough to climb through. She was staring into the distance with a look of defiance in her face.

"Don't stop me!"

I knew she couldn't possibly climb through before I could take hold of her, so I walked calmly up to her and gripped her arms firmly.

"Georgina. Don't do that. Let's talk about this," I whispered in her ear, not wanting to attract attention. "Let's go before somebody sees." I heard her quietly start to weep, and she went limp in my arms. I embraced her once, kissed her, and lead her quickly to the lift door.

"No!" she said under her breath.

"It's alright. He's gone. I followed him down."

When we were down we took a taxi straight to her sister's flat. I couldn't see any cars following. Georgina just sat despondently on the sofa while I made her some coffee. I sat down beside her on the sofa and put my arm around her.

"Georgina. Do you want to tell me what all this is about?" I said, after wondering for some time, what was the best approach, to get her to talk.

"You wouldn't understand. I am in terrible trouble. Oh I know you lost your daughter and you are in danger too," she said touching my hand, "But not as deeply as I am. I wish I could explain it all. But I can't."

"It involves the Jackals?"

"Yes. Of course it does," she said impatiently.

"Okay. No more questions. Do you want anything? Something to eat? Drink?"

"No. I couldn't eat, Just watch the television or listen to some music and let me curl up beside you."

Every word seemed to be an effort for her, so although I really didn't feel like it, I turned on the television, and watched an old movie that had just started. She was still tense for some time, nestled against me, but then I could feel her breathing evenly, and I guessed she was asleep.

Just after midnight my legs had gone to sleep, and I could bare sitting still no longer. I had to risk waking her. “Darling?”

"Umm."

"It's late. Let me carry you to bed."

"No. Don't fuss. I want to wash." She forced herself to her feet and padded off to the bathroom while I busied myself, tidying up in the kitchen. I followed her into the bathroom and after cleaning my teeth, I found her in the large bed with the sheets pulled around her neck. She smiled at me and I leaned over to kiss her. My hands discovered she was naked under the sheets.

"Hold me," she said.

As I put my arm around her she turned to me and kissed me – a long, warm and supplicating kiss. I moved gently on top of her, still kissing her.

"No," she said, so I stopped and pulled away. "Yes," she said. "Make love to me."

Sunday dawned long before *we* awoke. The sun must have risen as usual behind the veil of thin fog that usually covered Paris in those days, and the city must have slowly come to life. When I finally did wake, at first my thoughts were all about what I had to do that Monday, before realising it was Sunday, and then realising what Georgina had tried to do the previous day. Then I laid there wondering what I could do to make her feel better. I needn't have worried. When she woke, she seemed her usual perky self. I watched her closely as she quickly climbed out of bed and walked into the shower. I watched her as she dried herself, and asked me, "Coffee?" and I watched her as we sat sipping coffee, watching the early morning new broadcast. I could see nothing in her demeanor to suggest that she had tried to kill herself the previous day.

"Look!" she said, with a sharp slap to my wrist.

I looked at the television – at the news reader, and listened to the rapid French.

"Yesterday there was another murder with the victim apparently squeezed to death. The Gendarmes in Orléans are treating it as the work of a serial killer, and are asking witnesses who were in or near the Avenue de Paris around 1 am to contact them. All calls will be treated with the strictest confidence. Now over to our correspondent in Orléans, Paul Guiffrey. Paul. How are the locals reacting to this latest killing?"

"Georges. People are growing increasingly nervous about these murders. They seem to follow a pattern. Always late at night or very early morning, in a heavily built-up area, and around the weekend.

People are afraid to go out. Some wonder if it is not a crazy vigilante killer. One lady I spoke to is too terrified to go out."

"Orléans. The last one was Lyon! It's coming north! Maybe even to Paris," I said out loud.

"What makes you think that?" said Georgina, pulling away from my arm around her shoulder, and walking out to the kitchenette.

"Don't you think so? I mean you just have to look at a map. Its coming for me!" I laughed. "I guess you think I am paranoid!" I laughed again.

"Oh! We are out of waffles. I want some! Wait here!" She rushed past me, pulling on the afghan coat over her completely naked body and slipping on a pair of high-heels. "Have you some change? I know a little pâtisserie that is open on Sunday mornings."

"You are not going out like that are you?"

"Why not? Does it excite you?"

"Um hm." I could swear she was trying to distract me from my question. Just as she passed me, I felt a cold shadow pass over my heart, or perhaps my soul. It was like seeing a wraith walking across the dusty floor of some long-forgotten crypt. I reached out and grabbed her wrist. "Don't go out. Something bad is going to happen."

"Why? What is going to happen?" For a moment she looked scared, but then she smiled. "Don't be silly. I am just going around the corner."

I let her wrist go and heard the door shut behind her. For a moment I just sat there, thinking about the strength of feeling that I had at these times – when I knew something bad was going to happen, but then I noticed her handbag on the shelf. Thinking this time that it was an opportunity, I carefully unzipped it and peered inside. Sure enough there were the wire-cutters I had been expecting – with yellow plastic sleeves on the handles. She must have planned the whole thing. The gun was there too. Then I noticed a neatly folded slip of paper, out of place among the other neatly arranged make-up cases. I couldn't resist a quick look. In neat and strangely familiar handwriting was a short note. "Need to visit London for a few days. Have found something fascinating. Catch you later darling. xx BB"

'BB', I wondered. Who could that be? I was sure I had seen the handwriting before, and I searched my memory but I couldn't place it. Then I heard steps outside the door and quickly replaced the note. It was lucky for me that Georgina took so long to do whatever she was doing, before knocking on the door.

"Coming!" When I opened the door, however, she was holding a white envelope with blood-red writing on it. Her eyes were wide with fear. "What is it?"

She pushed past me and I closed the door behind her. She dropped the waffles on the sofa and sat down. "You open it. It's from the 'Concilium Putus Visum'.

"Did they give it to you? Where did you see them?"

"It was under the door. Not there when I left."

I lifted the envelope to my nose and smelled the surface. "Is it blood do you think?"

"They always write in blood – their own I think. It will turn brown soon."

I slipped my index finger under the stuck-down edge of the heavy cartridge paper, and carefully slit the envelope open. I read the single paragraph of neat classical script in the centre of the page.

'Come to Notre Dame tonight at eight. We have some information that you need, to save a man's life.

Concilium Putus Visum'

I read it out loud to Georgina. She remained silent. "You are not going to go of course? It's a trap"

"Of course." Her answer left some scope for doubt.

"But you're not going?"

"I will go. They mean you. Why do you think those things happened, or nearly happened at the Eiffel Tower?"

"I don't know baby. I have been asking myself that question over and over again. I wanted to ask you but I don't want to upset you."

"I am in a bad place. I am scared. I have done bad things and now somebody wants me to do worse things – to you. And I can't. And it's because of you, that I have hope for the first time since I was a little girl."

I walked over to her, and she stood to face me, her coat falling open revealing her pretty young body from neck to feet. I put my hands around her delicate waist and kissed her long and lovingly. This didn't feel like the moment for sex. Her soft vulnerable eyes looked pleadingly at me.

"I want to help," I said. "Why don't you tell me who is making you do these things?"

She was silent for a moment. "I will. Soon. Now I am going in the shower. Why don't you make the breakfast for a change?"

I picked up the paper-bag of waffles and set to work in the kitchen. I checked the fridge and decided on waffles with cream and butter, coffee and orange juice. Putting four waffles under the small grill, I set about working he percolator for the coffee. I had just stood back after boiling the water, and loading the percolator, when I noticed out of the corner of my eye some suspicious movement at the cooker. I leaped over and caught the hot grill as it slid out of its shelf, and lowered it to the cooker top, two of the waffles sliding off gracefully on to the floor. In my pain I tried to catch one, but only succeeded in flipping it over to the shelf of glasses above the work surface opposite, and one of them came crashing down, showing glass all around my feet. I shouted in pain and frustration.

"What happened?" Georgina called from the bathroom.

I ran the cold tap and stuck my hands under it, while I swore under my breath. Georgina emerged and ran over to me.

"Stop!" I shouted. "There is glass all over the floor" She nearly slipped as she jerked to a halt just outside the kitchen doorway.

"I burned my hands trying to save the waffles. I saved two." I grinned at her through the pain.

"Wait!" she said and returned wearing slippers. She looked funny naked, but wearing big furry slippers. I laughed.

"You stupid boy! What have you done?"

The grill slid off the shelf. I was watching the coffee, and just saw it out of the corner of my eye. I grabbed it, to lower it to the cooker, and two of the waffles flew off. I tried to grab one but it hit my hand, and hit the glass!" My voice must have sounded hurt.

"Tch!" She had taken a dustpan and brush, and was quickly sweeping up all the glass, along with the two lost waffles.

"It's started," I said.

"What's started?"

"You know. I feel so cursed at times like this." Then I laughed. Yes, cursed was the best description I had ever thought up for what happened to me. The thought occurred to me, that maybe I had done something terrible when I was a little boy, or in previous life.

"Let's look at your hands." She pulled them from under the tap and inspected their rosy red palms. She gently touched with the tip of her finger, a couple of white patches that looked like nascent blisters." Umm. Keep them under the tap for half an hour."

"Half an hour! Are you sure?"

"If you don't want blisters, yes."

Sure enough when I finally turned off the taps, my hands had returned to their normal colour and only one tiny patch looked like it might still become a blister. In the mean time Georgina had put on two more waffles, grilled them, and had fed me two, while I sipped coffee from a cup in her hand.

"You are like a little child," she said, chiding me. I giggled.

"Seriously though," I said. "Bad events often start like this – with little things. I feel it now. There is a force in here. It never normally happens with somebody else around though. Can't you feel it?"

"No. I don't feel anything. My life is bad anyway though at the moment."

"It's nearly lunch time. What should we do today? I don't feel safe going out."

"It's a lovely day. I think we should go out. I just want to go for a walk. Not much. Then maybe a film. I don't think they will bother us if we are together. Anyway they know I will be at Notre Dame tonight. Why would they bother us now?"

"But you mustn't go. I am telling you it's a trap and now I feel even more strongly you mustn't go!"

"I must go. Perhaps they have some information that will help you."

"I doubt it. And even if they do, there will be a price, and it might be a price I don't want to pay."

She looked at me for a moment, a curious far-off look in her eye.

"If you are going, then I am coming with you."

We slipped out of the flat and strolled the tiny back streets of Paris, under the noon sun, and as early afternoon passed, Georgina took to window shopping, while I offered useful comments about her potential purchases.

She was looking at a suit, tailored for a woman, with broad shoulder pads, in a display of clothes by a designer I had not heard of, and I lifted her hair into a cascade above the nape of her neck and kissed it. She looked down at something and I followed her gaze. I scruffy kid about five years old was silently tugging the hem of her dress. She crouched down, and gently ruffled the hair of the little boy. "You are hungry, you poor thing." He nodded silently, pitifully.

"Have you some change?" Georgina asked me.

I reached into my trouser pockets for whatever change was there.

"I will owe you," she said, smiling at her deft use of colloquial English.

As my fingers trawled for coins, I glanced over the narrow cobbled street. I could see a few hopeful heads of other children in the cool shadow of a side street, watching us. I glanced up at the narrow slit of blue sky high above, and then to the upper end of the street which sloped quite steeply towards us, and on down to a junction further on.

“Here you go.” I handed over the coins I had managed to retrieve, but there were more. I placed them in Georgina’s hand and she passed them to the little boy. He swiftly turned and ran towards his friends.

"There's more!" I said.

"Wait!" she called to him. He hadn't stopped and she started off after him.

At that moment, out of the corner of my eye, I saw a white flash moving towards her. I didn't have time to shout. I just ran after her and caught her dress hem flowing out behind her, just in time. I yanked it and she stopped as it ripped. The white car whistled by only inches in front of her face, knocking her hand to the side with a loud whack, which made her lose her balance and fall over.

"Georgina!" I cried. As I stooped over her fallen form, I looked at the car, as it rolled silently down the street, and saw the faces of two children leaning from the car window, laughing with delight. I noticed that the car appeared to have no driver, but I guessed another child was at the wheel. "Are you alright?" I asked, turning back to Georgina.

"Merde. My hand is broken I think."

"Let me look." I gently felt all the bones and although it was swelling fast, and she cried out in pain as I touched the back of her knuckles, it all seemed intact. "Maybe a fracture but nothing more."

"Don't worry. I will buy you a new one.

"My dress is ripped." Then she silently started weeping. She clutched my arm as if it were a log in white water, and I hauled her to her feet.

"Bloody kids. Joy riders!"

"It was children? Oh! Merde! I wish I could get hold of them!" She was angry. " I wondered why I didn't hear it. "You saved my life!"

She was sobbing now, convulsing, partly with shock from the sudden impact."

"They must have just pushed it down the hill."

After a few minutes, she stopped shaking and dried her eyes. "They are a nuisance." She was silent for a moment. "Is that what you mean by chaos? Was that one of those events?"

"Maybe. Yes. Evil possibly, but in a random way. It is Evil but in its raw form, like a whim – not really planned or carefully thought through. Not assisted, as it is when carried out by the Jackals."

"I felt it, yes. It was out of control. Tell me more about it."

We walked and talked, until we found ourselves back at the flat at around four. We had intended seeing a film Georgina wanted to watch, but never quite arrived at the Cinema. I told her as much as I could about my experiences, and what explanations I had for any of it.

She listened attentively, clutching my arm all the time, like a little child. After I had finished talking, she said simply, "It's around us now isn't it."

"Yes."

"I can feel it. It's like a darkness."

As we walked back to the flat, I looked around us and the shadows in the streets seemed just a little bit darker than usual.

I bathed her hand in disinfectant, to clean the small cuts, and then lightly bandaged it. She seemed quite sleepy when I had finished, so we curled up on the bed together for a doze. "Wake me in time to go," she said, before falling asleep.

I really didn't feel sleepy at all and just lay there looking at her hair, and at the wall above the window, overlooking Paris. I wondered what she had meant when she said she had done bad things. I wouldn't know until she told me. I wondered again if I had done something bad when I was young, which might explain why I was cursed now. I looked at the clock on the bedside table – it was nearly six. I considered briefly not waking Georgina – leaving her to sleep through her appointment at the Notre Dame. I knew something bad would happen if she went. I closed my eyes and my thoughts drifted. Perhaps I had done something bad in a previous life. An image formed in front of me. A robed and hooded monk was walking across an inner courtyard of a marble building, from my right to my left. His sandaled feet seemed to make no sound on the cool marble, and I could see olive trees and vines through the various porticos around the courtyard. He was moving so slowly that time almost stood still as I watched for each foot fall. I couldn't see his face but I wanted to. Finally he reached a step which lead down to a path which lead through a portico, and he stopped. His hands slowly raised as if to remove the hood from his face.

"Wake up!"

I recognised the voice but it couldn't be the monk. Then something was shaking me and I looked at Georgina's face.

"You were asleep," she said.

"Huh? What time is it?"

"Nearly seven. We have to go now."

I was disappointed that she had woken up in time but I hid it. "I was having a weird dream."

"What about?"

"I don't know. A monk I think. I really wanted to talk to him."

"Come on. Get ready."

I swung my legs off the bed and sat there, rubbing my eyes. "I only need to wash my face and comb my hair. We are not going to dinner."

"We might. Anyway. Just hurry up."

Within five minutes we were out of the flat, Georgina looking nervously about, as we stepped onto the pavement. Nobody seemed to be watching us. Within one block, she had stopped a taxi and we climbed in.

"Notre Dame, s'il vous plaît," she said.

As we crossed Paris I felt as if I was losing something – control, life, light. Something intangible was slipping away from me. "Darling, we are early. Let's walk the last half mile?"

"Why? It's not safe to walk."

"But we are early. It will be even more unsafe to be standing around for half an hour outside the Cathedral."

"No. I want to drive. Stop being so negative!" Her voice was tense, her words terse, and I stared out of the window. It was the closest we had come to an argument.

An image flashed into my mind – vivid and insistent. I tried to ignore it but it appeared again. A car hitting a pavement and crushing someone underneath. The car was white and I thought it was just the joy rider's car. I ignored the image. It flashed in my mind again and I saw that it was a man driving the car, dressed in black. I pushed it out of my mind.

"We're nearly there," said Georgina absently, looking out of the window, away from me.

Another image flashed into my mind – worse than the last. It seemed to be inside Notre dame, with the cool evening light blazing through the stained glass windows, and I could see several monks standing by the main gallery parapet, looking down at something. I followed their gaze down and saw something twisting on the end of a rope. There was a movement from one of the monks and fire leaped down the rope, igniting the object twisting on the end. Then finally I could see what it was on the end of the rope. It was a body and the rope was around its neck. It was Georgina! In the taxi, I jerked at the image. "Stop the car!"

"Why? No!" said Georgina.

"Trust me baby. We are not going to Notre Dame tonight. I just saw what will happen to you."

She looked confused, and the taxi driver was staring at us in his rear view mirror. He stopped the car and we paid him. I quickly ushered

Georgina up the nearest side street and into the shadows. I was sweating.

"What's wrong?"

"Don't ask. We havE to get away from here. We are too close. I took her hand and started up the gradual slope of the street, between the high sides of private apartment buildings. Only the occasional small window broke the grey concrete surfaces. The occasional car roared past, its engine sound echoing as if in a small box. I found myself humming 'Onward Christian Soldiers' yet again, as I always did to calm my nerves, but quickly changed it to 'This is my song', from the Tom Thumb film. We turned at the top, into another street, lined with small shops and wrought-iron balconies. With more people moving, I felt safer. A few streets later, moving in the direction of the flat, I began to feel that we really were safer, and slowed down. My heart was still thumping though, as if something were wrong. I looked around us. Everyone in the street us seemed suspicious. If I saw any man with dark glasses on, I found myself staring intently at his face, for signs that he was watching us. We only walked a few paces more and I heard the sound of a car engine being gunned. We both swiveled towards the direction of the sound, and I saw a white Peugeot crossing over the road, moving straight towards us. We ran and as I looked back, I saw the car crash into the wall behind the spot where we had been standing. There was a terrible sound of glass smashing, and metal rending, and then the sound of the engine running out of control, like a wailing animal. The driver was slumped over the wheel, motionless. As a crowd gathered, we turned down another side street, and I started looking for a parked car.

"We have to get out of here! We are being watched. We need a car."

My own car was still in Paris, parked in a bay I had often used when visiting, but it was too far away and anyway, it would be watched. My training from M.I.6 cut in and I looked for one of the types of car which I knew were easy to break into. After zig-zagging for a few blocks, I still hadn't found any of the cars I was looking for,, but we stopped outside a small boutique.

"Go in there, try something on quickly and bring out a coat-hanger – one of those metal ones," I told Georgina.

I straightened out the hanger and slid it between the glass and the rubber strip on the driver's door of a battered old Citroën I found in the next street. It was partially in shadow but Georgina stood in front of me to block the view from the windows of the flats opposite. In only a few seconds, I heard the click of the door unlocking and I climbed in. I ducked down to hot-wire the car and the old engine sputtered into life.

"It's no racer but it will do!"

"You really were in the Secret Service then? Either that or you are a criminal!" Georgina laughed, as we pulled away. "Where are we going?"

"I don't know. I don't think it matters. We just need to keep moving." After her little laugh, I was surprised that she suddenly went quiet. I glanced at her and could see her looking morosely out of the passenger window.

"You saved my life again."

"You don't seem very happy about it." I immediately wanted to bite my tongue. Given her suicide attempt the night before it was a particularly stupid thing to say.

"No. It's not that. It's just that it's only you that is keeping me alive! I can feel that I should have been killed already twice today, both times by cars."

"Oh the first one was just kids playing! It was close but you probably would have survived. But it is twice. I haven't told you the image I saw in my head about what might have happened to you in the Cathedral. I saw the second white car, exactly as it happened, so I am sure about the Cathedral too."

"I don't want to know. Don't tell me. You see! It's just your will keeping me alive. You have become like a light in the dark for me." She clutched my arm and was silent for a few moments. "Somehow you are managing to avoid fate, maybe for a few hours, who knows? But you can't escape it forever. I have done bad things and even God has abandoned me now. Oh its no use! Why do you even bother trying to save me! You will get yourself killed!"

I was barely hearing what she was saying – just concentrating on driving, constantly looking in my mirror for signs of cars following. "Yeah. Sometimes it goes like that. It will pass eventually." I was driving steadily North East towards Courvbevoie – the only suburb of Paris I knew well, using as many side streets as I could. The little Citroën was very easy to manoeuvre in and out of the heavy early evening traffic. Several times I thought cars followed us too long for it to be coincidence, but as we crossed the second strand of the Seine, I knew we were being followed.

"Christ! How the bloody-hell did they find us?"

"I told you it's no good. They have allies in Les Gendarmes."

"Somebody must have seen us get into this car. We have to switch to another car." Even as I said it, in my soul, I knew it wasn't true. They could see us. Or at least something could see us. I could feel its eyes on us – but not in the material world. In the spirit world, vague shapes drifted in and out of focus, but we were exposed and somewhere, far off dark, smoldering eyes watched us. A powerful mind seemed to know my every thought. I felt helpless and hopeless.

"They seem to know our every move. I think its the Serpent. I think it is beginning to read my mind."

Georgina looked at me, her eyes full of curiosity.

"We need to find a way to block its sight or something," I suggested.

"Okay. So how do we do that?"

"I don't know. Let me think about it."

The black Mercedes that had been following us was still there, almost like a shy stalker, crawling around corners about two-hundred yards behind us, before slowly catching up, and then falling back again at the next turning.

"Why do you hum that silly tune."

"Which one?"

"You know." She mimicked me and it was a pretty good rendition. I hadn't noticed that once again, I had been humming that same tune from Tom Thumb.

I don't know. Its from an old Hollywood film – 'Tom Thumb'

"Oh. I don't know it but I love films. I would like to see it."

"You will. I will take you to see it next time it shows in Paris. Do you have a cinema that screens old films?"

"Yes. Of course. Paris has many small cinemas."

"What's your favourite film?" I didn't know many basic things about Georgina – her favourite colour, film and book – and I was just about to launch into a question and answer session with her, when an idea came into my mind. "Of course. That's it!"

"What?"

"I think I know how to get these bastards off our tail."

"How?"

"Okay. Paris has had many famous films, filmed here, right?"

"Um hmm."

"Okay. So I suggest a film and you give me directions to go there, one street at a time. If I don't know where we are going to, nobody else will know until the last moment. Maybe it will work."

"It sounds crazy but let's try it! I may not know some of the films though."

"How about 'The Red Balloon'?"

"Oh I know that one! That was one of my favourite films when I was in school, because they showed it all the time in England, and it reminded me of home. I know where it was filmed too. Everyone in Paris would recognise it."

"Good. Don't tell me. Just take us there, but in a very roundabout fashion. Okay?"

"Uh huh. Let me think. Okay. Turn right at the next set of traffic lights."

We drove for perhaps a few miles North, on one of Paris' main roads before Georgina, sucking in her cheeks, pointed to the right.

"Turn there!"

All the time I was trying to think of ways to lose the Mercedes. For a moment our luck changed and we crossed a set of lights just as they turned to red, leaving the Mercedes stopped in the queue of cars. "Now's our chance!" I said. I took the next turn to the left and continued to weave through the maze of residential streets, heading roughly in the same overall direction as before. After about twenty minutes we hit another main road heading almost due North, and Georgina told me to take this road. There was no sign of the Mercedes. Dusk was falling over Paris and drivers were turning on their headlights. We followed the road around the Northern reaches of Paris until it headed South West.

"Somewhere near here we need to turn left. It's a while since I have been here." She seemed more relaxed now, and her face was fixed in total concentration, as she sought the right road.

We turned into another wide road but as it headed north, the streets became more narrow, and when we were driving alongside a row of trees on the edge of a park she asked, "Don't you recognise it?"

"Umm. Not really."

She laughed. "No. It's changed a lot. This park was once the waste ground, where the battle took place. Over there was the staircase leading up to the bakeries." She pointed ahead of us to some buildings with lights twinkling, on higher ground. We continued to drive around for some time, Georgina pointing out many locations in the film. Only the Church reminded me of the film.

"Okay. I think you have seen it all. Shall we stop?"

"No. Let's keep moving. How about 'Last Tango in Paris'?

"Oh *that* movie! Really, I am surprised at you!" She formed a moue with her red lips, pretending to be offended. But then she laughed. "I bet your wife didn't approve."

"I don't know. I didn't see it with her. Well? Do you know where it was filmed?"

"Most of it – no. But I know the bridge where they met, and I think I know the restaurant where they had the last tango."

"Okay. Let's go."

"Well. Just keep on going down here and then first right."

I followed her directions through a few dimly lit streets and then we turned South onto the only main road in the area, and I soon recognised it as the road we had come North on. On a street corner, I inadvertently saw the name of the street – the Rue de Belleville.

"Damn. I saw the name of the street."

"Do you think it's important?"

"I don't know. We better turn off it and try a different way." I took the next right, and after a few blocks we were lost.

"Damn. I don't know this area at all. I guess just head South for now."

"Which way is South?"

"Oh. That's right. We don't know do we. God I am hungry. Can't we stop for something to eat?"

"No. I don't think it's a good idea."

"I don't like being hungry."

"Neither do I. We just have to put up with it."

She smiled at me. "You know you bring out the little girl in me. Its been a long time since I was able to do that. I have been selfish most of my life, and haven't really got close to anyone. But now you are my shining White Knight." She was silent for a moment. "Do you ever think about having more kids?"

"That's a strange question."

"I don't know. I have been thinking about it. I don't feel as if I have much time left, and I never have had the chance to discuss it with anyone."

"Don't worry baby. You will be fine. I am going to look after you."

"I am not so sure. But don't change the subject."

"Well. I haven't thought about it really. To be honest I am just focused on finding out what happened to Annie. She is still my daughter, and I owe it to her to find out what happened."

"I know where we are now. Okay. Just follow this street."

Soon I started recognising places too. I knew we were approaching the centre of the City. We turned onto the North bank of the Seine and headed west. Eventually we passed the Eiffel Tower on our left and then I recognised it.

"That's the bridge isn't it?"

"Um hm." Turn right and follow the street."

"Oh yes!" I said as we drove. "This is cool! We are in the film!"

"I hear that the flat is up here but I don't know. I have never tried to find it."

We both peered up at each building as I slowed the car to walking pace. A car behind kept honking its horn before driving past.

"I don't know. I am not sure. I don't remember the front of the flat at all!"

"No. Me neither."

"Well that's it I guess. What time is it?" I asked.

"I don't know. About ten I guess.

"I am tired now. I really would like to stop."

"Stop then. Just for a few minutes."

"No. It's not safe."

"Where now? I could sleep right now."

"You decide. But don't tell me."

"Okay."

We drove on for two hours or more and the fuel gauge on the dashboard was showing almost empty. Even I was starting to think seriously about stopping. It seemed as if perhaps they had lost us. I didn't feel the eye on me as strongly as before. We were climbing up a steep hill and I guessed where we were. At a set of traffic lights my eyes closed momentarily and again the image of Georgina twisting on the end of a rope in Notre Dame flashed into my mind. This time, after laughing, one of the men in robes spoke to me. "She is not what you think she is. She is not a member of the Ordo Lupus. Ask her about the Ordo Loup-garou. She is your enemy." I jerked awake and when the lights changed, drove on. I puzzled over what had come into my mind. It had a strange resonance but I didn't want to think about it.

"Sacré-Coeur!" I said. "Let's stop. There are loads of people around and it's really late now. We will be safe for a few minutes."

With the crowds thronging around the great Church, even this late, I thought we would probably be safe. I parked the car and we walked hand-in-hand around the white Basilica. Apart from the great age-gap, we could be just another romantic couple – just like many of those around us. For a few moments, we felt normal – as if we belonged. We faced each other and kissed, holding hands.

"We *are* going to survive, aren't we?" she said.

"I think so. But we must be cautious. We walked for quite a while, hardly talking, but enjoying the sociable atmosphere, and the pleasant burble of people talking. On the North side of the Basilica there is a bridge. The brick-paved street passes over another street, lined with houses, and on the bridge, a young American couple stopped us to take their photo. I shied-off but Georgina was game, and the shutter clicked, as the couple from Idaho locked hands and grinned for the family back home. I had been behind them and Georgina walked back towards me as they walked the other way.

She was in a small crowd of people moving the same way on the pavement and I looked away for a moment. I remembered what the monk had said to me in the Notre Dame scene in my head and for a moment I doubted her. As I looked back, she smiled at me. Then I thought I saw an arm extend towards Georgina, and she lurched to her right, on the very precipice of the bridge. There was a low railing – at waist height, but it was rusty and loose, and she pitched over the edge with it, yelling out.

"Georgina!" I cried. I reached for her but she was gone. Her body vanished into the night. I yelled "No!" at the top of my lungs, and ran in what seemed like slow-motion to the spot from which she had fallen. A crowd was peering over the edge. I looked too, but I could see nothing. "Oh God! Does anybody know how to get down there?" I asked. There were lots of shaking heads. Desperately, I ran away from the bridge, heading back past the Basilica, and took the first road on the right. By luck and instinct more than anything else, and a few turns later, I found myself on the street that passed under the bridge. There I saw what I dreaded. A small crowd stooping over a crumpled shape on the road. I ran up to them and pushed them roughly aside. "Out of my way. She is my girlfriend!"

I could hear a murmur but couldn't hear what they were saying. Then a voice spoke up.

"Somebody is calling an ambulance."

"Where?"

"Over there." He pointed to a house with an open front door.

"Georgina?" I bent down and put my hand on her lips, to feel for a sign of breathing. There was none. She looked almost as if she were asleep, in a foetal position, apart from the dark pool which was spreading from under her right cheek. I wanted to lift her and hold her, but I knew if there were any chance of saving her I should leave her. When the ambulance finally came, siren wailing, I climbed in and accompanied her to the hospital, but I knew she was gone.

"I am sorry," one of the paramedics said. I sat beside her still body until finally, at 3 am, the Gendarmes arrived to take a statement. An officer accompanied me to a quiet little room and gave me a statement sheet and a pen. "Can I have some privacy please?" I asked. When he had gone, after writing only a few lines, I quietly slipped out of another door and left the building.

On the sheet, signing it illegibly, I had written, 'We were on the bridge at Sacré-Coeur. Georgina had just taken a photo for some American tourists and was walking towards me in the crowd. Suddenly I thought I saw an arm reach out from the crowd and push her. I am not sure. Anyway she fell against the rusty railing, which gave way and she went over the edge, hitting the road below. A crowd had gathered by the time I reached her and somebody had called an ambulance. She was not breathing but I thought there was a weak pulse. That is all.'

In the end, I wasn't sure if she fell, or was pushed.

* * *

Chapter Seven

2512, 2149, 3008, 4840 205, 2753, 58, 2164

"Georgina! Georgina! What a mixed up girl but for a while she had filled the space that Rose had left empty. For a while. She would love to have been here in the Secret Chapel, exploring ancient and esoteric symbols. Her death was such a blow to me – not because we were close – we had only known each other a few days, but because I had let her down. I believed I could keep her alive – keep her from Pastor Michel, and I had told her so, but in end I had failed. I shook my head slowly at the desolation that had come into my life lately. All seemed so dark. Now I have finished reading Rose's note, I reflect on it. It hurt to read the parts about not including Rose in my deepest thoughts, and Henry. Both are true. And yet there was so much warmth in the statement it made me remember how much I cared for her. The fact that it had taken so many words for her to express her feelings, also touched me and made me smile. She was clearly struggling to come to terms with her own feelings. Only such a passionate woman as Rose, and one who's relationship with me had been formed under such difficult circumstances – in War, in the Balkans and fighting together, could care enough to try and make the pain of separation as little as possible. I think about her comment that I am a tenacious seeker of truth. I remember how I took the next step to discovering the location of the Crypt – meeting Ayshea."

I took a taxi back to the flat, and nervously approached the door to the block. I need to get my things, and find answer to a few questions, but I had no idea if the flat was being watched or not. A man I had seen on the stairs before, walked out of the night and up to the door. I pretended to rummage in my pocket for a key, and followed him in. He smiled at me. "Bon soir."

There was no alternative but to force Georgina's sister's door. I did it as quietly as I could, but there was a loud crack as the lock gave way, and then I was in the flat. I stuffed my books and papers back into my bag and as many of the new clothes as I could. I put my jacket on and went into the bedroom. I grabbed the little black notebook, brown leather scrap book, the copy of the Malleus Maleficarum and a few other books at random and put them in the bag too. Finally I grabbed her handbag, stuffed that in the bag, and left. Already as I descended the stairs, I could see a few doors ajar – suspicious faces watching me. No doubt the Gendarmes would be here soon and I thought briefly that I should have covered my face.

Where to go now? I was still reeling inside from Georgina's death and I desperately needed somewhere private to let out my emotions. I thought about my car but dismissed it as too risky. The only thing I could think of was a café and a hot drink. There would be food too, but I knew I would have to force myself to eat. I walked for about thirty minutes and entered the quietest bistro I could find. It was 3 am – dawn would not be far off. I forced down a veal goulache and had the waiter bring me one coffee after another. I must have looked a mess because he eyed me suspiciously. I didn't get the smile he gave the other customers, but perhaps they were regulars. I wasn't the only one in the bistro who was simply passing time. An old guy with white hair and a long Gallic nose, which dipped inside the rim of his glass, sipped something clear in a glass, in the corner of the room at a masterfully slow pace. I wished I still smoked, so that I would have something to do with my hands. I wanted to take out the books but it wasn't safe. Finally, the pale, early morning sunlight fingered the carpet beneath the front windows. The waiter told me it was 7.45. I paid the bill, and left. My only plan was to walk the few miles to the Bibliothèque de l'Arsenal, find the 'Encyclopedia of French Medieval History', and see if there was a reference to Le Pilon in it. It seemed such a small plan, like a white bone left on a plate after a huge meal had been eaten, but it was all I had left.

I reached the Library before opening, time but I was too tired to walk anymore so I stood silently in the short queue, before being admitted. It didn't take long to find the 'Encyclopedia of French Medieval History', which was a reference book, and not available for loan. It was about three inches thick, with thousands of colour illustrations, and after briefly marveling at them, I turned to the index. My finger traced down the entries for 'P' and suddenly it was there. 'Le Pilon' was right in front of me, and for a moment I wasn't sure what to do next. I turned to the page reference, and there was a beautiful photograph of a Cathedral, one I did not recognise. I felt sad somehow that Georgina was not here to see it as I started reading.

'Born in 1456, Jeanne Laisné, also known as Jeanne Fourquet was a heroine of Beauvais and nicknamed Jeanne Hachette ('Jean the Hatchet'). She is known for a single act of heroism on 27 June 1472.

At the time the town of Beauvais was defended by only 300 men-at-arms, commanded by Louis de Balagny. Jeanne Laisné prevented the capture of Beauvais by the troops of Charles the Bold, duke of Burgundy.

The Burgundians had launched an assault on the main garrison, and one of their number had actually planted a flag upon the battlements, when Jeanne, wielding an axe, flung herself upon him, threw him down into the moat, tore down the flag, and thus revived the failing courage of the soldiers of the garrison. Louis XI was so grateful that he instituted a procession called the "Procession of the Assault," and married Jeanne to her chosen lover Colin Pilon, also known as Le Pilon, bestowing on them many favours.'

So the hero was actually a heroine! I had never heard of Beauvais. Did it even have a cathedral. It sounded like some small village somewhere in rural France. I remembered the inscriptions on the base of the bronze statues – B'vs or BV. That seemed to support it. But I certainly needed more information. I wondered what the 'sk' in the inscriptions and also the name Piere Drang Clenn meant. I looked for that name in the index but found nothing. I looked also for a name that would have the initials S.K. but again found nothing. I was idly looking at a map of France to see where Beauvais was, when one of those moments of serendipity that are so rare in life, happened. Until then, my luck had seemed to be all bad, but perhaps now it was about to change. I jumped as an alarm bell rang metallically, throughout the large hall of the library. All the visitors looked at each other, wondering what was going on, and soon the library staff were ushering us out of the library, and into the street.

"Vite! Vite! Quittez la bibliothèque."

"What's happening?" I asked a young man waving his arms at us.

"It is probably nothing monsieur. Probably a member of staff smoking in the storage rooms. Quick now!"

I quickly stuffed my notes into the bag, and stood up while he looked on disapprovingly. As I did so I put my hand inadvertently on the Encyclopedia which was already on the edge of the desk and brushed it off of the table. I caught it clumsily before it fell and placed it back on the table. I noticed that something made of card had half fallen from between two pages and I quickly snatched it up before being ushered with the crowd, to the door. We assembled on the pavement and I looked at what I had found. It was a business card with the words Concilium Putus Visum scrawled on the reverse side. For a moment I was stunned. I couldn't believe what I was seeing. Then I tucked the card into my pocket and quickly walked away from the library. I found a telephone box and called the number on the card.

"Allo?"

"Ah. Bonjour. Do you speak English?"

"Yes."

"Erm. Are you Ayshea Aikborne? I found your business card in a copy of the 'Encyclopedia of French Medieval History' in the Bibliothèque de l'Arsenal today with the words 'Concilium Putus Visum' written on the back.

"Oh, yes. I must have left it there."

"Well I am researching the 'Concilium Putus Visum' and wondered if we could meet?"

"Really? You have heard of the 'Concilium Putus Visum'? It's a very obscure area of research and I have not found many others who are interested."

"Well I definitely am. Can we meet?"

"Okay. Where are you now?"

"A few blocks from the library."

"Okay. Wait outside the library. I will be there in thirty minutes. Okay?"

"Yes. Fine. I will be there. I will be holding a black bag and wearing an overcoat."

"In this weather? Okay."

I couldn't believe my luck. Not only had I found somebody else who knew about the 'Concilium Putus Visum' but she was willing to talk.

After forty minutes or so, a young woman wearing a green dress, with severe looking spectacles balanced on her freckled nose and the tight bun on top of her blonde hair, waked straight up to me and held out her hand like a dagger. I noticed that she was wearing blue plastic flip-flops and I laughed to myself. *Wow! She is really weird.*

"Ayshea," she said.

I told her my name and we found a quiet café nearby. A waiter brought us coffee but I swept the cup and saucer aside, clearing the small table for my notes which I set out facing the pretty blonde opposite me.

"Ceci est à vous?"

"So you know something about the 'Concilium Putus Visum'" she asked.

"Yes, and they have been chasing me for the last twenty-four hours."

She looked surprised. "They are here?"

"Yes. As a matter of fact they are."

She smiled warily. "I don't believe you. I have plenty of experience with men like you trying to get my attention. It's a nice trick but it won't work."

"I have never seen you before!" I said, indignantly.

"You might have seen me in the library?" She didn't sound sure.

"The Ordo Lupus. Does that name mean anything to you?" I saw her eyes widen just slightly at the sound of the name.

"Does it matter if it does?"

"Well actually I don't know why I am trying to persuade you of my intentions. I am actually interested in what you know. Are you an historian?"

"Why try to persuade me then? You are wasting both your time and mine." With that parting shot, and pushing back her glasses on her neat nose, she started to stand up.

"Huh!" I said to myself. Then a thought came into my head. "Piere Drang Clenn," I said out loud, but she had passed behind me and left the café.

It's no use.

It did seem an incredible coincidence that she was researching something so close to my own research. Just then I jumped.

"Spell the name please."

I turned and there she was leaning over me, looking at my notes in front of me. I could smell a faint floral perfume, delicate but rather cloying. I spelled it out.

"Have you thought that it could be an anagram?" she said.

"No. Why do you say that?"

She pushed her glasses up her nose as she leaned over. "Oh, just a theory. Well. I have a few minutes. Let me try." She took my pen as she sat down in the chair opposite me and started scribbling. As she tried various combinations, she asked, "What period?"

"Thirteenth Century."

"Huh! Good," she said as if she were a doctor and I had just told her I was taking the pills and feeling better.

"France?"

"Yes."

"Anagrams first became popular in the mid-thirteenth Century in France and were popularised by poets such as Guillaume de Machaut and Christine de Pizan. They would often use them to identify themselves, their patron or the poet's lady. The common people who they were writing for, wanted heroes to identify with, but often – given the adventures they had in poems, it was simply too dangerous for them to reveal their true identity. Monks used the same techniques to conceal their own identities or those of characters in their stories. Theobald of Marly springs to mind and then of course there is Eustace!" She suddenly let out a shrill laugh. I gathered Eustace, whoever he was, gave her some amusement.

All this was delivered while she was writing, head down.

"Umm. I am not sure of this one and I have to go. Here." She handed me the pen and stood up. "You try."

"I am no good at anagrams." It was a small lie. I was actually quite good but I wanted her help. Without a knowledge of naming conventions of the period, I stood little chance of deciphering it.

"I have to go Monsieur. I am not very impressed with you but you need help don't you? You don't seem to have shaved for days, and I think some terreeble things have happened to you. You can call me if you wish. Good bye." Then she was walking away rapidly, her flip-flops making a clacking noise as her footsteps receded.

I felt indignant, grateful and amused all at once. There was no point me staying after this strange lady had left. I was out of ideas and my brain wasn't working properly anyway. I drank the coffee and left. As I was walking away from the café I saw a Gendarme standing on a street corner, looking towards the library and very bored. He didn't glance at me as I walked quickly in the opposite direction. I needed a base for the night and I decided an even cheaper hotel than my earlier one, was the answer. Looking up a few side streets I found skulking, one Hôtel de Paradis, advertising itself in faded 60's style lettering on a yellow board. I wasn't optimistic as I climbed the steps and walked into the dimly lit vestibule. The receptionist was friendly enough though, and the room, at the front on the second floor, was basically clean. It had bars on the window – I wasn't sure if this was meant to keep the inmates from escaping without paying the bills, or stopping undesirable neighbours from climbing in. I dropped my bag after paying him for the night, and collapsed on the bed. I fell asleep immediately and woke in darkness, my stomach gnawing and my throat parched. For a few blessed moments I couldn't remember what had happened to Georgina, and then I rolled over to feel for her body. I opened my eye at the absence and then my heart sank as I remembered. I wanted to go back to sleep but couldn't so, I swung my legs over the edge of the squeaky bed and sat there in the dark for a while feeling glum.

"Can I use the telephone please?" I asked at the reception desk. It was late morning and I wanted to call Paul.

"Non. We don't have one Monsieur. Down the street to the right, one block."

"Hello. Paul Dubinski here. If you wish to leave a message, speak after the tone."

I put the phone down and looked for the nearest half-decent café. After a half-dozen coffees, and fish and chips, I felt better and called Paul again."

"You bugger! Where have you been? Rose is out of her mind and half the police in France are looking for you. You are in real trouble mate."

"I thought Rose was back in London. She wasn't at the house when I visited. Actually she left me a little present."

"Yes. I know about the present. She told me. Sorry mate. She went back to Nevers, and the Gendarmes came looking for you. In fact they had practically staked-out the house. Remember that old cat used to sit on the wall?"

"The son or the original."

"Oh well. The son I guess. Well he has gone. Never see him again. Some local copper is hopping mad you have skipped town. He is after you. Apparently you are suspect in some murders. I hear a rumour he is in Paris looking for you."

"You mean Parcaud?"

"Yes. That's the man. Very determined he is."

"How is Rose?"

"Oh you know. Holding up. What on earth are you up to old boy?"

"Well I can't tell you much but I guess you know my theory of what happened to Annie."

"Not that again."

"Well I think I may have proof. I know it's all a bit weird but it's all that keeps me going these days. I just have to find out."

"But these deaths. It's serious. You have to at least talk to the police. Things might get really serious. Something bad might happen to you and even with my contacts I might not be able to help you. It might all be over in a moment. The French police don't mess about you know."

I know Paul. Listen. Can you pass on a message to Rose. Just tell her I am fine and Paul?"

"Yeah?"

"Can you do me one other favour?"

"Depends what it is." He laughed.

"Call my secretary Cosette and ask if there has been any letters for me or unusual phone calls. Anything unusual. If there has, try to get as much information as possible. I don't want to call as I am sure the office phone will be bugged."

"Well. Alright but if this goes on much longer you must hand yourself in."

"Alright. I know. I will. Bye"

With a full stomach and a mind drenched with caffeine, I felt as if I could do anything, or at least anything I could normally do. I decided to call the flip-flop girl, but then, at the last moment, I hesitated. Should I get involved with another young girl? Probably not. I went back to my hotel room and started to go through Georgina's notebook. I wanted some answers. What I found was pages and pages of observations about The Ordo Lupus, but these were all rather remote, as if made by someone who was a secret observer, rather than a participant. The handwriting was of course that of Georgina's father. Only the last few pages were in her neat, rounded handwriting. Some of it read more like a journal:

"February 19, 1947

Met with the Interfeci again. Of all the Lupus Angelus he is now the most deadly. He has been too effective of late, and killed two serpents in 20 years. He has one of The Weapons of myth. His end will come. We will engineer it."

In another place the journal said:

"Sometimes I think there are too many of the wolf-angels. We are outnumbered."

Further on:

"Met under the Great Council in Nice. So many of us there. Some said it was the greatest meeting ever. Hope to gain some kind of elevated position as a result. Shaking the right hands and greasing the right palms."

There were so many pages of symbols, examples of magic writing and cryptic diagrams, that it all started to blur, and I skipped forward to the last few pages in his hand.

"1972 July

In the next few months I intend to confront the Interfeci again. I know now the nature of The Weapon and I think I know its weakness. I will follow him one night when he least expects it and surprise him. The Weapon is too large to conceal, so he cannot carry it always. I do not think he will be a match for me, unless he can get to it. It's a risk I am prepared to take for the Concilium Putus Visum. They have promised me great wealth if I can do this."

There were some more musings after this, but only two pages, before a large gap, and then Georgina's hand took over. Apart from noticing the scrawl which read 'Father died – 14 September 1972', on the first page of the new section, I didn't have the stomach to read any of it yet. So here at least was proof that her father worked for some cult that opposed that of my grandfather's. They seemed bent on destruction of the Ordo Lupus or the wolf-angels as they called them. The awful truth that Georgina probably had taken over the quest of her father, nagged at my consciousness, but still I dismissed it. I vaguely wondered about the identity of this Interfeci, but for some reason, the date of 14 September 1972 was now ringing in my ears. I lay back on the bed to consider it. It seemed familiar but I just couldn't place it. My head swum with memories. Then, again I saw the monk.

There he was again, exactly as before, robed and hooded, walking across the inner courtyard of a marble building. Again it was all in slow motion, his sandaled feet making no sound on the marble and again he reached the step down to the path, and raised his hands to his hood. This time I noticed he had something shining on one of his fingers. Perhaps a ring, it seemed to be emitting a powerful, piercing light. This time he did pull back the hood slightly, and I saw a long, slightly hooked nose, that of an old man, but I woke before I saw the rest of his face. Jerking upright on the bed, I was filled with a sense of purpose, and a feeling that truth was somehow washing over me. I picked up the black note book, and, holding my breath, turned to the second page in Georgina's hand. It seemed mostly the incoherent musings of a ten year old girl and I turned the pages quickly. There was a date of 1980 at the top of one page and my eyes immediately were drawn to the paragraph underneath, the writing seeming bolder.

"I have discovered the identity of my father's killer, the Interfeci. I resolve on this day to kill him. I will find a way. I have approached members of my father's cult, whose name is secret but goes under the alias of The Ordo Loup-garou. I have been initiated as a Sorceress, along with two others, a girl from Nice and one from near Orléans. They said they would help me. It's so good at last to feel that I belong to something, and something that my father belonged to, too. It connects us. Even from the grave."

I felt a bitter taste in my mouth and I wanted to cry out. So Georgina was, after all some kind of sorceress. I had suspected it, but hadn't wanted to believe it. Perhaps she had just seduced me. Probably she had. I slammed the book shut and threw it against the wall. How could I have been so stupid? No wonder such a beautiful young girl had been interested in me. I was a fool. I rose from the bed, and paced the room, going over events of the last few days. I stopped at the barred window and looked out at the spangled lights of Paris. It had just started to rain. Suddenly my attention was drawn to a faint blue flashing patch of light, a block away. I couldn't see the source, only its reflection on the side of a building. I was ultra-sensitive to any signs of the Gendarmes these days. I peered into the gloom below the hotel, and what I saw horrified me. There was a group of armed Gendarmes cordoning off the street outside the hotel,, and a few seemed to be looking up towards my window. A large crowd of pedestrians, held back by tape, was building up about fifty yards to the right, nearest the main street. So Parcaud had found me. It was time to move. The only way out would be over the roofs. I stuffed the books back into the bag, zipped it up and closed and locked the door.

There was no lift in such a cheap hotel, so I took the stairs up to the top floor and looked for a fire-exit. Nothing of that description met my eyes. Looking up at the ceiling on the narrow top landing, there was a very dirty looking skylight, but no way to reach it. Looking up and down the short corridor I could see nothing that would help. Desperation took over at this point and I listened at one of the doors. Hearing nothing I knocked loudly. There was no reply. Leaning against the door with my shoulder and all my weight, I gave it a good push. It flexed but the lock held. Fortunately the corridor was narrow enough that I could place one of my feet on the wall opposite and then I pushed as hard as I could. The door gave with a cracking of cheap timber and I fell into the room. Seeing nobody in the bed I ran to the window and peered out. There was no balcony or fire-escape but there was a heavy, blackened drain-pipe. I turned the light on and looked around the room for something to stand on. A chair was the only possibility, so I carried it out to the corridor,, along with a large towel and climbed on to the chair. Throwing the towel over my head and left hand, and wrapping part around my right fist, I reached up and punched the pain of glass which shattered, showering me with shards. Pulling the towel off my head but still with it around my hand, I pulled the loose triangles of glass from the edge of the frame and jumped down from the chair. An old lady with rollers in her hair and a kitchen roller in her hand, confronted me.

"Que faites-vous ? Êtes-vous un voleur?"

I told her in my best French that I wasn't a thief and that she should go back in her room and she wouldn't get hurt. She threatened to call the Gendarmes, which seemed pretty ironic to me.

Throwing my bag through the black gap in the ceiling, I took hold of the frame with both hands and hauled myself up and out into the night air on the roof.

The skylight was in a small, flat area on the roof, flanked by a chimney on one side and an old rusty railing on the other. The railing ended a few feet ahead of me at the top of an equally rusty ladder, which led down onto the slated sloping roof. Putting my arm through the straps of the bag, so that it became like a shoulder-bag and gasping for breath, I climbed down the ladder, which suddenly started to come away from its brackets. I swore under my breath. At the bottom of the ladder, and a few feet above me to the left, I could just make out the crest of the roof, and I clambered up onto it. Sitting astride it I inched forward, my feet clattering on the tiles, and dislodging a few. The roof hadn't been maintained properly and every part of it seemed ready to slide into the abyss, that lurked somewhere to my right beyond the edge of the roof. The edge of the roof was suddenly highlighted by a strong beam from below. I guessed that the women with the roller had called the police and they now knew where I was. It would only be a matter of time before they followed me out of the skylight. My best hope was to stay hidden so that they wouldn't know which was I had gone. After an interminable length of time I reached the end of the roof, and my stomach leaped into my mouth as my hands clasped the edge of the roof and I peered over. There was a building beyond this one but it was at least a story lower. It looked as if it would be possible to jump from the lower edge of the roof that I was on, so I carefully started to slide down the incline. The slates were wet from the rain and my feet kept slipping.

From the corner of my eye I saw lights coming from the location of the skylight and a voice shouted in French, "Stop! Come back or we will shoot!"

As if in slow motion I saw a slate slide from under my foot, and then for some reason the slate wasn't moving any further away from me. I realised that I was sliding too – towards the edge of the roof. There was nothing to grab hold of! I tried to lay flat and spread my arms out but the bag on my back stopped me, and if it is possible, I am sure I prayed in a split-second. I slowed but I didn't stop although my heart seemed to, as the edge of the roof came towards me. I felt the very lip of the roof beneath my heals and then I stopped. My feet had landed in the gutter on the edge of the roof. The old lead piping held together just long enough for me to crouch, and jump onto the next roof, before it bent away from the roof and fell to the street below. I had landed on a flat roof covered in gravel, and there were other flat roofs ahead of me. I started running, the lights from windows of a high building, opposite, lighting my way. After some time and out of breath, I came to an intersection, where the road turned ninety degrees to the right and the tops of the row of building I was on intersected in a 'T' with those of another row of houses. I turned to the left and kept running. 'They won't find me now', I thought. It was time to get down. I looked for a way down, and found a door set into a column, on top of a house with a nicely tended roof-garden. I forced the door with a trowel and tip-toed down the stairs. When I reached the front door, I lifted the latch and I was out onto the street. I quietly closed the door and disappeared into the shadows. I thought the best thing to do was find a car and get out of Paris. It was getting too hot, with Gendarmes, for my liking.

* * *

Chapter Eight

1821, 592, 5006, 2672, 1899, 3093, 2762, 3726, 4480, 4402

"It is stifling in the Cathedral roof now. The chinks of light between the leads, that seem to move across the roof tell me that the storm outside is still in progress. I imagine that the clouds have become even thicker and more angry-looking. What looked like a giant whirlpool of clouds in the sky, I was sure, was connected with the Serpent who sought the same thing as me – the Sword in the Secret Chapel. It had used me. It was I who had led it to this secret place, and now I know that even if I could find the Sword – the one weapon that could kill it, that this is what the Serpent wants. It had not been able to find it for its self, but now it would take it from me. I am dying for a drink and as I wipe a drop of sweat from my forehead, I remember how I had finally learned the location of the Cathedral where the Secret Crypt of the Ordo Lupus had been hidden."

"Bonjour – vous etes bien sur le repondeur de Ayshea Aikborne, historienne. Merci de laisser un message bref et je vous re-contacterai des que possible."

Roughly translated, the answer phone said, "You have reached the number of Ayshea Aikborne, historian. Please leave your number and a brief message and I will get back to you as soon as possible." It was eight-thirty in the morning and I had just parked the stolen Renault in which I had spent the night, to call the number on the scrap of paper, that the flip-flop girl had written on. Aikborne did not sound like a native French surname so I guessed she was at least third generation emigrant from England.

Opposite to Georgina.

The morning had started badly. Apart from having to wash in the toilet of a cheap café, where I also downed a fried breakfast of bacon and eggs with two coffees, I had discovered that I had made a big mistake. Parked in a secluded street in the outer suburbs, I had started to go through my notes again. I wanted to get away from Paris but wasn't sure where to go. I found my notes on Beauvais, but one of the pages was missing. It was a page I had been looking at late the previous evening, just before I opened the little black notebook. It must have become separated from the rest of the notes, and was probably somewhere on the bed in the hotel still. This would give Parcaud a clue as to where I might go. For this reason alone, I needed to be double sure that really was the place to go before I did. I needed to speak to the flip-flop girl, and find out if she had solved the anagram yet. I left a message, saying I would call back in one hour and then I caught a nap in the car. I awoke, feeling like kicking myself for my mistake, and then I called the number again, not expecting much luck.

"Allo?"

"Ah. Hi. Its the guy from the library – the one with the anagram problem." I laughed nervously.

"Oh yes! How are you?"

I lied. "I am fine. But I am running a little short of time. Have you had any luck with the problem?"

"Well, it's a bit early but I was up anyway. No I haven't solved it. Why is it so urgent?"

"Ah. That would take some time to explain."

"I have some time."

"Well." I had been about to hang up and then I thought that really, I had nothing to lose.

Here goes.

"My area of research is around the 'Concilium Putus Visum'. I know them as the Council of Pure Vision or even the Concilium Putus Visum. My girlfriend and I called them the... Oh well, never mind that. The reason I am researching them is because my daughter was murdered years ago and I was with her. I can only say at this point that it was something supernatural that took her and I believe the 'Concilium Putus Visum' have something to do with it. My wife has left me, most of my friends think I am insane, and the Police are chasing me because they think I killed my own daughter. Sorry, I wasn't going to tell you that. The thing is, I really need to prove something to turn all this around. Now I think I have only a little time left. On top of all this I have these little statues – in bronze, which I bought in Bulgaria, showing flying wolves called warg and – well, one of them is fighting a snake, and I believe there is a secret cult called the Ordo Lupus, and there is a secret weapon to fight these snakes. I know there is no reason for you to help me, and I guess you are thinking that I am mad as well, but I would really appreciate your help." I paused, half expecting her to hang up. She didn't. "I know you know something about the 'Concilium Putus Visum'." I stopped again, waiting for her reply.

"Well. That is quite a story. Flying wolves and serpents? We have to meet." Her voice seemed to have risen half an octave.

"Okay. Where and when? I think I have to leave Paris today. So it has to be soon."

"Leave Paris! Why? Where are you going!" Her voice was almost a screech.

"I don't know yet. That is where you come in."

"Can you meet me now?"

"Yes but where? It has to be quiet. In my car would be best."

"Your car? Well, where are you?"

"In the north of the City. Can you come north?"

"Yes. I can meet you at the Station on Avenue Victor Hugo in one hour."

"Fine. I am driving a white Renault. I will drive past the station at five minute intervals and sound the horn and stop when I see you."

"Okay. Good bye."

She was there on time, this time wearing dainty little boots, which might have been Victorian, but still the green dress. I drove north, out of the City.

"On the back seat are all my notes. There is paper and pens there."

"Let me read what you have. You say Serpents? And a secret weapon?" Her eyes were like saucers.

"Yes." While I drove. she read, until two hours later she had finished, and I stopped in a picnic area, in some woods.

"You know it's quite incredible," she said in careful English, but with a heavy French accent. "I have been studying this obscure subject for years. I did my thesis on it at the Sorbonne. Nobody else has been interested. I have had to make my living doing research on completely unrelated areas of history. But this area interests me the most.

"Your father I guess?"

"No. Why do you say that? No. The Knights Templar was my first area of interest, and it has grown from there. It seems that you and I are looking for the same thing. I have wondered about these Serpents for a long time although I have never met somebody who has seen one.

I looked at her and she looked at me. "I have seen one," I said.

She slowly nodded. What are they like?" I must have grimaced because she immediately added, "Oh. Sorry. How stupid of me. I can be a little insensitive sometimes." She gave that shrill laugh again. "Do you have one of those statues with you?"

"No. Wait. Yes I do. I reached into the pocket of my jacket, lying on the back seat, and pulled out the little statue which I had been carrying around with me for almost a week. Its weight had become so familiar to me that I didn't even notice it any more. I climbed out of the car to stretch my legs while Ayshea turned the statue on its head to look at the base.

"B'vs IV sk," she read out loud. "Any idea about the 'sk'?"

"Not really. A historian friend of mine – Henry de Silva, thought they were something to do with Piere Drang Clenn. Maybe it's an alias?"

"Hmm. Maybe. It's very good workmanship. Do you think it's original?"

"Well, I am not an expert, but I do have an antiques business, and I have been looking at these things since the War. In my opinion that one is genuine – yes. Of course there are a lot of fakes."

"It would have been very difficult to make in the 13th Century. Only a few craftsman could have made it. I am thinking of all the top craftsmen I know from that period."

After scribbling for a few minutes she called out, "Piere England rcn."

After another fifteen minutes scribbling and murmuring to herself she came up with another unscrambling of the anagram.

"Regne clin adn pre. That means 'reign pre covering joint DNA'."

Every few minutes she would come up with another one.

"Gendre lancer pin."

"Cendre rang pin le."

After nearly two hours she came up with one last one. "Cendre panel ring. That means 'ash panel boxing ring' in English" She laughed shrilly. "Oh. I don't know. It eludes me!" She put the pad she was writing on, and the pen, on the shelf formed by the door of the glove-compartment, closed her eyes and leaned back. "Does this chair go right back? I think I need to sleep. My mind is tired now."

"I am sure it does. Ayshea. I am running out of time. I just have this strong feeling that I have to find this secret weapon, where ever it is, very soon – perhaps in the next day or two. And then there is the Gendarmes and also Concilium Putus Visum, although to be honest, I am not sure if they are chasing me. They were certainly chasing my girlfriend.

"Why isn't she helping you? I am not sure if you need a historian. Perhaps you just need a linguist."

"She is dead."

"Dead? How? When? Oh, I am sorry."

"Erm. The night before last – Sunday night. She died near the Sacré-Coeur. I still don't know if it was an accident or not. But we were on the run from the servants of the Concilium Putus Visum."

"The Gendarmes know about it?"

"Oh yes. I gave a statement. She fell from a bridge. You see it could be an accident. I want to believe that it was."

Ayshea sat up and looked at me. "You must be very upset, you poor thing. No wonder you haven't shaved. Or eaten properly. Have you eaten?"

"A little."

She was silent for a while. Then she looked again at the pad. "You know scholars have probably been trying to decode this for centuries. What makes you think we can do it now?" I was surprised at her sudden change of tack but then I thought it must be tact.

"I don't know. Because I have to?"

"You! Ha! It's me that is doing the work."

I looked around me. The birds were singing in the trees. A few sparrows and a crow hopped around the clearing among the tyre tracks, picking up tasty bits of litter, and sticking their heads inside crisp packets hopefully. The wind rustled the leaves in the trees gently to create that soft summer song of nature. It all seemed so calm and I wished I was in another life and that I could just enjoy it. But I was in the centre of a maelstrom, and soon this moment of calm would be gone. From this moment of reflection came a new determination.

"You know Beauvais is my favourite candidate at the moment for the place where this Temple is?"

"No. Well why do you say that?"

"I didn't want to mention it because I didn't want to influence you, but also because I hope it's not Beauvais."

"Why?"

"Because I made a mistake. Last night I left some of my notes in a hotel and it mentions Beauvais. If I go there, the Gendarmes might be waiting for me."

"Well. If that is the correct place, then that is where you have to go. What is your evidence?

"Well. There was a poem. Here. Let me find it." I opened the rear door, pulled out the bag and searched for the translation. I read it aloud to her.

"Alone upon the wall
With axe, throws assailant in the moat

he who removed the flag,
Again the flag was bright
Our hero's reward Le Pilon"

Apparently it's about somebody called Jeanne Laisné, born 1456 who was a French heroine known as Jeanne Fourquet and nicknamed Jeanne Hachette or 'Jean the Hatchet'. And all this took place in Beauvais."

"Where did you find the poem?"

"It was hidden in the chapters about the Ordo Lupus in a book called the 'De Secretis Scientia Occultis'."

"Ah. I have heard of this book, most definitely. It is very valuable – if it exists at all."

"Oh it exists alright and I own a few pages from it. The rest is in the Richelieu Library."

"Really! I didn't know that. I have been wanting to see a copy for years."

"I will show you gladly what I have, later, but right now, there isn't time. Anyway, I think that the secret weapon is in a Crypt and that this may be at Beauvais."

"Beauvais Cathedral is quite famous for its gothic architecture – and its height. I believe it's the highest cathedral in all of France. Of course its been falling down since it was built."

"When was it built?"

"Mid 13th Century I think. An architect friend of mine – Bertrand, knows much more about it than I do."

"So who was the architect?"

"Oh I don't know." Her words petered out quietly as she seemed to focus inwardly on something. Then her voice started up again, rising in volume. "But I do know one of the artists who worked on the Cathedral. His stained-glass windows were the best anywhere. Now what was his name? Something like England. Yes. What was that first silly decoding of the anagram that I wrote down?"

"Yes! That was England something."

"Wait." I could hear the furious rifling of notepad pages from the car. I walked over and leaned in.

"Here. Piere England rcn. Well that's not right. And I think it's Engrand but I can't remember the rest. Oh we will have to call Bertrand."

"Do we have to? It's not really safe."

"Oh it will only take a moment. He will be in his office."

We drove on to the nearest village and next to a village shop, there was a public telephone. While she called Bertrand, I bought a few packets of biscuits and chocolate cake – what girl can resist chocolate cake? I also bought a newspaper and a few cans of Fanta.

Ayshea was smiling when I reached the car. "Engrand Le Prince. Famous stained-glass artist but also, I think, an artist who worked in other mediums. I told you Bertrand would know. He says Le Prince would be working in late 15th Century and did definitely do the stained glass at Beauvais. He also said that Beauvais is one of the first Cathedrals in France which we now think of as Gothic."

"Here. Eat something. You must be hungry." I passed her the carrier bag and she peered inside. "That's great. So Beauvais it is! You didn't tell him where we were?"

"No. Bertrand is cool. We were at college together. Ooh! chocolate cake. My favourite. Beauvais means 'handsome face' you know."

"Really?"

"Um. Let's go"

"Where?"

"Beauvais."

"Wait a minute Ayshea. You can't come with me. This is dangerous. The Gendarmes are after me. Anything could happen."

"Yes I know. Isn't it exciting?"

I was busy trying to think of something even more dire, to put her off, but she saw my what was coming.

"You need a companion – somebody to help you find the Crypt. You know you do." Her words were slightly muffled as she had a mouthful of chocolate cake, and I smiled, as I looked at the flakes of chocolate around her lips.

"Well okay but as soon as it gets dangerous, you have to step aside."

She clapped her pale hands together, making a very thin slap sound. "Oh great! We are going to find the Secret Crypt of Legend – and the Magic Weapon." She paused. "Don't worry. I have no intention of fighting the Serpents."

Beauvais was only about 50 km North from the picnic area in the woods and Ayshea navigated. As we drove I watched her from the corners of my eyes. She was not unattractive, even with her glasses and hair in a bun, but she wore no makeup at all, as far as I could tell, and seemed unaware of her looks. Her face was very finely chiseled, with pale – almost white skin, and freckles. Her blue eyes darted tirelessly this way and that, taking in all that she saw, but giving little away of her deeper emotions. She seemed to hold these permanently in check, and I guessed she found it difficult to really trust people. Perhaps her bookish nature was a form of defense. But then she surprised me. I glanced at her just after we had turned onto a main road, and were easing into a stream of traffic. She had formed her hands into the roof and spire of a church, as kids often do. When she noticed I was watching her, she suddenly turned her hands upside down and formed the batman mask with goggles over her eyes. She looked at me like this and we both laughed. She was very disarming, but her childlike pranks seemed to be a form of genuine naivety. I wasn't quite sure what to make of her. Back at the picnic area, I had, for a moment wished that I could stay there forever, even with Ayshea. Yes, I was slightly attracted to her. But now she seemed so young and naive, I wondered at my own attraction to her.

As if she sensed what I was thinking she asked, "What was Georgina like? Was she very beautiful?"

"Well yes. She was. Very dark haired and very beautiful."

"Was she nice?"

I laughed. "Nice!"

"What's so funny?"

"Well – nice! Umm. I don't think you could really describe her as nice. But she had her good qualities. She was very troubled. Yes, I think it would be fair to say that."

"Oh."

She seemed as sad as I was at my answer. We were both silent for a while, the gentle roaring sound of the tyres on the road and the wind around the windows, drowning out my own thoughts pleasantly. After a while I actually felt like talking, and I didn't think I had give her enough.

"I don't remember much of the Serpent really. What I remember is a sense of enormous strength – it was certainly big – taller than a man. I remember it was like being confronted by a body like fire, and yet at the same time it was completely dark – as if absorbing the light around it. Its surface seemed to shimmer.

"I see. Can I write that down?"

"If you want to." I didn't want to say anything but I wondered if she thought I might not be around much longer for her to record my memories. We were about thirty minutes from Beauvais now, and my thoughts became darkened by the prospect of Gendarmes all over the town. I didn't know whether Parcaud would equate a stolen Renault in Paris with me or whether he would find the notes on the bed and take a chance I might go to Beauvais, but he might. "We have to lose the car."

I took the next turn-off to the right and followed the narrow lane until we reached a small village. There I found what I was looking for. Driving through the village, I saw a white Volkswagen Beetle among a row of cars. The owner was probably some distance away and Beetles are easy to steal. A white one was the most anonymous of all. I drove back out of the village. "Can you drive?"

"Not very well."

"Good. Drive back to the main road and wait for me there."

I easily broke into the Beetle, hot-wired it, and drove casually off in it, back to the main road. It had all the familiar paraphenalia of a family car – cushions, toys on the back seat, empty and half-full packets of sweets, and colouring books.

"Follow me," I shouted to Ayshea when she wound down her window.

I turned onto the main road and drove south, back the way we came – through one village, and then turned off onto a lane, out into open country. I took the next turning to the left, so that we were travelling south again. Ayshea followed in the Renault, until I saw a muddy track. It disappeared under some trees, between two fields. It was not the best place to leave the car – half way to Beauvais, but it would have to do. I stopped and told Ayshea to wait. I drove the Renault into the track, making sure I left heavy tyre tracks on the side of the road, making it clear we had been travelling south. I threw some branches over the car to conceal it a bit more.

"Okay. Let's go to Beauvais."

Just outside Beauvais I saw what I head dreaded – police cars lining the roads. Fortunately they were only stopping cars randomly at this point, not quite confident that I would be here.

"Quick. Swap!"

We swapped places, with the car still moving, and then I hid on the floor, as Ayshea drover past the row of police cars.

"They hardly even looked," she said.

Beauvais is a very large town, almost a city by English standards, with the south side laid out in almost a circular pattern of roads, and the north side a more rectangular grid. Most of the buildings are only two-story, so we could see the Cathedral long before we reached it. Somehow we had to drive past the Cathedral before we did anything.

"Wow! It really is quite special isn't it?" said Ayshea,

It seemed incredibly tall, and is in fact the highest vaulted Cathedral in Europe, the vaulting in the choir reaching forty-eight metres. From the outside, the Cathedral of Saint-Pierre, as it is officially known, is faced with an impressive array of flying buttresses, which reach to its full height.

"Its just so enormously high!" I said.

"Can we go in?" she asked.

"We can try. Let's park somewhere." While looking for a space in a side street, I saw a couple of Gendarmes lazily leaning against a wall. We noticed four more on the way to the Cathedral entrance, more than one would expect, and I tried to keep my face turned away.

"Sorry. You cannot come in tonight. There is a special service in progress", a clergyman explained on the door in French. Ayshea explained politely that we only wanted a glimpse of the choir vault, and that we were just passing through. He relented and let us walk up to the railed-off portion of the choir, where the service was taking place. I looked up and was astonished at the height of the vault far overhead. For a moment I was dizzy, and felt something like vertigo, as I imagined what it would be like to be up near the vaulted ceiling. The black and white tiled floor seemed somehow to add to the effect, making the vast space fluctuate.

"We can't stay. Come on. Let's go," I said.

We reached the corner of the Cathedral just in time. Two Gendarmes were just rounding the opposite corner and approaching the huge wooden doors to the Cathedral.

"Damn. I need to get in that Cathedral as soon as possible. Where do you think it iS, do you think?"

"The crypt?" Ayshea shrugged. "Usually they are in the basement." She laughed, and I laughed at her use of the word 'basement'.

We found a small restaurant in a side street and I treated Ayshea to a four-course meal with wine, coffee and after-dinner chocolates. It was pleasant enough, with candles and soft, lush orchestral music, playing through hidden speakers.

"Now we have the problem of where to stay tonight, " I said.

"We could drive out of town and sleep in the car?"

"No. We would probably be spotted and anyway, that's not a fit rest place for a young lady." She giggled. "No. We have to find a hotel but you will have to smuggle me in somehow."

Driving across town in the car, I suddenly had an idea. "I have to do something before we get a hotel." I drove around for a few minutes, trying different streets before i saw what I was looking for. I parked the car, took my jacket and left Ayshea, mystified in the car for a few minutes. I returned with a carrier-bag and smiled at her as I placed it on the back seat.

"What is it?" she asked.

"A tape-recorder."

"Ah I see."

"Do you? It's for Rose as much as anything."

"Yes but it's a good idea anyway." Her face was creased with concern.

The Hôtel de Royale was what I was looking for. Modern, with plenty of large windows, and large sections of flat roof. It was also only three floors so there was a good chance we could get a ground floor room.

"Here's the money. Two-hundred francs should be plenty for two nights. Find a good room, unpack and then, when you are ready, go out for a walk. I will be waiting for you. Remember. Get a ground floor room if you can."

"Okay. I have never booked a hotel room before. My alias is Madamoiselle Cheuvelle?"

"Yes."

Thirty minutes later she left the front entrance and turned left, towards the town centre. I followed her and when we were out of earshot from the Hotel, I caught up with her.

"Hi!"

"Hello. Who are you?" She laughed. It was the first time I had seen her without her glasses, and her hair was down. She had even applied some blusher and lipstick – God knows where she had hidden that, as I hadn't even seen so much as a purse on her, let alone a handbag. Women have an extraordinary talent for having the right things with them when they need them.

"You look lovely."

"Thank you. You are kind."

"I need a shower. I must look awful," I said.

"Oh. Don't worry. It's a lovely evening. Let's just walk."

She was right. It was warm with just a faint breeze and the many planted flowers, in beds alongside the road, gave the air a sweet tang.

I looked up at the moon, and remembered what time of the month it was. The last quarter had started the day before and the waning gibbous moon looked slightly yellow. I shuddered and tried to put it out of my mind. Ayshea entwined her arm in mine, and we walked like that, past many couples enjoying the evening.

"You are very tense. Are you worried about what might happen tomorrow – in the Cathedral?" she asked.

"Yes. Of course. But I am more worried that I might not get to the Crypt in time. I didn't tell you the whole truth the other day."

"I know. I know tomorrow is the last day."

"You do?"

"I have been following the 'crusher' murders as they have crossed France. The first one was twenty-nine days ago – thirty tomorrow. I know about the heartbeat of God and I know that the Serpents have a thirty day period when they can exist on the earthly plane."

I looked at her in astonishment. She seemed about to tell me something more but something was stopping her. I waited but eventually she looked away.

"You know a lot," I said.

"I should do. I have been studying the subject for years."

"Are you a sorceress?"

She laughed and this time it was shrill.

"One of those. No! I know what you mean though. The followers of the dark cult – they call themselves servants of the Concilium Putus Visum."

"They use another name too. Sometimes they call themselves the Ordo Loup-garou." I laughed bitterly. "Isn't that funny. It's so similar a name it caught me out." I stopped, knowing I had said too much.

"You mean Georgina? She was one of them?"

"I don't want to talk about her," I said quietly.

"I have researched this. The French name for a werewolf, is loup-garou, Obviously you know the Latin noun lupus meaning wolf. The 'garou' bit is thought to be from Old French garoul meaning 'werewolf'. This in turn is most likely from Frankish wer-wulf meaning 'man-wolf'."

It's clever. Most people wouldn't realise it was a counter-cult. It would allow them to insinuate themselves into The Brotherhood. And yet I don't even know anybody in The Ordo Lupus. Not for sure. I think my grandfather was a member. No, I know he was. But he is dead now. I haven't met anyone else." It occurred to me that Ayshea might be. "Are you?"

"Noooo. I am just a historian. My father had no interest in these things, if that is what you are wondering. Neither did my mother."

"Oh."

There was an awkward silence but she ended it. "I haven't met anybody in either cult. My life has been very boring – until now."

"How about your childhood? Do you have brothers and sisters?"

"No. I am an only child. Spoiled really, I suppose."

"No. I don't think so. I have met many spoiled women and you are not like them. You are thoughtful and caring."

"I wasn't in the Library."

"Well, I was rather cheeky with that piece of paper. You probably thought I was chatting you up."

"Ah. That English phrase. You mean making a pass at me?"

"Yes."

"Yes." She blushed. "Err. I am not very experienced with men. There have been a few – especially at college, but I was always too impatient with them. I expect too much, I expect." She laughed nervously at her own little joke.

"Gendarmes!" I whispered and took her hand in mine.

"Oh!"

Her little hand seemed cold to the touch, almost as cold as the metal band on a ring she wore. I kept her close as the Gendarmes on the other side of the street passed us, without really noticing us.

"Tell me a little about yourself – how you came to be here," she said.

"I wonder myself how I came to be here." I told her something about my childhood in Highgate, my two sisters, who I rarely saw these days but talked to on the phone, my time in the War and M.I.6, and life in Bulgaria. I told her how I met Rose, and about life in the Civil Service. Lastly I told her about the statues we had found – Rose and I, and how they had formed the basis of a hobby, which had grown into a business, and now had become a matter of life and death.

When I had finished, she gently withdrew her hand from mine – I had forgotten I was still holding hers, and said, "Let's go back to the Hotel. I am tired."

"Yes."

The room was on the first floor, and when she opened the window, I climbed in quietly with the carrier-bag. It was a large and comfortable room with an en-suite bathroom. I took a shower while she dozed on the bed.

I came out with just a towel around my waist and she was still lying on the bed, but with an impish grin. "My turn. I had a quick shower earlier but I like to soak in a bath every night."

"Yes. I noticed we had a shower *and* a bath."

I collapsed on a stiffly upholstered chair, hooked me leg over an arm, and let my eyes close. I was exhausted.

"Wake up!" It was Ayshea shaking me gently. "I have been out of the bath for an hour! I ordered some coffee from Room Service and they are coming so you better hide in the bathroom."

"What's that noise?" I could hear a tap-tapping somewhere.

"Wind. A branch on the window. The weather has changed while you were asleep."

I came out of the bathroom after the waiter left, and Ayshea, fully dressed again, was busying herself with a tray of coffee. Served in white porcelain with a cute little sugar bowl, and cream, I thought the hotel service was better than I had expected.

"Now. If only we had a wood-fire," said Ayshea.

"Well, we can imagine it. It is very warm anyway."

"Yes, but its getting colder. Can't you feel it?"

I could hear the gentle pitter-patter of raindrops on the window panes. "A storm do you think?"

"Probably. Sugar?"

"One please."

"Cream?"

"Yes please."

"You sound like a little boy!"

"That's not fair. I am not properly awake yet. You are taking advantage of me."

"There is something I want to talk to you about. So drink your coffee and then we will talk."

After I had finished that cup, she refilled it.

"How much do you know of this 'Magic Weapon'?"

"Not much. Just that it is large – too large to conceal in your clothes. I know that there were two of them and that they were brought out of Montségur by the two monks, just before the siege in the 13th Century. Oh yes and the Crypt was built shortly afterwards. That is about all I know."

Hm. That is quite a considerable amount of information, considering that most people have not heard at all of the weapons. There is more though." She pulled her legs up underneath her on the other chair, and settled herself, cradling her cup of coffee on her knee with both hands. "The weapons, which are swords the size and shape of Great Swords, were made from a casket of pure silver which was blessed by Jesus. They were lost, or hidden for many centuries. " Her voice soothed me and as she spoke, I closed my eyes to listen.

"Vos fossor! Quare did vos dico Abbatis nos es leprous! Iam nos es damno pro umquam!"

"Exsisto quietis quod servo pedes!"

The two monks were just dark shapes in the gloom under the battlements of the castle. It was darkness like that's rarely glimpsed in the 20th Century – no candles, no street lights, no faint glow from a city on the horizon. Like wriggling artifacts in a grainy black and white photo, they moved across the mossy rocks towards the steep grass slope, that would lead them down off the rock bluff, upon which the castle was perched. The latin they spoke was crude.

"You fool! Why did you tell the Abbot we were leprous? Now we are damned for ever!"

"Shut up and keep walking."

"What's in these boxes anyway?"

"How should I know? Who cares. They needed mules and we are it! Just thank God we are out of there!"

"I will, when I get a decent meal, and a barrel of ale."

Montségur loomed like a jagged tooth against the faint star-light above them. The siege of 1244 was almost at an end – there was no more food, precious little water, and most of the Cathars were ready to risk surrender. On the darkest night, with black clouds obscuring the sliver moon, the two monks had slipped out through a hidden tunnel, carrying their precious cargo. For monks, they were brawny, and hefted the five-foot long crude wooden boxes on their shoulders with ease, as they negotiated the rocks and came to the grassy slope.

"Shh! The enemy lines are near. The buggers will eat us for dinner if they don't burn us."

Huddling low on the rocks, so as not to show a silhouette against the sky, they crawled and scrambled between two large boulders, and found themselves between a tent and a row of tied-up horses.

"Nice horse," whispered the leading monk to a horse, patting it's nose, fearful that it would give them away. They crossed a roughly defined causeway between two rows of tents, and saw a sentry leaning lazily against a rock, flagon of ale slung lazily over his arm. He was looking from side to side, but was on the lookout for superior officers rather than the enemy. He didn't notice the two shadows, close to the ground, fifty feet in front of him. They passed alongside another tent with voices within, and then chose a a path cutting obliquely across the steep continuation of the slope on the other side of the causeway. This part of the slope was too steep for tents and soon they were safely out of earshot of the camp.

"Gratiae exsisto ut Deus" The rearmost monk offered up a prayer to God. "We're through." A small town lay only half a mile below them but they didn't head for it. They started for a large cave they knew that cut into the rocky hillside, a few miles further down the valley.

"Will we ever see any of the other again, do you think?" said the leading, and more lanky monk?"

"I don't think so. If they surrender they will be burned or at least tortured. Lord Raymond will be burned for sure."

"It's a shame. He's a noble Lord."

"Yeah. Not a bad type."

And then they were gone into the night. When they reached the cave, they found a niche deep inside, dug a trench into the dusty soil beneath their feet, and buried the two long boxes. Then they went their own ways, each seeking shelter with a Cathar families they knew in the area."

I felt I was in a dream. Perhaps I was listening to Ayshea's voice and perhaps it really was a dream. I started, and suddenly I was listening to her normal voice again.

"Probably, they were hidden in the Crypt which if it is in Beauvais Cathedral, would have been built at the correct time. In any case, some time early in this century, a man who is now known as the Interfeci- meaning 'cruel slayer', found one, and began using it to fight, and indeed, kill the Serpents. He since became the most successful Serpent Slayer of modern times – perhaps of all time. However it is not known if the other Weapon still exists."

"Where did you find all this?"

"Oh. It has taken years to piece it all together."

"Do you know anything more about The Ordo Lupus?"

"Only what you probably know already."

"Well, tell me. You would be surprised how little I know."

"Okay. Another coffee?" She was kneeling on the thick rug next to the low carved oak coffee table, pouring another for herself – black.

"Mmm. Maybe one more. I really should get a good night's sleep."

"Really! You don't know much about flattering a woman do you?" It was such a playful and intelligent flirt, that I knelt on the rug on the opposite side of the low table. I was probably old enough to be her grandfather and when I had come out of the bathroom with just a towel around me, I had sucked my sagging belly in – more to save her sensibilities than my own embarrassment, but now, flirting seemed harmless, and even necessary, to calm both our nerves.

"One thing I was going to ask," I said. "You said these Swords are in the shape of great swords, but made of pure silver? So presumably they are completely useless as real weapons? I mean they won't cut very effectively."

"Yes. That is true. But they are not purely ornamental. Silver is believed by many to have a sort of purity – hence the legend of killing vampires by impaling them with a silver knife. In fact these Swords may well be the origin of that legend."

"So they are for stabbing the Serpents with?"

"I don't know. Maybe."

"So you were going to tell me some more about the Brotherhood."

"Well it is only what you probably know already. The story goes that the winged snakes are really demons and that they are fighting these winged wolves who are really fallen angels, and trying to get back to heaven by killing the snakes. God gave them the form of wolves, so they would be different from the snakes, and he also gave them the silver swords. Of course you know the rest. The snakes are invisible normally, and 'constrict' the fabric of the world, making evil things happen to people, and living off the souls of the dead. Every sixty years, the fabric of space is torn for a period of thirty days,s and the snakes have to survive but actual killing and they take real bodies."

"That bit about the snakes 'constricting' space and making bad things happen to people – it sounds exactly like a quote I have heard before. Henry was reading from the 'De Secretis Scientia Occultis'."

"Really? Probably is the same text, but from another source."

"So I guess these wolf-angels have something to do with The Ordo Lupus."

"Yes. Exactly. I would think that the Interfeci was a Lupus Angelus. Sorry. I forgot your coffee!" She laughed and poured the now luke-warm coffee. She leaned over the table to hand it to me but then she lost her balance, and her elbow crashed into the glass top of the table. "Wo!" she cried, and then there was a gasp as her back hit the floor. I rushed around the table.

"Ayshea! Are you alright?"

"Merde! How stupid I am!" Then she laughed the most shrill laugh of all those that I had heard from her. I scooped her up, and helped her onto one of the chairs. "I suppose I am a little bit tired," she said.

The branch outside was hammering on the window now, the wind beginning to howl. In pulses between the sound of the wind, I could hear rain lashing down.

Tired, I was just drifting off when I heard Ayshea's little voice. "You know you are a wolf-angel?"

I was alert again and I smiled at her. "I am not sure about that but it's time to use that tape-recorder. Will you help me?"

"Of course."

I took the small box out of the carrier-bag and unpacked the mini cassette recorder. It was a dictating cassette recorder with a built in microphone and I had bought batteries and ten microcassette tapes too. I loaded the batteries and one of the tiny cassettes, and did a quick test recording. I played it back and listened to my voice which sounded muffled. I moved closer to the cassette recorder, pressed record and said, "Tape one. Ayshea, I am going to tell the whole tale, as best I can and I want you to stop me if I am unclear and ask questions. Is that okay?"

"Okay."

I recorded for nearly five hours, switching to new tapes at appropriate points in the story, after labeling them. When it was done I had eight recorded tapes. It was close to dawn.

"Ayshea. Look after these tapes okay? If anything happens to me, I would like the tapes to be given to Rose and published too, if possible. Here is Paul's number." I wrote it down on a scrap of paper. "He will get a copy to Rose and might be able to help with publishing." I loaded a blank cassette into the recorder and put it in my jacket pocket.

"Okay. I will. Now you need to get some sleep at least."

While she lay on the bed, I pushed two chairs together and curled up on them, falling sleep almost immediately.

I woke up wondering about her comment about me being a wolf-angel. My dreams and waking thoughts had been a sea of doubts, and vague images of things half-forgotten – half-imagined. Could it be that I was some kind of spiritual warrior or something? It seemed too ludicrous and I kept dismissing it with a smile. But the thought would still be there, lingering.

I wasn't uncomfortable on the two chairs but I was restless. I couldn't get back to sleep and Ayshea's light but steady breathing seemed to mark out time, so that I was too conscious of its passing. I quietly picked up my bag and went into the bathroom, switched on the light, and closing the door. Unzipping the bag I rummaged for my shaver and took it out. I put in two new batteries I had bought in Paris, but I wasn't hopeful that it would work. It buzzed into life, bringing a smile to my face.

At last, some luck.

I spent a happy half hour washing and generally repairing the damage of the last few days, until I found myself staring intently at my own image in the mirror, my, mostly grey hair, outlining a rough, craggy face. I didn't even notice the difference in colour of my two eyes any more – at least I didn't notice that it was unusual. Beauvais means 'handsome face', I remembered Ayshea telling me. This thought went around and around in my mind, but I could only see the face of a troubled man. I knew what I might have to do that day, as at times during the War, conviction – absolute and utter conviction that I had to do something, made thoughts – fear of death, shrink to almost nothing. Of course I didn't know exactly what I would have to do that day, but I thought – almost hoped, that it would involve a fight with the Serpent – he or it, who had been stalking me for the last month, and perhaps for years.

"Are you finished in there Monsieur?" called Ayshea from just outside the door.

"Almost. Be out in five minutes."

Later, she ordered breakfast in her room, enough for what must have seemed like a very large woman. Two round of everything and a large plate of bacon, eggs, fried bread, tomatoes and mushrooms.

"Eat it all," she said. "I only want a slice of toast. I am not hungry." She watched me eat my way through just about everything on the tray. "What is the plan today?" she asked.

"Um. To get into the Cathedral and somehow, find this crypt. Then after that, I don't know. I suspect the Serpent will find *me*."

"And you think it will be difficult to get in?"

"Well yes. The Gendarmes will probably be there and Pastor Michel."

"Pastor Michel? Who is he?"

"Ah. You haven't met Pastor Michel yet?"

"No."

"He seems to be the main agent on my case from the Concilium Putus Visum. He chased Georgina and I in Paris. I only know his face from an old photo."

"Oh."

"Ayshea. I need to make a quick call. I wrote the number down. Can you get reception and ask to be put through?"

"Okay."

When she was put through, she passed the telephone to me, and I heard my lifelong friend Paul's familiar voice."

"Hello."

"Paul. Its only me. Just a quick call."

"Where the deviL are you? Rose is going out of her mind!"

"Oh really? Well. I can't tell you actually but I am not in Paris."

"You really have to hand yourself in old boy. It's no joke any more."

"Yes." I knew I sounded vague.

"Listen. Remember in Sofia during the War when I called and we knew three was a crowd?"

"Oh yes." I paused to think. "Lovely girl."

"Well I heard from her again just now."

"Oh. Well, just before I go, have you heard anything from Cosette?"

"No. Not a thing."

"Oh. Alright. Bye then."

"Cheerio."

"We have to leave now," I told Ayshea. "His telephone was bugged. It's possible the Gendarmes will be on their way here now."

It was eight-thirty. I took a few items from the bag, and stuffed them in thE pocket of my jacket, putting it over my shirt to keep me warm. It was quite a cool day for August, with the wind still rustling leaves around the window, as I climbed out. "Meet you near the car in half an hour," I told her. I had parked the car well away from the hotel, nearer to the Cathedral.

When I reached the car, I waited on a street corner nearby, for only a minute. Two Gendarmes were guarding the Beetle, and what looked like some plain-clothed police, were casually leaning against walls or smoking or reading magazines at other places along the street. I retraced my steps and waited on a corner of the street I hoped Ayshea would come down, well away from the car.

"What is wrong? she said, when she arrived.

"Gendarmes watching the car. Let's go."

We soon reached a small open space – smaller than a park, near to the Cathedral. I couldn't see any plain-clothes, or uniformed police, anywhere. I sat Ayshea on a bench. "Listen Ayshea. Things are getting really hot here. I have the Gendarmes after, me, the Concilium Putus Visum, and a snake. As I told you, I am a suspect for murder, and its entirely possible somebody might shoot at me when I get to the Cathedral. I can't take you with me. It's just too dangerous."

"But that's not fair!" She stood up suddenly and faced me, with that imperious look I had seen in the library. "You drag me away from Paris, bring me here, and make me stay in a hotel for a night – with a complete stranger, *and* run away from the Gendarmes, and now you want to just leave me? Huh! No." The 'no' was adamant.

I had to admit to myself, it was going to be really hard to get in to the Cathedral. "Okay. You can help me get in, but when I say you must go, you must listen to me. Is that a deal?"

"Hm." She didn't sound happy, but I took that as a 'yes'.

"Okay. Let's go. I glanced up at the sky. Storm clouds were gathering in a weird cyclonic swirl, which seemed centred on Beauvais.

The Cathedral was in the plan-shape of a crucifix but a very truncated, with the upper stem very shortened. The choir, or long stem, was very wide, with the apse – the dome shape over the altar at the end of the long stem, also very wide, giving the whole Cathedral more of the plan-shape of a filled-in 'U'. It had no tower. One had been built, of immense height, but had fallen on Ascension day in the 16th Century, minutes after the congregation had left, and remarkably,nobody was killed. As a result, work on the Cathedral had been halted, with no tower being rebuilt.

The main entrance was in the left of the two arms – or transept, of the crucifix shape, and consisted of two huge, carved wooden doors, atop a flight of stone steps. It had no plaza or wide open spaces around it, and the little houses crowded around the old lady's skirts, as if listening to a winter's tale. The contrast of size between the houses and Cathedral made it look even more imposing. It was a web of column upon column of flying buttresses – towers which rose to the roof, supporting its immense weight which pushed outwards.

Author's note: This marks the end of the story which was taken from the tapes. The rest of this tale is gleaned from several sources including an extensive interview with woman who is here represented by Ayshea Aikborne, a woman who has only recently come forward, making this story possible.

* * *

Chapter Nine

5:1, 1:2, lonely, time, alternatively, ventilated

"Alone in the roof-space I am thinking about Rose's note once again. I can tell too, that there is still, burning in her, a spark for me. What Paul had said to me the last time we spoke on the phone, comes back to me. "Rose is going out of her mind!" That doesn't sound like a woman who has lost all feelings for me. That thought gives me strength. Perhaps there is hope for us after all, Perhaps, if I could find the Sword, prove that the beast had killed Annie, Rose, would believe me at last. I will look again for the Sword."

We crossed the wide open road in front of the cathedral,, and walked around the side to the main entrance, which was opposite a narrow approach road. As we crossed the space, I felt something looking at me from high up on the Cathedral – perhaps on the roof. Instinctively I looked up. "Do you see anything – on the roof? Something is watching us. I think it's the Serpent."

"I can't see anything."

I looked up again and noticed something move near the top of the flying-buttress on the southern end of the Cathedral. I concentrated on the spot but my eyes wouldn't focus. That area seemed blurred somehow. "Look near the top of the buttress."

"No. I can't see anything."

We reached the steps and started up towards the doors. It was immediately apparent to me that the place was swarming with plain-clothed police. Every other person was single, male and looked completely disinterested in the building above them. I grabbed Ayshea's elbow and steered her back down the stairs and across the road to the open space. "You have to go Ayshea. It's no good. You could get shot. I have to get in there."

Her shoulders sank and she let out a little sigh. "Be careful then. Give me just one little kiss." She reached up and gave me a chaste peck on the cheek.

"Wait for me at the restaurant we went to last night." At that point, she seemed very reluctant to leave, so I had to be firm. I gave her a little wave. "Bye." I turned and headed back towards the edge of the open space. I looked behind me and Ayshea was just disappearing from view, around the corner of a building. I let out a sigh of relief and stopped to consider what to do next. I had no idea how I was going to get into Beauvais Cathedral. After about ten minutes, watching the movements of the plain-clothes I could see, the only thing I could think of was to pretend to be a guide, and attach myself to a group as they approached the steps. I saw a likely-looking group and made my way across the road, trying to look very formal. I wished I had a clipboard in my hands.

"Bonjour mesdames et messieurs. Si vous visitez notre belle cathédrale aujourd'hui, vous aiment un guide? Pour un prix raisonnable je peux vous dire tout au sujet de l'histoire de cette cathédrale gothique du 13ème siècle." I laid it on thick about value for money and my expert knowledge, in my poor French, but they weren't impressed. Apart from one matriarch with a blue rinse who eyed me appreciatively, they all looked at me as if I was a cheap vacuum-cleaner salesman. They turned and continued up the steps leaving me alone. In a crowd of clusters of people and single men, I was the only single man who wasn't a Gendarmes. A bead of sweat formed on my forehead, as I looked for any other groups that I could try. There were none. I felt my throat tightening as a young, well-dressed, but formal looking guy approached me.

This is it.

"Don't turn around. Just follow me," spoke a familiar voice behind me. I felt a hand on my shoulder and I followed her up the stairs, trying to look as relaxed as possible, and ignoring the man who had stopped, and was looking at us both suspiciously.

Ayshea led me back around the corner of the building to the side we had approached from, and I noticed she had a straw-hat on. "I am glad you are here. That was getting a little hairy. What's is the hat for?" I said.

"Disguise. Here try this."

From, a carrier-bag, she handed me a long curly, brown wig, and I didn't hesitate. Nobody appeared to be looking, so I turned towards the wall and put it on.

"Try these too." She handed me a pair of thick, black-rimmed glasses, and I willingly put them on. "Where did you find them?"

"A second-hand stall in the market."

"Let's go."

I followed her and we breezed past all the Gendarmes, and into the Cathedral as if it were any normal couple going into a Cathedral. A Gendarmes in the doorway, even smiled at us.

"We're in!" I resisted the urge to laugh at our success.

"Yes. Thanks to me!"

"I know. Thanks baby." I squeezed her arm.

"Baby?"

I didn't reply. A service was in progress, and the great organ pipes boomed in the vast space that stretched out before, and above us. We turned right into the great nave of the Cathedral. The black and white, checkered tiles, seemed to make the vast hall shimmer, in and out of focus, in a way that accentuated the height and made me dizzy.

"Wow! Look at that." Ayshea looked up at the vaulted ceiling way above us and laughed. "Did you know it's the highest vaulted ceiling of any Cathedral anywhere?"

"Yes. You told me. It's pretty impressive."

"Oh, you Engleesh. You are so.... so... controlled!" Her French accent showed when she was excited or amused.

I had to admit, the vaulted ceiling was more than impressive. It was mind-boggling – and stomach-churning.

"Let's find the crypt," I said.

"Umm. Over there I think," said Ayshea pointing to a set of wide, well-worn stone steps lead down. There were other people following their curiosity down to the basement, along with the usual plain-clothes, and Ayshea said we looked inconspicuous, although I felt that I must stick out like a sore thumb, with the long curly brown hair.

"Relax. Nobody is looking at you." We hunted around, not really quite knowing what we were looking for. I even lifted a few of the long, heavy red drapes, aside in some of the alcoves, but there was only bare 13th Century stonework behind. I even found myself tapping one of the masonry blocks. "Mad," I said to myself. It was solid stone.

Then we found ourselves circling around a large bronze tomb near the very back of the crypt.

It must be from the very earliest years of the Cathedral.

Gradually we both realised the significance of it. As if out of a trance and suddenly awake, we both exclaimed at once.

"Look!" Ayshea said.

"Wolves!" I said.

Around the base of the large bronze tomb, which was itself about ten feet high, perhaps twelve long, and four wide, at the corners were four wolf-men statues. Like satyrs and at first, you would have mistaken them for such, it was only when you looked closely that you could see, behind the horn drinking cups which they held to their lips, that they were wolf-men. Not only that, but they were attached to the tomb itself by what I could then see were highly stylised wings, which at their tips, became part of the decoration of the tomb. We eagerly sought the name of whoever was interred. A Knight perhaps? Finally we found a name but it was not one either of us was familiar with. 'Guillaume de Grez, died 1293'. We looked all around the tomb, but nothing more was said of him.

"Hmm. Well I wonder who *he* was" I said. I noticed a face out of the corner of my eye – one of the crowd. His face was strangely familiar. At first I couldn't place it and then I realised who it must be. Yes, older, but undoubtedly that face from the old grainy photo was staring at me. It was Pastor Michel. He was looking at me, and for the briefest of moments, our eyes locked and then he looked away. I didn't say anything to Ayshea.

"I don't know. We could ask." she said.

"What?. Oh, let's look some more." We continued our search, and I found myself trying the handle of a door, hidden in an alcove, but it was locked. Slightly frustrated, we decided to find somebody to ask about the tomb. It seemed that nobody who worked in the Cathedral was in the crypt, so we ascended back up to the ground floor, and walked the great nave itself, where the service we just concluding. A verger was standing dutifully at the end of the aisle, waiting to accept donations from the worshippers, and we asked him about Guillaume de Grez.

"Yes. He is a very important Bishop of Beauvais. A local man, he actually added nearly five metres to the height of the great vault," he said reverentially, pointing to the space above us. Again we peered up to the mighty cream-coloured scallops of the vault, 158 feet above us.

"Interesting," I whispered to Ayshea as we walked away. "What do you think?"

"Well yes. Interesting but where is the Crypt that we are looking for."

"I don't know. It's here somewhere. I can't think."

"Let's get a coffee."

"Where?" I said, confused.

"Over there." She pointed to an area at the far side of the transept, opposite the door we had come in through. There were some tables and what looked like a small canteen. I laughed with delight. I had never thought to find a café in a Cathedral.

"How civilised."

She smiled.

With two coffees, and an almond biscuit-like cake, native to the South of France, and something I am fond of, we set about solving the riddle.

"Well. If it's down there, we are not going to get access without help."

"Yes. I don't know who to ask, but maybe we could try a bribe?"

"Bribing the Church? Are you crazy?" I said.

"Oh well. Everybody has their price."

Ayshea! I am shocked. That doesn't sound like you. Are you sure that is not blind optimism talking?"

She laughed at the metaphor. "I am sure we could try one of those vergers. They must be poorly paid, and perhaps I could even try a little charm on him." She had a naughty twinkle in her eye.

"Oh now you really are being optimistic." I laughed. She kicked me hard under the table.

"Listen!" she said. "Have you heard what people are talking about?"

I listened but it was hard to make out individual conversations. "What are they saying?"

"They are talking about the storm. They say it is supernatural – perhaps a visitation by the Devil, or some great religious event. They say it is right over Beauvais. Typical superstitious French Catholics!" She let out one of her familiar shrill laughs.

After another coffee each, and many caffeine-fueled blind-alleys explored, we were out of ideas. We both stared at our empty coffee cups. I glared at the nave and I could see the Bishop approaching, behind the last of his flock of worshippers, preceded by the Dean of the Chapter who was himself preceded by the Head Verger and some other vergers. The organ was just a murmur now, playing the church equivalent of muzak.

"Wait! Perhaps the Crypt is not below!"

I nearly jumped out of my skin. Ayshea's voice was like a shout. "What do you mean?"

"Did you notice? The four wolf-angels each had a hand pointing to the sky."

"Yeah? Is that significant?"

"It could be. The meaning of the word crypt is from Greek, meaning 'hidden' or 'secret'. She paused.

"Yes?"

"So it doesn't mean it's 'down below' or 'below ground'."

"I suppose so. Where could it be then?"

"Up there? Above the vault."

"I craned my neck. Above the vault? What is up there?"

"Well, normally not a lot. A lot of wood that is. Not much else. It *could* be up there."

"Hmm." I thought about it for a moment. At first it seemed like a crazy idea, but then again, if there was an enormous space up there that nobody would normally see, it would be a really good place to hide a secret crypt.

"Okay. So how do I get up there?"

"I don't know but perhaps we really should ask one of the vergers. Think about it. If there is a whole secret crypt up there, then somebody who works here would have to know about it."

"Oh no." Just then, I noticed another familiar face across the transept. Parcaud, in full uniform, was talking to the Dean of the Chapter. "That Officer. I know him. He is from Nevers and he has pursued me for some time." I looked studiously at my coffee for what seemed like an age, but when I looked up, he was not even looking my way.

"Don't worry. He has looked at us several times and he is not interested."

"Let's speak to the Head Verger. You are right. He would be the one to ask."

"There he is."

We were two of many, swirling around the clergy of the Cathedral, and it was a while before I could speak to him. I asked him politely if he had heard of the 'Ordo Volatilis Lupus'. I used the Latin version for discretion, since we were in public. Both Ayshea and I saw the result. He looked from one of my eyes, to the other, and I could see recognition in *his* eyes. His face turned white, and beads of sweat formed on his forehead. It seemed as if he would stay silent, and I was about to walk away, when he uttered something.

"What was that?" I said in French. "Can you repeat it please?"

He said again in old French, "He who is Good, is pinned to he cross when he looks into the Serpents eyes – he who is damned, feels himself emersed in the cauldrons of Hell". His words delivered, he apologised, turned and walked away in a hurry. For a moment I was too surprised to speak.

"Come on." I took Ayshea by the elbow, and we walked away from the crowd, down one of the aisles to the side of the nave. I whispered to her, but my voice sounded too loud – the sound carrying in the vast, chamber. "What do you make of that."

"The poor man looked terrified. What are we getting ourselves into?"

"Not 'we' – me. I am not going to let anything happen to you. What did you think he meant?"

"Well it's a quote from somewhere, but I don't know where."

"He must know something. At least he knows about the Brotherhood. Somebody has put the fear of God into him and I think I know who."

"Who?"

"Pastor Michel. He is here. I have seen him. He really *is* evil. Garrotting is his speciality."

"Where? What does he look like? Is he one of the priests?"

"No. He was in plain clothes – a suit I think. I saw him in the crypt."

"Oh God. They are all here for you! They are all out to get you! This isn't going to work! Something terrible is going to happen."

"Probably yes. I won't lie to you but I have to do this – for Annie and for myself." She looked away from me. At first I thought it was fear, but she wouldn't meet by gaze. There was something else, but I didn't have time now to find out. "We must find the way up to the space above the vault. Where do you think it would be?"

It was a few moments before she spoke, sounding irritated. "Did you notice those turrets at the ends of the transept wings? They go right to the top and have little windows in them. I guess there are spiral stairs in them. Perhaps you can reach them from the gallery or the – erm – what do you call the upper gallery?"

"Clerestory?"

"Yes."

"Well. Lets look." We walked back towards the transept, and I noticed the great wooden buttresses, behind the last pillars of the aisle, that had been built in this century to keep the Cathedral from falling down. There were also huge wooden cross-braces high up in the transept between its two walls. We turned to the left, towards the door we had come in through, and then left again, into the aisle where there were many alcoves, some with doors.

"There!" I pointed to a door which the Dean of the Chapter had just opened. Beside the door was a plain-clothes Gendarme. "I need to get up there! I need to talk to the Dean and see if he knows anything! Can you distract the Gendarme for a moment?"

"Well I don't know. I have never tried anything like that. I am just a normal girl you know." She looked slightly indignant, and slid her glasses back on her nose with her forefinger.

"Please try."

"Okay. Wait just over there."

I stood near a pillar, pretending to look up at it's great height but I was watching Ayshea out of the corner of my eye. Whatever she was saying to the Gendarme was working. She had taken her glasses off and was shaking out her hair. He appeared to be giving her his full attention. Then, she appeared to slip on her high-heels, and went to sit down on a ledge, rubbing her ankles. He was very attentive, and with my heart in my mouth, I approached the door, opened it, and was through. I quickly shut it, and started up the narrow stairs, which turned through ninety degrees to the door and then went straight up. Bare stone and badly worn, they were the width of my shoulders, and lit by a bare bulb about every ten feet. The stairs went straight up in the main wall of the Cathedral, until they reached a curtained-off area of the Gallery. Any moment, while I had climbed the stairs, I had expected to hear "Arrêté!" from below. The stairs turn through ninety degree again, at the top, and I looked left and right along the empty Gallery. I couldn't see where the Dean had gone but there were several heavy wooden doors on the inner side of the Gallery, set into edifices that looked like large pillars, set apart from those that stretched to the roof of the Nave. I turned left and tried the handle of the first door. It was locked. Then the next – locked. The third opened with an ancient creak and I found myself facing the Dean, who was startled, half disrobed.

"How did you get in here!" he said in French. He was tall, had a rich, deep baritone voice, and wispy white hair, which had become matted with sweat under the mitre he had been wearing. His penetrating blue eyes had assessed me instantly as no immediate threat, but a problem.

"I am sorry for the intrusion. I am in great need of information and help. Otherwise I wouldn't be here. As you probably guessed, I had to negotiate the Gendarmes to get up here." I spoke in French.

"Indeed." His eyebrows showed his disapproval. "You seem to be a man who is not easily put off when you want to speak to someone."

This impressed me. He was cautious, but curious. "Have you heard of the Ordo Lupus?"

He laughed. "Well. You are very direct. In fact I have, but they are an ancient cult, and I don't think they are active any more. Why do you ask? Are you an academic?" He removed his Bishop's scarf and turned around a chair, before sitting facing me, arms crossed, and with his long legs set out elegantly in front of him. "Please. Sit down." He indicated the other chair at the small table. The room was polygonal – I couldn't tell how many sides, but probably eight or ten – and only about eight feet across, with its furnishings specially shaped to fit the unusual room. The table was shaped to fit two sides, and opposite, to my left, a blue drape covered one of the other sides. A few religious paintings hung on the walls, and a small wash-basin was against the wall to my right.

I wasn't sure how much to tell this man. A man of the cloth, nevertheless, I didn't know how much to trust him. After all, Pastor Michel was also a man of the cloth. "My daughter was killed by a demon, and as I understand it, the Brotherhood have a reputation for killing these demons."

"Do they? I only know them in a clerical sense. They kept good records of their times, and as a historian, I have taken an interest in them."

"So I came to the right place then?"

"I can tell you a little, but others can tell you more." His eyes glanced to something near the blue drape, for just a moment. I wondered what he was hiding. I was tiring of this cat-and-mouse game. I stood up, as if to go, but glanced over to a small bookshelf near the drape. On the lower of its two shelves were a neat row of bound volumes, like ledgers, and instantly, on one, green, I recognised a wolf's head, embossed in gold-leaf.

"Do you know the password?" he asked me.

"What?" This seemed a change of direction and I guessed that he had guessed what I had seen.

"No I don't."

"Well then I can't help you."

"But just now you said.."

He interrupted me, standing up and pushed me with his hands outstretched. "You must leave now. I am sorry. I cannot help you."

I wasn't going to leave that easily, and I reached for the green volume, but he was quick. He reached for a gold-threaded chord that hung from a slot in the wall. It was clearly some kind of bell-pull that rang in some other office – a form a communication common in medieval buildings. Before he could pull it, I lunged at him and jabbed with my fingers up under his rib-cage – an attack taught us in M.I.6. Although it hurt my fingers because he was still wearing a tightly bound sash, the jab penetrated far enough, and he crumpled to the floor with a moan and lay still. He would be badly winded or unconscious for a few minutes but no other harm would be done. I didn't like to do it but my need was great.

I picked up the green book and opened it. It did indeed appear to be a ledger, with pages and pages of accounts and a few unrecognised names throughout. It mainly appeared to be costs for stone-work and transportation, and appeared dated from the early 1700s onwards. The sheets were in fact photocopies of much older sheets, whose ragged edges were faithfully reproduced in the facsimile. In leafing though the book, I became vaguely aware of a door behind the blue drape but at first the book held my full attention. Once I realised it was of little value to me, the door became more interesting. I couldn't wait around long so I tried the handle and the door opened onto a darkened stone stairway. I fumbled for a light-switch but found none in the stairway. Pushing aside the drape I finally found one and flicked it on. A bulb lit in the stairway and I could see that it led up in a straight direction. I wasn't sure of my directions within the Cathedral now but I didn't need to be. It went up and that was what I wanted. I went up the stairs, which were even more narrow than the ones up to the Gallery, but hardly worn at all. After about twenty feet, they doubled back on themselves, and this repeated several times until I was faced by another door, guarded by a stone basilisk peering at me from its lintel. I tried this door too and it opened, this time into an enormous space, which could really only be discerned as enormous by the odd chink of bright sunlight jabbing into the gloom though tiny slits in the sloping walls. This had to be the roof space above the vault. "At last," I said under my breath. I was standing on a small wooden platform above the rafters, and a panel on the wall to my right had a few notice-boards, warning of various dangers, and that hard hats needed to be worn. There were various switches and I pressed the first one. Instantly the space was lit up by a long row of bare bulbs hanging on both walls. I would guess the distance to the end of the space was about two-hundred feet or more, fifty wide and about the same high. It was truly a dizzying sight. What looked like acres of oak as far as I could see – like an odd, but beautifully shaped forest. My awe was quickly displaced by disappointment however. I could see no crypt up here. From my little platform, there were wooden boards, laid across the joists, which led to a small raised platform, perhaps a third of a way along the space, where workmen were clearly working on one of the beams that braced the roof internally. Their greasy mugs and piles of sawn wood could just be made out in the gloom. I took one last, disappointed look around, and then went back down the stairs, and entered the Bishop's room, pushing aside the drape.

"Ah. At last." It was Parcaud, standing in the small polygonal room pointing a gun at me as I emerged from the stairs. I could see no sign of the Dean. "The wig and glasses are slightly absurd, but I recognise you now. Please remove the glasses.

"It's been a long time Officer. You have been chasing me I hear."

"Yes. And I nearly caught you in Paris."

"Paris? Ah. The hotel."

"Yes. It was me that shot at you on the roof."

"You missed."

"Sometimeser we choose not to kill Monsieur."

"You mean you missed deliberately?"

"Let us just say I am not satisfyed of your guilt just yet. I am not prepared to be your executioner."

This gave me hope. "Listen. You have seen those great swirling clouds outside?"

"Of course. The whole town is worried about it. Hysteria iz building."

"Haven't you wondered why I am here in the Cathedral?"

"Before the Dean was taken aware for medical attention ee said something about a cult. Ee said you were askinger about it – The Ordo Lupus."

"I believe that cult has a Secret Crypt in this Cathedral and that the clouds are caused by something – some creature, which is here to find the Crypt and perhaps take something. I believe the same creature is the one who killed my daughter in Nevers all those years ago." My voice rose gradually almost to a pained shout as I added, "I saw it! I saw it!"

"Alright Monsieur. Calm down. There are many Gendarmes who believe you are a killerer and they want you dead. If we to get you a fair trial – and I *do* want a fair trial, you have to trust meer. Pleeze.. sit down." He indicated the Dean's chair with an outstretched hand, but at that moment, through the doorway to the main corridor came another familiar person – Pastor Michel. He was wearing a plain, dark grey suit, with a waist-jacket. I just caught a glimpse of a wet patch under the waist-jacket pocket before he pulled the jacket over, to cover it.

"Monsieur," said Parcaud, acknowledging the other with a polite nod.

"Ah. You have him. At last." said Pastor Michel. It was strange to hear this mysterious man speak at last. So familiar had I been with his face, and rumour of his character, that I had scarcely imagined his voice. Even so, I shuddered slightly when he spoke. It was quiet, melodic and cultivated, but cold. There was something coarse, hidden there – almost completely concealed by practice. I thought from his accent, that perhaps he was not French originally, and perhaps as a boy he lived in the country. His eyes darted this way and that, only touching for the briefest of instants on my own. I could not read what was in his mind.

I could see he was breathing heavily though. He stepped away from me, and closer to Parcaud.

"Did you find anything?" he asked quietly, pointing to the open door behind the drape, which was still half pulled aside."

"No."

"I thought not." He seemed on the verge of a snigger and his lips curled in a smile. "It has been a wasted journey for you my friend. "We nearly caught you in Paris, but unfortunately you escaped from us just long enough to kill that lovely young woman – what was her name? Georgina wasn't it?"

"You bastard. It was your Council who had her killed. It may well have been you that pushed her!"

"You are a liar Monsieur. Also a very dangerous killer. Monsieur Parcaud knows that you killed the Head Verger."

"What? He was alive when I last spoke to him. Petrified, but alive."

"He was killed a few minutes ago. It appears he was strangled or perhaps something similar. Perhaps his neck was crushed, like the other victims you are responsible for?" Parcaud seemed to be goading me but there was a strange look in his eye.

"Me? No. I know who it was." I pointed to Pastor Michel. "He was garroted and I can tell you that this man – Pastor Michel kills frequently – by garroting."

"Absurd." Pastor Michel had a sickly smile on his face as he denied it.

"Check his waist-jacket pocket. You will find a blood stained rosary in it."

Pastor Michel laughed but I could see Parcaud was interested.

"If he has nothing to hide, let him show you." I said

"Monsieur. Just to assure our capteeve, please show your waist-jacket pocketser," said Parcaud.

"Don't be absurd. Is this a joke?"

"Please."

"No. I am leaving now. I have to leave." He took a small step towards the door, but Parcaud pointed the gun at him for a moment, before pointing it back in my direction.

"Please," said Parcaud to Pastor Michel, pointing the gun back at me.

Pastor Michel seemed rooted to the spot, but as Parcaud slowly pulled aside his jacket lapel, revealing the dark stain, his hand was brushed away viciously and the gun pointed away from me for a moment. I moved towards the door and Parcaud shouted "Stop." I guessed that he wouldn't shoot me now and I ran out through the door, and back to the stairs.

"Wait!" I heard Parcaud shout. Then there were muffled shouts as I guess the two men started a scuffle.

As I rushed down the stairs I heard the servant of the Pastor's acid voice, one last time. "You have no powers. You cannot fight the Serpent. Despair! Heretic! Heathen!"

As I reached the door at the bottom of the stairs I slowed to a walk and calmed myself. A plain-clothes would probably be outside the door. I opened the door and stepped out, but there was nobody there. I couldn't understand it. Looking for Ayshea I walked towards the little canteen, and was surprised to see hundreds of people on their knees, even in the canteen praying. Half of Beauvais seemed to be there. There was a deep rumble from somewhere and the Cathedral shook. I nearly lost my footing. People screamed, perhaps fearing the building would collapse, perhaps fearing for their souls. I couldn't see Ayshea anywhere, but then I felt something brush the back of my hand lightly. I turned and it was her.

"You took so long! Did you find it?"

"No. Where were you?" I almost had to shout to make her hear me, over the praying and moans which followed the screams.

"I was hiding – behind a drape. What are we going to do?"

"I don't know. I saw the roof-space. There is nothing up there! It's empty. The Crypt must be somewhere else. Let's try again. Just look for anything that might be relevant – a painting or statue maybe." I took her hand and we started down one of the aisles. I knew it would be only a matter of a few minutes at most before we were caught. I decided to take off my wig. Maybe now Parcaud had seen me they would be looking for someone with long hair. It itched anyway. We searched desperately for something – a sign that would trigger some memory, or recognition in some other way. I looked up at the old religious painting here and there, but nothing struck a chord. I found myself looking at a small relief-painting, just above head height – that is, a painting on wood that is carved or shaped to suggest the scene. Very common as religious works in the middle-ages, survivors are very rare now. This one had two panels bordered in gold, one above the other, with layers of wood to suggest the shape of two eyes. Suddenly I squeezed Ayshea's hand tight. "This is it! Look!"

The top eye, with a blue background, had a man crucified inside it and the bottom eye, largely in red had a man being dipped in cauldron of boiling oil, with flames all around – suggesting that he was in Hell.

"Oh yes! Yes! You are right."

Immediately I started feeling with my fingers for a catch or lever. The wood was thick with many layers of varnish, and smooth to the touch. I had to stretch to reach the top border but I could find nothing there. Then out of sheer frustration I pushed on the upper eye. It was a terrible act of desecration but it gave. The background of the eye, a flat panel of wood hinged by its top edge, opened, and I could see a lever inside. I pushed it and heard a click. A large panel near the floor moved outwards slightly. I peered in, but the door cut off the light to the space beyond. "Are we being watched?"

"No. Everyone is panicking."

The Gendarmes had their hands full now, controlling the crowds, which were beginning to make movement difficult in the main part of the Cathedral. I pushed the panel, which was really a small door, about chest high, and peered inside. I could see nothing. "This is it. I am sure this is it! I have to go Ayshea. You cannot come with me. Stay here." I squeezed her hand and tried to let go, but she held on.

She looked as if she really wanted to say something but didn't know how.

"The Serpent is here. Up there! It was on the roof. Whatever that thing is I have to face it."

"I am scared. I am scared for me and for you." She squeezed my hand harder.

"Don't worry. I am not scared."

She hesitated, but then let go my hand, after one last squeeze. "Good luck!" she said.

I closed the door behind me. It clicked shut and I was in darkness.

I felt for a switch but could find none. The cool stone on both walls, shoulder-width apart, was nice to touch, given that I was sweating profusely. I still had on my long jacket, and although it was an exceptionally cool day for August, the exertions of the last hour had taken it out of me. I sorely regretted shutting the door now, as I couldn't even see my nose in front of me. The corridor smelled damp and uncared for. I took a hesitant step forward, expecting steps leading downwards, ran my hands over the cool stone, and then took another step. My foot hit something hard and raised. I lifted my foot to feel for the edge. It was there, and another flat surface on top had a similarly raised shape at the back. The stairs led upwards! Just like the other steps up to the Gallery, these turned through ninety degrees. The door had been much further down the aisle though and perhaps half as far from the altar. This flight went on and on, turning back on itself twice so that at the end, I was facing towards the altar. If I had been claustrophobic, I couldn't have gone on, and it seemed an eternity before I my feet finally hit something wooden – a door. I felt for a handle and there was a loop or iron which when twisted lifted a lever to open the door. I stepped into a large space, dimly lit by thin spikes of light between the leads of the roof, just as in the other space. As before, there was a light switch in a panel next to me and I flicked it on.

The sight that met my eyes was beyond my wildest dreams. It was like a church within a church. There were the familiar rafters, and the height and width looked the same as the previous roof-space I had seen. But I was only a few feet from the Western end. It stretched in one great concave arc around to the other side of the Cathedral roof. Immediately I knew what it was, and smiled. An optical illusion! I had seen the trick so many times but hadn't imagine it could be used by early Gothic builders. The true Eastern end of the Cathedral was curved, over the great stained-glass windows designed by Engrand Le Prince. This curved wall was false and because it was a smaller diameter, I guessed that on the other side of the wall was the roof space I had been in previously. The sides which I had looked at in the other roof-space, must converge slightly to give the illusion of the whole length of the Cathedral when in fact they only stretched about two-thirds of the distance. This space made up the rest – perhaps seventy feet long. The space was brightly, although sparsely ornamented with gold paint, and a long red carpet ran down the middle, with many coats of arms woven in to it, again in gold. Large, ancient iron chandeliers, empty of candles, hung in two rows either side of the carpet. At the far end, directly over the main altar in the Cathedral below, was another altar. This one had a very large version of the statue I had bought, of a wolf-angel fighting a snake-demon, both supporting a round disk, upon which was the figure of Christ. At first glance, I took this to symbolise the struggle which The Ordo Lupus undertook in the name of God. Just to the left of the altar, beyond the furthest sarcophagus was a jagged hole in the roof. Leads lay in a pile below it on the floor. Around the space, hanging from the beams, and in places, the sides of the roof, which sloped in to the point perhaps forty-five feet above me, were all sorts of paraphenalia of war – shields, spears, swords and parts, or whole suits, of armour. What fascinated me the most was a row of perhaps seven stone sarcophagi down each side of the chamber, lain at right angles to the sloping roof beams. On plinths perhaps four feet high, they formed alcoves, within which were many coffins of wood. Almost everything in the chamber was covered lightly with dust, some of it by many, many years of dust, replete with cobwebs. I walked hesitantly down central walkway, along the red carpet, reading names on the stone sarcophagi, none of which were familiar.

So this must be The Crypt.

I stood staring at the altar for a few minutes. A large table in front of it draped in green, held a very large bronze basin which was empty, and two candelabras on either side. Within panels on the green cloth, were embroidered symbols and scenes within panels. I couldn't decipher the bowl's purpose and after looking at, but not understanding any of the symbols and images on the green cloth, I turned and walked back down the carpet, reading the names on the stone sarcophagi on my left. At the second one from the end, I stopped, stunned. The name on it was very familiar to me and very precious. It was my grandfather's name. So here he was. I looked closely at the sarcophagus. It was perhaps seven feet by three and four feet high, with each side divided into quadrants by large crosses in relief. Between the arms of the crosses were carved scenes involving battles with Serpents. A sword was in the hand of my grandfather. Around the base were carved strange masks, some of which were interwoven with what looked like ivy, or leaves of other plants. Around the top, just under the stone lid, was a simple pattern of orbs. The lid held an effigy of my grandfather laying flat, fully suited in armour, with hands clasped, as if praying, and under them, a long sword. In my sudden grief at finding his interred remains, as I was sure they were, I was still somehow delighted at the image of him as a Knight. This fitted my memory of him. I placed my hand gently on the sarcophagus.

"Grandfather. I miss you. Now I know just what you were up to all those years. I really wish you were here to advise me."

An answer came back to me but I was sure it was my own subconscious speaking. “Where is the sword?” Yes, where was the sword. I reluctantly turned away from grandfather’s tomb and walked back down the aisle to the altar, without even glancing at the last two sarcophagi in the row. I looked closely at every sword I could see – some I rubbed the dust off, but none were silver, or special looking in any way. Behind the last sarcophagus to the right of the altar, and behind the dusty rack of wooden coffins, I noticed something I hadn’t seen before – a builder’s hoist. Perhaps ten feet square, the rafters were there formed into a frame, surrounding a platform, suspended from four heavy ropes at each corner, which were themselves joined above to one lifting rope, perhaps an inch thick. Also at each corner of the platform was a wooden post, with a thin rope chord passing through eyelets at the top of each, to form a safety rope at about waist height if you were to stand on the platform. This was suspended by a system of pulleys, from a tie-beam above, and a loop of the rope was knotted around an oblique beam, leaving a large coil of rope on the floor boards. I sat, leaning against the cool stone of the sarcophagus, took off the sweat-stained jacket and lay it beside me. My fingers absently played with the end of the rope, feeling how supple it was although its roughness prickled. I thought it was probably hemp. I remembered the cassette recorder, took it out and turned it on. That was when I found the divorce papers, half out of my jacket pocket, and reread the note from Rose.

I walked nervously around the great Secret Chapel, for I felt a presence now. *Not much time left.*

In my wandering I finally arrived at the last two sarcophagi nearest the entrance doorway, which I hadn’t even glanced at before. Stopping at the second-to-last one, I glanced casually at the name carved there. Astonished, I had to bend down and run my hands over the stonework to confirm the name. To my astonished chagrin, I recognised my own name. I laughed a stone-cold laugh. “Who knows of my death here?” I shouted to the sloping roof above me. My head hurt, not at the thought of my own death but that I myself, must be a wolf-angel. ‘Like my grandfather’, I thought, but the thought also occurred to me – ‘not like my father’. The fact that it was only alternate generations that inherited the gift, was borne out by my own sarcophagus, next to that of my grandfather. I did not understand, however, why my grandfather had not inducted me into the Brotherhood. There had been no ceremony, no private talk, no mention of it even.

I heard a deep moan somewhere behind me and swung to face it but I could see nothing. I knew the Serpent was here but I had to find the silver Sword. I was almost at the end of the aisle and noticed a Latin inscription on the lintel above the door through which I had come. It read, "Is quisnam est Bonus est pinned ut is crux crucis ut is vultus lumen leptos, is quisnam est damno sentio sui emersed in lebes Abyssus," but of course I couldn't translate it. I looked down at the last sarcophagus but at that moment I heard or felt an ungodly roar from somewhere near the altar. It was followed by a long drawn out and blood-curdling hiss.

I crept around my own sarcophagus, and crouched behind that of my grandfather. I searched desperately across roof timbers and wall-hangings with my eyes for the silver Sword – symbol of my Brotherhood and the only means to kill the Serpent – possibly.

This is it. This is my end.

Something shimmered on one of the timbers high above the altar. I stared hard and at first could only see the air disrupted, like the heat haze above the desert, which reveals a mirage to the unwary. Then I felt I could make out something. It seemed like a large snake, and yet perhaps a very large man at the same time. It moved with the intelligence and dexterity of a man and yet the reptilian smoothness of a snake. It was moving along a beam towards me. I gradually became aware too of a deep rumbling murmur, as of countless thousands lost souls, lamenting. It was a deeply disturbing sound, and the temptation to close my eyes and give in to the strangely hypnotic song was great, but I focused hard on the approaching shimmering form. Then it was gone. I couldn't see it any more! I turned this way and that but I couldn't see it. Fear was rising in my knotted throat now with an intensity I had never felt before. I had certainly feared death before but never for the loss of my soul – for that was what this creature or monster could perhaps take from me. Eternal damnation in Hell suddenly seemed a possible end for me. Then I felt that familiar sense of foreboding – my gift, as of something bad approaching, only from behind me. I knew it was about to strike, and I waited until the last moment before leaping aside. Something huge and heavy crashed into the tomb and its lid cracked. Pieces of white stone went clattering across the floor boards and a dust cloud filled the air. In the cloud I could distinctly see the shape of a large serpent with wings. It also appeared to have arms, and turned to face me, but I didn't wait. I ran as fast as I could towards the altar. Where was this damned Sword? I swore to myself and then crossed myself for swearing in a holy place.

Then into my mind came clearly the words from Rose, ‘I still know this about you however – that you loved Annie deeply and would never harm her. I also know that you have a greater capacity for getting to the truth than anybody else I have ever met.’ For a moment my mind was completely clear and I heard the voice of Henry spelling the initials ‘sk’ on the bottom of the statues. We never had figured out who that was. Perhaps he was a Knight who lived shortly after Guillaume de Grez and was involved in the manufacture of the statues. It seemed suddenly important somehow and I ran back to the first Sarcophagus furthest back on the right from the altar and opposite the door. I felt as if I was moving in treacle – as if the Serpent would be upon me at any moment. I wiped the dust from the name plate of the stone tomb. To my great relief it fitted – sort of. ‘Simon de Cleves’. I knew ‘C’ in old Latin as spoken by French was pronounced ‘K’, so it would make sense that, if the tomb had been made much later, they may have used a ‘K’ to represent the old family name. It was close enough for me. I wiped more dust from the side of the stone tomb, and found a large inscription upon a quartered shield, on the side facing the altar. It read ‘My brother is buried with he who wielded him. Wake him not unless you have the strength to fight.’ I didn’t know who the brother of Simon was! Panic made the knot in my throat tighten still more. I swallowed and forced myself to think clearly, and then realised how beautifully simple the clue was.

I knew that the brother of a shield would be a sword. So the Sword must be entombed with the last person who wielded it – my grandfather. What was more, the Serpent had just cracked open the tomb for me. Perhaps I was not completely alone. I remembered that the whole purpose of the Serpent had been to use me to find the Sword so that it could be destroyed. Therefore I had to keep the location of the Sword secret until the very last moment. My terror subsided slightly for a moment, as a plan presented itself in my mind. I would lure the Serpent away from the sarcophagus, and then circle around, get the sword and stab it. Now I had hope in my heart at last. I would kill this Serpent and prove to the world – and Rose that I wasn’t mad, or a killer and that this beast was the killer of Annie and all the other victims across France. Perhaps it wasn’t even too late to save my marriage! Again I was drawn back to the altar but this time I was calm. I feigned curiosity about the design of the altar – my examination would give my enemy plenty of time to attack. I had to trust that my gift would warn me at the last moment. I didn’t think in any case that it would kill me before discovering the Sword. The large statue of the

Wolf-angel fighting the Snake-demon looked as if it was bronze. I tapped it and it sounded metallic. This bottom half of the statue was perhaps four feet high and balanced on the head of the snake, and held up in one of the hands of the wolf-angel or warg, was a dais. In the warg's other hand was a long sword, pointing at the heart of the Snake. It reminded me of George and the Dragon. It was upon the dais that stood the figure of Christ, again about four feet high, so rising in total to some eight feet above the altar cloth. Christ's head was adorned by a halo, sculpted cleverly to look separate from his head, but no doubt attached at the back. His arms were spread wide with hands palm-up – forefingers and thumbs touching, in a gesture of benefaction. The bowl in front of it, had figures intertwined with foliage around its sides and looked vaguely pagan. I picked it up and tapped it. This surely was bronze. Its age was hard to determine. I wondered for a moment why there was even an altar here, and why there were so many sculptures of wargs in the world. Were they worshipped as Gods? I supposed that as well as a crypt, Guillaume de Grez had intended this space as a secret chapel, at the time of great persecution for the Cathars, and presumably the Brotherhood, in the 13th Century. As for so many warg statues, for now I didn't know the answer. What I noticed next seemed completely out of place. In the centre of the altar was a large ornate silver chalice about a foot high, and it was filled with a slick red liquid. I looked closer and smelled it. It had that sickly metallic smell of blood. The chalice was the only thing which broke the spell of frozen time that the crypt exuded and it must have been placed there by the Serpent. But for what purpose? On the front of the altar cloth, stretching down to the floor, were depicted two processions. One had adepts and wargs, flanked by helpers, male and female. The other was a procession of snakes, flanked by what looked like male and female succubi. I looked at the central panel on the green cloth for clues. There I saw something else that surprised me. It was the Garden of Eden scene but as well as a snake, there was a wolf behind the legs of Adam, looking up adoringly to its master. There were dark blood-stains on the altar cloth and drops of blood on the floor.

The hairs on the back of my neck stood up. I leaped to the left just as something large darted past my right shoulder and hit the green cloth. That something was shaped like the head of a Serpent, perhaps two feet long, but as if made of water. I hit the ground hard and knocked the wind out of myself. There was a loud, pained hiss from the altar. Now was my chance. Although I was heaving for breath, I stood up, ran to my grandfather's tomb and inserted my arm through the large crack in the top. The impact of the Serpent had dislodged completely a triangle of the lid, about six inches along each side, and sent a crack along the top of the sarcophagus, from the apex of the triangle to the other side. I felt around for anything cold and metallic but my hand touched only stone. I tried to force apart the two halves of the lid, and to my relief, the right-hand piece moved a few inches with a grating sound. I peered inside and I could see something glinting there on the side nearest me. There were also the grim remains of my poor grandfather, wrapped in cloth. Seeing the Serpent's shape only about two coffers away from me, with one last desperate lunge, I reached in and grabbed the sword. It was incredibly heavy but using my elbow to move the right half of the lid further away from the other, I forced a gap big enough to pull it out with the last bit of oxygen still in my lungs. I thought I would pass out but at that moment, I drew a long gasping breath, and stood defiantly facing the Serpent, the long silver Sword held vertically in my clumsy hands.

My enemy stopped a few feet in front of me, and something I had vaguely noticed earlier, filled my senses. A foul stench filled the air. I knew I had smelled it before – several times. It made me want to gag, just at the moment I was drawing my first breaths.

"You have found it now. That is good." From a series of hisses, I could just make out words, and then realised the Serpent was speaking to me. "I thought you had found it and concealed it from me. Thank you. Your work is done now. You have fulfilled your purpose little spirit. The Great one will remember you." Its voice was truly awful to listen to. As well as a hiss, it seemed to be simulated from the voice of many others, a gravelly rasp that hurt my ears.

I cleared my throat and waved the Sword slightly, in warning. Sweat was blurring my vision and I wanted to wipe my brow, but the Sword was too heavy to hold in one hand. I wasn't sure I could hold it up for long. "What do you mean?"

Suddenly the Serpent solidified, from the watery shape of before, to the solid form of a living creature, and rose to its full height, towering above me. Easily ten feet high, its scales were of many colours, shimmering iridescently, and its eyes burning pits of restless fire. In the instant I looked into its eyes, I felt extreme pain, as if my flesh were being seared, and I screamed in agony. Then an instant later the pain was gone. Its mouth, when it opened, was of a deep red that seemed to drip blood, like saliva from long white fangs, onto its chest and from there, onto the floor around it. Its tongue darted this way and that, and as I looked more closely in horror, its ends seemed to be made of smaller serpents but with faces of tortured men. Then I noticed that the scales of this monster were also the forms of men and women, curled up in agony, and occasionally one would throw up its arms in supplication, Perhaps theirs were the voices that made up the one voice it spoke with. I had to look away. Even with my eyes cast aside, the whole smelled foul.

"I have revealed myself to you, as I can, now I have fed sufficiently on the flesh of men. My body is real – for a while."

"Why don't you just go back to the pit of Hell, where you came from?"

"Indeed I will in a short while. But in answer to your first question, you are a servant of the Great one too."

"Don't be ridiculous. My whole life has been a fight against the forces of Evil."

"Ah, Evil. What is Evil? Am I evil? I was a wolf once – like you. Of course the snake and wolf forms are just physical symbols for our deeper, spirit-selves. These are mutable, like everything else in this Universe, or without." It seemed to laugh. It was a long drawn-out terrible sound. "I tried and failed to kill snakes, until I lost favour with God, and felt abandoned. I was recruited by snakes, as the Order are, and finally became one myself. Who is he, who can judge who is good and bad? Nobody is completely bad. Can you redeem me?"

"No, I am not God and no kind of saviour. You have to redeem yourself!" I rested the pommel of the sword on the edge of the sarcophagus.

Again the monster before me seemed to laugh. "In fact, you are evil. Have you not realised?"

"If I am evil, why is it the servants of the Concilium Putus Visum, servants of yours, have tried so hard to kill me?"

"We allowed them to believe we wanted you dead, to give you better cover, but in fact we have been watching over you."

"No." I shook my head.

"Do you remember the Cemetery in Highgate? That was where you were recruited. But you were weak and ready for it anyway. You remember the suicide attempt of that nice female teacher? Engineered by you. It was only your guilt that made you report it and save her at the last moment. Your Squadron that was wiped out over the Dutch coast and that girl in Paris – all your doing. You imagined it and it happened. You have a gift for it. That is why your grandfather never inducted you, and was so reluctant to even tell you about The Ordo

Lupus. I have saved the best for last though. It was you who killed Annie. Yes! You killed your own daughter."

"No! That cannot be."

"What did you feel when you looked into my eyes?"

"Pain. Extreme pain."

"As if being burned? As if being boiled?"

I remembered the few lines that the Head Verger had recited to us. I moaned in anguish. "No! No God. It cannot be!" But I knew it was so.

"Think about it. Think hard, and when you are ready, give me the sword," the Serpent said. I looked up the great Serpent body, to the head far above me. I looked into those terrible eyes, feeling acute pain but there was no emotion there. The Serpent turned to slink off down the aisle, creasing the red cloth into 'S' shapes as it crawled towards the space in front of the altar. I noticed for the first time the intricate designs on the blade of the large ornamental sword in my hands, but bitter thoughts were filing me with despair. I lay the Sword on the sarcophagus and leaned against it, panting.

A small voice still fought it. 'No! It can't be! Surely just another lie by this snake. Everybody knew the story of the Garden of Eden – how snakes deceive'. I fought in the darkness of my mind, in that moment. But in my heart I knew it was true. With a searing white light, the truth burned through my head. 'I *was* Evil'.

I remembered how Miss Silver had told me off for talking in class earlier on the day she hung herself, and how much I had hated her for a moment. It was an intense and vitriolic thought, that I had quickly banished, and thought no more of. But yes, I had wished her dead, for just a fraction of a second. And why had I chosen the path that would allow me to see her hanging in the storage room? Was it luck, as I had always thought – my 'gift', or a wish to taste the revenge which I myself brought about. I thought about the mission over the Dutch coast. I remembered seeing the 'box' in the sky and knowing the AA would be centred there. But did I just know this or did I plan it? Did I in fact steer the whole Squadron into the box, giving myself just enough time to escape? Now, suddenly, from the darkest corner of my mind came a memory – a memory so bad that I instantly wanted to die. I remembered laughing to myself, knowing where the box was, from intelligent reports I had sneaked a look at, while drinking tea with Paul, months earlier – reports nobody but Paul and I knew that I had seen. I remembered steering for the box and making sure I was right at the front of the row of bombers – making sure they were line-astern.

"No! No!" I moaned to myself. "How can this be? Annie? Did I even kill Annie?"

I must have. 'How could I do this? I was cursed. I should die.

For a moment I wished the Serpent would kill me. Why did neither Paul nor Rose realise I was Evil? Why did M.I.6 ever recruit me? Surely they must have known something was wrong? But then again perhaps I was too clever. Perhaps they did suspect something, and wanted me under close observation'. My mind was a mass of rushing thoughts, and I felt my whole world falling away from under my feet. I felt unsteady and had to sit down. I leaned against the sarcophagus and let the Sword fall to the ground. I buried my head in my hands and moaned, "No! No!" I heard the Serpent laughing some distance away.

But in my despair came another thought. 'No. I couldn't have killed Annie. The Serpent was there'. I knew it was because of that foul stench. I knew I had smelled it before, and now I remembered that it was there – that day in Nevers. The altar cloth reminded me too that the Serpent was lying – at least about Annie. Perhaps, even I could redeem myself. I might have caused the death of hundreds of men during war – allies, but I still had free will. Now I knew what forces were at work inside me, I could more easily choose, and I chose to kill the Serpent.

"There is someone else who has come to meet you – another ally," hissed the Serpent.

From behind one of the drapes which formed a backdrop to the altar stepped a young and beautiful woman wearing a simple black dress, like a shift. I recognised her at once and my mouth fell open.

"Georgina?" She walked towards me, bare-footed without uttering a sound. Against her skin were contrasted unfamiliar patterns drawn in blood. Something like a cross, but with a curved stem, was at the top of both arms and a series of cursive shapes like numbers ran down her arms. Her legs were similarly decorated as was her cleavage. I had little time to take in any more. Breathless and almost in tears I mouthed the question I wanted to ask, "How?"

"How am I still alive?" she said in her familiar voice, but sounding as if far off. "Did you miss me?"

"I shook my head. "You know I did!"

"I am a Sorceress. You must have seen the pictures on the altar-cloth. There have been many of us down the generations, helping the Serpents do their work on Earth. We have power over the physical world. I left my body for a while. That is all. I told you I had done many bad things but you didn't want to believe me." She was only six feet away.

"I tried to save you!"

"Yes you did and I am grateful. I am.. fond of you." She reached me and leaned forward to kiss me. As she opened her mouth I could see that her incisors were like those of a wolf, long and pointed. They both laughed at me. "Now you see me as I really am. Am I still attractive? She was achingly beautiful. I felt my will being totally and inexorably drawn from me. I knew of course the myth of succubi; that they were irresistible to men and drew their life force from them, and I could no more resist her than I could stop breathing.

"You are.. You are.." I closed my eyes and gave in. But she didn't kiss me. I opened my eyes and shouted, "No!" in anguish.

"Give me the Sword," she said.

"If I can't persuade you, she can," hissed the Serpent behind her.

"No!" I shouted. I couldn't resist her body but I could resist her demand for the Sword.

"Give it to me and I will give you anything you want." She sounded less patient now.

My whole body and spirit ached for her. It was something beyond endurance and I fell to my knees. "Please."

Somewhere deep inside me, I resolved to kill her with the Sword when she kissed me, as I knew she must, but I laughed at myself. I knew I could never do it.

"Please what?" she said.

I shook my head slowly but she leaned leaned towards me. her hair seemed to writhe, and danced like smooth jet serpents, and yet when I looked closely I could see none. I seemed to see her as she was on some demon plane with an inner eye and as she was in reality with the other, all at the same time. She leaned closer and took my lips with hers. I cannot describe the feeling but it was most like being washed clean of all pain and longing but losing oneself completely. My hands let go of the Sword and it was in her hands.

She pulled away "Yes!" she shouted, triumphant. "Yes! I have it." She walked away a few paces and climbed on the nearest intact sarcophagus. Standing, legs apart, she held the great Sword overhead, with a strength beyond that of the Georgina I knew. "Serpent. I command you. Do my bidding."

The Serpent looked surprised, if it is possible for such monstrosity to do so, and seemed to pull back slightly. If anything its redness paled slightly and I started to see that it was afraid of her. So she had wanted it for herself! She had forgotten one thing though. While she was watching the Serpent, I was released from her spell. I quietly picked up one of the heavy shards of stone from grandfather's sarcophagus with both hands. The Serpent was looking at her but I knew it could see what I was doing. It was watching and waiting. It seemed she had wanted the sword for herself; for the power that it held.

"I command you chalcathgna!" she repeated.

It answered her. "What do you command?"

With tears in my heart and my heart in my mouth I took the best position to knock her down and then to launch the stone at my lover's head. I was just behind her and I would not miss. Part of me was listening to their exchange as I leaned towards the back of her knee with my shoulder. At the last moment, I glanced at the Serpent and I thought it looked tensed, as if itself it was ready to charge her.

"Go from this place and never return to Earth!" she shouted. I stopped and the Serpent hesitated for a moment. I had expected her to tell it to kill me, not to flee. An instant later the monster had started to move and before either of us could move it hit Georgina full in the chest and she flew past my head as I ducked and rolled on the floor behind the tomb. The Serpent quickly came around the tomb and moved towards her with astonishing speed. She was sitting up as it reached her, but the Sword lay ineffectually beside her. The foul beast grabbed her in its jaws and I thought it was over for her but she was muttering something and the jaws of the beast flew open, dropping her against one of the coffers on the far side of the aisle. I rushed forward and picked up the Sword. I looked up just in time to see a flash of flesh and black cloth disappearing through the jagged hole in the roof as Georgina escaped.

I stood up and held the Sword out in the palms of my hands. "You can have the Sword now!" The Serpent was watching me and then started down the aisle towards me. Even now I could not clearly tell if it had arms or legs. By the way it moved, one would think not, and yet when it reared, it often appeared for a moment, to resemble a man and the shape of arms seemed obvious. But this could be imagined. It stopped a few feet from me, its foul stench filling the air again. I coughed.

"Give it to me," it said.

With all my strength and in one movement I grasped the hilt and swung the great Sword at the neck of the beast as it lowered its head towards me. "Here you are!" But the beast was too quick for me, pulling back its great head, and the Sword swung harmlessly below its nose, clanging uselessly on the stone coffer, and crushing my hand viciously. I screamed in pain but held on to the Sword. I had to try one last time. I climbed up on the sarcophagus and started to swing the great blade again. This time though, at the last moment, I changed the sweep into a thrust, aimed at the jaws of the great demon. Its jaw opened and it tried to swallow the blade, which disappeared up to the hilt in the beast's mouth. I let go of the blade, fearing my hand would be consumed too. The Serpent reared up, turning its head towards the roof, and opening its mouth wide, to try and swallow the blade. It had become stuck, the hilt too wide to pass between the fangs of the snake. It roared in frustration.

"Take it out! Take it out!" it screamed. "I'm not ready. It's burning me."

"I hope it finishes you!" I shouted through gritted teeth. My hand was bleeding profusely, and my arm felt broken. It was agony.

"No! Take it out!" A white incandescence burned in its eyes. "Even if you could kill me, I would let all that is in this room, fall into the Cathedral below. The whole roof would collapse, killing all who are praying there. Think of that!" it said, half choking.

Not knowing what to do any more, I simply said, "God help me!" The great beast suddenly thrust its head towards me, and I stepped back. I crawled behind the sarcophagus, and around behind the Serpent, trying not to get trapped between the beast and the back wall. It turned to face me, and I could see part of the tip of the Sword protruding through its flank. I had hoped that swallowing it would finish the beast, but it seemed that its plan all along had been to swallow it anyway. Perhaps it had some strong stomach lining that could consume holy metal. In any case, the blade was burning it now. Perhaps it would die after a while. Then I had an idea. Grasping my wounded arm, I made my way to the hoist. Perhaps if somehow I could kill the Serpent, and send it to its doom on the altar 150 feet below, it would not have time to bring the whole Cathedral roof down. I could hear the scraping sound of the Serpent dragging its body down the aisle towards me, the red cloth being pushed aside now as it struggled for grip in the slick blood and entrails that strung out behind it, some of its own and some of others. As I sat wearily beside my coat, I realised just how hopeless my situation had become. I didn't even have a weapon now. How was I to lure the beast onto the platform, which after all, was barely wide enough to hold it, and probably not strong enough? I felt very small and helpless. The end was near for me if my idea didn't work. Trying to open a way for the beast onto the platform, rather than make a weapon for myself, I wrenched one of the stanchions at the corner of the platform, this way and that, until it came free. Two long twisted nails protruded from the split base. If I could just cut the chord at the top I would have some crude form of weapon. A builder's toolbox lay beside the hoist and I flicked it open with my good hand. I saw a knife and quickly cut the chord with it. I pulled the club I had created towards me and the chord slipped out through the eyelets. Sweat was pouring off of me, and I could hardly see through my stinging eyes. The air seemed so dense and dusty in that roof space, that it was hard to find breath to draw.

Then there was no time left. The Serpent was close.

"You little fool!" I see you think that somehow you can be good again? Think again. It is too late for you. The girl you left behind in the Cathedral below? She is dead. Your wife will soon be dead. Pastor Michel will see to it. Pull this hot blade from my mouth and live, or else die!"

I lashed out with the club and caught the Serpent a glancing blow on the side of its jaw, but it pulled away and the club flew out of my hand. I fell back on my jacket and onto something hard underneath it. In a haze of pain, sweat and terror, I felt to see what it was. It was the little statue in my pocket which had been there all the time. I fumbled for it while the Serpent eyed me, waiting for an answer. Finally, I pulled the statue free and held it behind my back.

"Answer me!" screamed the demon in that unearthly voice. It thrust its foul head close to my face, and I thrust the upstretched arm of the statue into its left eye. For a moment, as its eye burst into a thousand exploding shades of red, it was stunned, and in that moment I withdrew the statue, and thrust it deep into the other eye. This too exploded into a myriad of colours, and blood poured from the socket.

The beast roared and then pulled back its great head. The blood and flesh-soaked statue, was wrenched from my hand. I cowered, waiting for the final thrust. It came a moment later but blinded, the Serpent was using smell alone, and raked my sweat-stained jacket instead of me, with its huge fangs. For just a fraction of a moment, the hilt of the sword was right next to my face, and I grabbed it with my one good hand. I heaved but it wouldn't come out.

"No!" The Serpent screamed in frustration, realising its mistake at striking the coat, and heaved its head up for another strike. Only the beast's own strength could have pulled the sword free, and then I scrambled to my knees and forced the long blade into the chest of the bewildered beast – in where I thought the heart was. The snake gave a hideous roar and shuddered.

"No!" It screamed again, but this time it was the scream of defeat. I was exhausted and all I wanted was for the beast to die, and for me to lie here still forever, but I knew there was something I had to do. What was it? I had to force my weary mind to work through the fog of exhaustion and finally I had it. To the left of my hand, only a foot away was the end of the hoist rope. It might have been a thousand miles away. I didn't think I had the strength, or the time to reach it. I looked to where the Serpent was coiled, half on and half off the hoist. I couldn't tell if it would be able to hold onto something if the hoist fell, or not. It seemed in the last stages of its death rattle. Then I heard its bitter voice, uttering something so foul that it must be some kind of curse. I kicked with all my might against its flanks on the floor beside me, and at the same time pulled the end of the rope as hard as I could. For a moment I thought the knot would hold, but then I saw daylight around the edge of the platform as it tilted precariously. The Serpent didn't stop uttering its curse. Then dust stung my face as the loops of rope on the floor were whipped around my legs. The knot had come undone, and the platform started its swift journey to the Cathedral floor below. A few seconds later I heard screams, and a great crash, as the wooden platform, with the Serpent upon it, hit the main altar of Beauvais Cathedral.

* * *

Epilogue

1808, 1343, 1098, 1568, 1214

It was some time before anybody found me in the Secret Crypt. At first I lay half-conscious and troubled thoughts visited me. I seemed to be floating in a half-light world and many voices whispered around me. Then from the gloom I heard a familiar voice. Like a whisper on the faintest breath of cold winter air, came Georgina's voice. "Don't forget me." I felt my heart being clasped as if by two cold, clammy hands and then I could feel no more. I must have been asleep for a while, and my dreams were troubled before voices called my name and I found myself being lifted up by brawny arms. One of the voices was strangely familiar and then I remembered a girl called Ayshea. Could she be the one talking to me? But she was dead, surely. I opened my eyes and at first I couldn't see anything clearly. Somebody wiped dirt and sweat from my eyes.

"He is coming to!"

"Hello. Hello. It's me. Ayshea. Are you alright?"

"No. No. I am not alright." I smiled. "I am not alright but I am alive. I thought you were dead! Are you alright!"

"Oh, I am fine. Apart from having a strange demon fall onto the Cathedral altar, it has been quite boring really." She smiled back at me. I found that she was holding my hand and she squeezed it.

The journey on the stretcher down the secret stairway, was pretty unpleasant, and I was somehow surprised to see the bright afternoon sun, as we crossed the open space to the waiting ambulance outside the great Cathedral. I felt as if I had been in there for many hours. Looking up at the blue sky, my vision was framed by the bold towers at the end of the ancient Gothic Cathedral, and I watched with affection as the towers bobbed up and down, until they were out of sight. Both Parcaud and Ayshea accompanied me to the Beauvais Hospital.

"You are quite a hero now!" said Parcaud. "I was never quite convinced you were a murderer."

I gritted my teeth against the urge to laugh bitterly.

Ayshea squeezed my hand again and leaned over to whisper in my ear. "Your first."

There was silence during the rest of the journey. It seemed a strange thing to say to me, and I thought about it. I remembered the two processions on the altar cloth in the Secret Crypt and I remembered the female helpers next to the wolf-angels.

My arm was broken in two places, and I had lost quite a lot of blood from deep wounds on my hand. In the three days that I was kept in hospital, I had plenty of time to tell Ayshea everything that had happened in the Crypt, and get her to repeat the story of what happened to the Serpent when it fell. Later, I regretted telling Ayshea much of what had happened in the Crypt and swore her to secrecy.

"We were all cornered by the Gendarmes at the other end of the Cathedral," she said. "They had formed a ring around us. I think they had called in all The Gendarmes in Beauvais. A lot of people were screaming that this was the Apocalypse. Several times the Cathedral shook, and we thought it would collapse. Eventually the Gendarmes themselves took cover in the aisles, and most of us hid under the benches, or in alcoves. I wanted to come and find you but I remembered what you said, and I waited next to the little door. Then somebody near the front of the benches shouted, "Look! The roof is coming down!"

"Weren't you scared?"

"I was – a little, at this point. I believed the Cathedral was about to collapse. Many have said it would, for a long time. I peeped out from behind one of the columns and I could see a square of the ceiling had separated. I hadn't seen a door there before so I too, thought that the roof was falling in. Then slowly the square of ceiling detached, and then quickly came crashing down, right on top of the altar. We all screamed. On it was what looked like a giant snake. I saw it with my own eyes. I ran towards it, thinking that you must be there too. I was so scared for you." Within a minute there was a big crowd of us around the thing. Gendarmes too. It was not moving and then slowly, as if it was dissolving, its flesh turned to a liquid mess. It was as if it was putrefied already. The flesh ran out over the floor and seemed to burn everything it touched. There was a moan from the crowd. Nobody could believe what they were seeing. And the smell! It was terrible. I couldn't see you but I just couldn't take my eyes of the snake. It was like something from Hell. From the Bible. Finally it was just a mess on the floor and the Gendarmes had to bring carts in with spades to scoop it up and take it away. They took a sample to analyse and then took statements from all of us. They forbid us to talk to the press, who were eager for any information about the Secret Crypt, and the silver Sword, and the Serpent."

"What happened to Pastor Michel?"

"Oh he has been arrested for the murder of the Head Verger."

Newspapers and esoteric journals as well as some of the scientific journals were full of theories about all three for months afterwards.

"That sword must be worth many millions. Especially given the theories about its provenance," Ayshea said to me.

"Yes and I suppose it must stay with The Crypt which is no longer secret."

"Yes. I suppose so."

The press were camped outside the hospital for the duration of my stay, but I left secretly in a car hired by Parcaud, and was taken to a secret location where Ayshea was waiting. The first evening away from the hospital, we had dinner together, this time brought from a restaurant to our secret hideaway, in an unmarked police car. Over the main course, we talked about my battle, some of the questions that were still left unanswered and I told her I had decided to tear up the divorce papers and try again with Rose. I thought she would be surprised but she wasn't. She seemed more interested in talking about Ordo Lupus though.

"I cannot figure out why there are so many wolf-angel statues everywhere, especially in the crypt. Were they worshipped?"

"Ah well. I have been doing some research there. Gillaume de Grez had the idea of furthering the influence of the Ordo Lupus to one of the few fertile areas for Religious indoctrination in Europe – the Balkans. There was a cult there, based on a wolf-god that many worshipped. He started the idea of presenting the wolf-angel as a minor deity, or prophet, within the Catholic Church. It was enough to recruit many more adherents to the Church and in fact, secretly, to The Brotherhood. Simon de Kleves merely came up with the idea of manufacturing these statues in very large numbers, in France, and exporting them."

"Ah."

It soon became apparent that the Gendarmes were starting to cover up what had actually happened in Beauvais Cathedral. They liked the story of a giant snake dying on the altar but they didn't like the story of a demon serpent who devoured bodies and souls. They published an official account in Le Monde, stating that the snake had caught light on the altar's candles and that the flesh had burned until it could only be scooped up with spades. Of course there were mutterings in the press about a cover-up and several eye-witnesses tried to sell their stories but they suffered from inextricable accidents like fires at their homes or burnt-out cars. At first I received friendly letters from fellow historians and academics seeking information but soon these turned to spiteful mail accusing me of publicity-seeking or worse, being a witch-hunter. I learned to keep silent and started to fear for my life from the public as well as for my life and soul from the Serpents and their followers.

The altar cloth had continued to fascinate me – especially the Garden of Eden scene and once I went back to the Cathedral to look again, having to climb over red-tape to get to the altar after getting permission from the Bishop, who was now only too pleased to help me. I had always been, in the literal sense, a passionate opponent of the creationists. Being myself a Christian, I did not believe the Bible should be taken literally, but the presence of a wolf in this design – something tending towards esoteric teaching, left me dumbfounded. If wolves really had been 'man's friend' from such an early time, then man could not have tamed them, as evolutionists had taught us. Try as I might, I could not square this image with my own upbringing, which flaunted Darwin's theory as the 'truth'. I would never see the world in the same way again, but then I had changed in other ways too. I no longer saw good and evil as so very far apart, or so opposed to each other. I even, on occasion, felt pity for the Serpent, but then I dismissed this as a sentiment I could not afford. I had to carry on with my life. When I finally had time to think, I wondered if the battle had really been in the roof of Beauvais Cathedral, or if it had been inside me. I went back once more, a year after that but the Bishop had been replaced and I couldn't gain access to the Crypt at all. In fact it was now out-of-bounds, and seemed, even to academics, to be considered some kind of abhorrent blemish on the life of the cathedral. The clergy spoke about it only in the most hushed of tones.

I still had the little black notebook of Georgina's. Somehow I hadn't been able to bring myself to throw away this sad little memento of our time together. Some weeks after the events in this story, in a quiet moment, I opened it again and read it from cover to cover. It made sombre reading. I gathered her father, already wealthy had been drawn to the cult overseen by the 'Concilium Putus Visum' out of greed. In fact that seemed to be their main motive, although they accumulated wealth as servants of the Serpents. Georgina had used the cult for her own ends of course.

On one of the very last pages, I discovered something which astonished me. There was a physical description of the Interfeci. Evidently Georgina had finally located him and seen him. She described him as having white hair, being in his nineties, and having a strange red birthmark underneath his left ear. He also had blue eyes, and a long, slight hooked nose. At once I recognised my grandfather in the description. He had a red birthmark under his left ear – in the shape of a crab with one claw he always joked to me – blue eyes, a slightly hooked nose and would have been the right age at the time. I finally remembered the significance of the date, 14 September 1972. That was the date my grandfather was supposed to have been mugged in Paris and suffered a bad knife-wound to his leg. The wound must have been sustained, after all, in the fight with Georgina's father. So my grandfather hadn't been so wheelchair-bound as we'd thought. It seemed that Georgina's father had been killed by my him. A grim but faint smile spread across my face, like the faintest winter dawn. So that was why initially she had wanted to kill me. I often wondered where she was but I never told Rose that someone else had been in the Secret Crypt with the Serpent and I.

* * *

Postscript

3066:8,3 3078:66,3 3086:25,5 3165:34,3 123:55,5 3213:19,4 9:5,2 214:12,4 3:1,2 2034:15,8

Author's note: Shortly after the events related by me in this story, the story-teller vanished without trace before he ever completed the final cassette. His whereabouts is, as yet, unknown.

Finally, years later, another mystery was cleared up. 1985 was the first year DNA analysis entered the courtroom and the Gendarmes had passed on the sample of Serpent 'flesh' to a lab for analysis. Rose received a letter via Parcaud which, when you finished reading all the numbers and caveats, showed that some of the DNA that had been extracted, matched exactly a sample taken from some of Annie's clothes, which the Gendarmes had taken from Rose all those years ago in Nevers.

All historical facts are accurate and authentic except the following, in most cases to conceal the identity of the story-teller:

1. The raid on the Netherlands by a squadron of Bristol Blenheims is fictional. In fact the Blenheim, a two-engined medium bomber, took the brunt of casualties in the early war and there is at least one well documented case of ten aircraft going out and only one returning, so heavily damaged that it had to be scrapped.
2. The name of The Jazz Club Gang is fictional. There were many resistance units in Bulgaria at the end of WWII and they communicated with locals and other gangs using posters; often for concerts by local bands.
3. Although there is speculation that two or monks did escape from Montsegur Castle the night before the defenders surrendered, it is not known for certain what they were carrying.
4. 'A History of the Supernatural and Mythical Beasts and Customs of Central and Southern Europe' by Edgar de Boulon is a fictional book.
5. 'De Secretis Scientia Occultis' is a fictional book.

For those interested in learning more about Ordo Lupus, go back and decode the chapter headings. They were written on scraps of paper by the story teller and are steps on the road to secret and esoteric wisdom for Ordo Lupus members.

* * *

Read The Chronicles of Baltrath, a novel by Gary Kuyper, another writer in The Inkubator group.

Following is an excerpt from the Epic Heroic Fantasy:

The Chronicles of Baltrath

THE

DARK

WIZARDS

By Gary Kuyper

PROLOGUE

'Death to the enemies of Kith!

May their blood further temper the metal of our swords!

Death to the enemies of the Empire!

May Dakur grant us victory or suffer us to die with honour!'

Kithian War Chant

Since the beginning of time, fear of the unknown persisted amongst all inhabitants of the savage and unpredictable world of Baltrath.

Death, the greatest unknown of all, being a state or condition that all living creatures must eventually succumb to, contributed to being the greatest cause of fear.

It was ages ago that the first of the great warriors dared to crawl forth from the mire of fear, and spat defiantly into the face of death. To him, tempting death was tasting the fruits of life. The more daring he became, the more flavourful and meaningful became that short existence between the cradle and the grave.

Through this perverted, symbiotic relationship, he learned to understand and control the great power that fear was to bestow upon him.

With fear and death to command, he was soon to carve his name into the flesh and minds of all those who dared to challenge his will.

This warrior was Kith, father of the Kithian nation, ancestor of Baltrath's mightiest empire.

CHAPTER ONE

Golden Dreams

Groad kicked his heels all the more harder into the sides of the mighty, tawny-coloured stallion. For the first time he cursed the fact that the Kithian war-horses were bred for their incredible strength and not for speed. Bred to carry the enormous weight of a fully armoured warrior into the glorious throes of battle.

Such were the Kithians themselves, a race bred and refined for the sole purpose of wondrous war and destruction.

The sound of sword upon sword is the sweetest music to a Kithian warrior. The foe's screams the loveliest of songs. The saltiness of perspiration, blood and leather mingled with the delicate aroma of fear, hatred and anger are heady and intoxicating, like that of a bouquet of freshly picked lavender.

The battle is the dance itself, a palpable sensation surrounding and filling the senses like too much good wine; coaxing the participants of its macabre drunken revelry into absolute ecstasy.

Truly a magnificent *banquet of death.*

Groad was one of the finest warriors to come out of the Kithian Empire. If he were able to stand erect (a difficult and uncomfortable feat for all Kithians due to their ape-like anatomy which causes their head and shoulders to slouch forward), he would stand approximately seven and a half feet tall.

He was not considered enormous in stature as the average height of the Kithian male was considered to be about nine feet tall.

In fact, Groad was considered to be rather short by his peers, but what he lacked in height he certainly made up for in sheer ferocity, skill, cunningness and, a trait most sorely lacking amongst most of the inhabitants of Kith, namely intelligence.

It was by choice and not some sort of genetic impedance that Groad, apart from his dark eyebrows, had no other hair upon his entire head. He had found that the long locks and beards displayed by many of the Kithians were merely a hindrance in battle and required too much attention to keep properly groomed.

Out of nothing but the purest of respect was Groad nicknamed *Gu Tibor* by his fellow warriors.

Although Groad considered the name degrading and an insult to both his physical and mental personality, for some inexplicable reason, he thought it best to remain silent about the matter.

The fact that Groad had survived the Ten Cyclan War against the Artanian barbarians with only so much as a small scar above his left nipple was proof enough of his prowess on the battlefields.

Unfortunately, he was not pleased with his situation. After all, were scars not the marks of battles fought? Were scars not the true signs of a great warrior?

The solace he received from fellow warriors sporting their limps, stumps and eye-patches was of utterly no comfort at all.

Groad saw only a dim future where his *gruntlings* sat in a circle, the campfire reflecting from their eager, expectant faces, begging for their father to tell them tales of his military exploits. But in how many ways can the tale of a single, small cicatrix be told?

When the war had finally ended, the Artanians forced back across their borders, Groad had returned to his home village in Bryntha. His brave and daring accomplishments had preceded him, making him a legend in his own time. A living legend to be respected and feared.

The expected hero's welcome awaited him, as well as a selection of beautiful young nubile maidens vying with each other for the attentions of the handsome warrior.

It is important at this point to note that the human concept of female beauty and male handsomeness, as opposed to the Kithian concepts, differ rather profusely.

For example, the male is primarily attracted to the female by the size and shape of her eyeteeth. The larger the fangs, the greater the attraction. Good strong teeth are a sign of a good strong healthy gruntling-bearing body.

Most females keep their *persuasive talents* hidden behind closed lips, displaying them only, and ever so subtly, in the company of *fair game.*

Compared to the female, the eyeteeth of the male are relatively small.

Under extreme emotional conditions a Kithians tear-ducts excrete small droplets of blood. This gives the eye a glistening red tinge.

In anger or pain it adds a terrifying ferociousness to the facial expression; in joy or passion it evokes, in other Kithian onlookers, a certain stimulus that promotes sympathy or physical attraction.

Marriage and gruntlings were soon to follow, but Groad being Groad, and Groad being a warrior born and bred soon felt the insatiable call to adventure. The homely life had begun to squeeze its fist on his physical and mental well-being.

His wife and gruntlings became the constant scapegoat to his frequent outbursts of physical and verbal abuse.

Groad knowing all too well that the fault lay solely in himself, arose early one morning, strapped his battle-armour onto his horse's saddle and without looking back rode off into the rising sun.

It took him the best part of two *moons* to lose his unsightly paunch. It had been an unforeseen necessity due to the fact that he had experienced difficulty donning the custom-made battle-armour.

It had taken even longer before he was able to move about in the armour without feeling faint or winded from its enormous weight.

But it had taken no time at all before he was able to wield his sword again like the true warrior he had once been.

Even Zarkas, the weapons-master, who had been Groad's trainer and mentor, was amazed and impressed at his uncanny ability to adapt most weapons to become a natural extension of himself.

Groad was truly the ultimate warrior; a death-dealing machine made of flesh and bone.

Four times the snows had come and gone since he had left his family in Bryntha. He at last felt that his appetite for adventure had been appeased, at least for the time being.

He sincerely longed for the company of his wife Lorra and their three gruntlings, Zemth, Groadlid and Lorralel.

Lorralel, literally meaning *daughter of Lorra,* was Groad's youngest gruntling.

She would be six *cyclans* now, but even at two, the evidence was clear that she was going to be the spitting image of her mother. Groad often smiled, thinking about how the young warriors of Bryntha and beyond, would one day flock to his door with gifts of tibor skulls and *mollok sap.* Adolescent female Kithians regarded the extent of their tibor skull collections and jars of mollok sap as extremely serious status symbols. These were, after all, a reflection of the owner's popularity and physical attractiveness. It was a rare occurrence for a young Kithian warrior to court a female purely because she had a stunning personality.

Quite often the fathers of the less attractive females were obliged to please their daughters by undertaking the arduous task of obtaining these coveted symbols of vanity.

Lorralel would pose no such threat to her father. Instead, the male that wished to marry her would fill Groad's purse with many golden pieces according to the ancient custom of *loballa.*

The price of the loballa is generally in proportion to the size of the daughter's tibor skull and mollok sap collections, which in turn is usually in proportion to the size of the daughter's eyeteeth.

Groad with wishful foresight had arrayed the walls of Lorralel's sleeping quarters with crude wooden shelves that he hoped would one day be filled with an abundance of perfume and putrescence.

Groadlid, literally meaning *son of Groad*, was the younger of two sons. But younger by only minutes. Lorra had blessed Groad with one of the finest gifts in the Empire. It was a known fact that one of the greatest honours that the elder gods could bestow upon a Kithian couple was the parturition of identical twins. They would be seventeen cyclans old when the next season of warm mists arrived. There were certain physical traits about them that resembled Groad, but already they were showing the natural signs of rapid Kithian growth.

Groad was pleased that they would not have to face the humiliating jeers and taunts about diminutiveness, which he himself had once been subjected to many cyclans ago by the other village gruntlings.

The twins were energetic and stalwartly gruntlings who would have little trouble passing the grueling initiation into *savden.* The initiation, also commonly known as the *Ana Iram*, consists of three dangerous and trying tasks.

Firstly, the youth to be tested, is taken by raft and under safe escort to the centre of the great *Ana Weezi*, a vast swamp lying on the northern border of Kith. Here he would be left alone, weaponless and stripped completely naked. He would then have to find and fend his own way back to the outskirts of the swamp, where the escort would set up camp to wait a quarter cycle of the moon for the young warrior's return. Should the youth fail to return within this set period, the escort would return to their home village. It is against Kithian law to send out a search party to retrieve any stripling undergoing the trials of savden.

The second task is to procure two large feathers from the aerie of an ana-*rod noc*. This fowl, although remarkably large, is rather docile by nature. Its domicile, on the other hand, is not quite as friendly. Having an enormous wingspan, ana-rod nocs are able to soar to great heights and so have a partiality for building their nests upon steep mountain crags; especially on the cliffs of the treacherous *Chaxer-ran.*

The magnificent spectacle of the Chaxer-ran mountain range rises abruptly and awesomely above the plains and valleys of central Kith. Only on a clear day is it possible to view the plateau's ridge, which is more often than not, hidden in the low-lying cloud formations.

Ana-rod nocs have a preference to build their nests where, for someone trying to negotiate the sheer rockface, it would be a similar experience to that of ascending the side of a steep wall.

It is strictly forbidden for a competitor, under penalty of death, to remove more than two feathers from a nest. The price of obtaining these feathers could literally cost an arm and a leg. Many times it has cost more.

The third and final task is for the youth to hunt and slay an *ana desh-gla.*

These beasts' habitat are chiefly amongst the close stifling foliage of the humid and oppressive *Kriti Dakur.* The ana desh-glas are primarily nocturnal hunters, making the task of finding, capturing and slaying these powerful predators the most difficult feat of the Ana Iram.

Once the final task of savden is passed, an honourary feast and ceremony is held, wherein the young warrior discards all possessions related to his past into a raging pyre.

This is considered an outward symbol of bidding farewell to the weaknesses of youth and gruntlinghood.

The stripling next presents the pelt of the ana desh-gla to his father as a token of gratitude for past services rendered and as a symbol that he is no longer dependent upon his parents for advice or security.

In return, the family of the new warrior gives honour by presenting him with a number of gifts. These gifts are mainly in the form of weapons that the young warrior can use in battle or hunting excursions.

Finally the father presents the young warrior with a necklace made from the ana-rod noc's feathers and the teeth of the ana desh-gla. The two large fangs of the ana desh-gla are considered to contain mystical properties that can enhance the virility of the wearer. In the centre of the necklace is hung a small scroll, fashioned from thinly beaten metal, onto which the father is obliged to engrave a written blessing concerning the future of his son. The small metal page is then rolled into a tube that is sealed at both ends with molten metal.

Not is it only against Kithian law, but it is also considered to be extremely unlucky to ever break these seals. This makes it possible, for any father harbouring a contemptuous attitude towards his son, to engrave instead of a blessing, a curse upon the beaten metal. This practice is not too uncommon amongst Kithian fathers who have suffered constant regret in the wake of a son's overegotistical behaviour (A practice not too uncommon amongst Kithian sons).

The feathers of the ana-rod noc are believed to produce pleasant dreams. It is also alleged that these feathers, symbolic of flight, will carry the warrior's spirit form to *the other side* in the event of his demise.

All Kithian warriors wear their Ana Iram necklaces with exceptional pride and possessiveness.

The most convenient opportunity to safely remove this hard-earned symbol of savden from a Kithian warrior's neck is only after being absolutely certain that he is entirely deceased.

With the completion of the feast and ceremony, the *lid* part, should there be one in the warriors name, would fall away. *Groadlid*, for example, would then become *Groad*.

It was just shortly after Groad himself had passed the Ana Iram that he experienced a great tragedy that would haunt him for a very long time.

Zarkas, the weaponsmaster, who had become Groad's best friend, had decided to take him along on his annual hunting trip. A journey which Zarkas normally endeavoured alone, enjoying the solitariness of the rugged Kithian panoramas.

It was said that Zarkas was proficient not only in the use of over thirty different types of weapons, but also in five different forms of martial arts, which he had studied in his many travels around Baltrath.

He had also painstakingly constructed a unique suit of armour for himself. The armour had long metal spikes that were strategically placed on the helmet, shoulders, elbows, gloves, waist, knees and boots. This enabled him, when in battle, to not only use his sword as a weapon, but his entire body as well.

To allow himself to become one with the armour, he would wear it as often as possible, removing it only to bathe or sleep.

He too received a nickname from the other warriors of Bryntha. They called him *Gu Shora*.

Once a cyclan Zarkas went on a major hunting expedition. The walls of his enormous log cabin in Bryntha were decorated with the heads of many of the most dangerous beasts that roamed the world of Baltrath.

This time he had decided to take his protégé along, not only for the learning experience, but also for the sheer adventure as well.

Their travels took them to the northwesterly quarter of Kith, half a day's ride from an area known as Grimwald forest.

The forest had become notorious as the domicile of the *zin-zas*.

The zin-zas are renowned for their ferocity as well as their stupidity. They are not partial or prejudice about who or what they eat. It is their lifestyle. Simple, yet effective.

They get hungry. They eat whatever is available. They get tired. They sleep. They wake up. They get hungry. So on and so forth.

Whether their prey is dumb or intelligent makes no difference. The zin-zas themselves are too dimwitted to make any distinction. All they are interested in doing is appeasing the anger of their primeval god, the rumbling in their bellies that frequently wake them from their serious and laborious slumber.

The fact that these creatures are able to procreate is a mystery to many of the learned biologists of Baltrath.

"Why do you not have a zin-za's head on your wall?" Groad had asked staring into the campfire.

Their journey so far had been rather fruitless. Apart from the few animals that they had killed for sustenance, there had been no real challenges. No prize worth taking back to Bryntha as a victory trophy.

"I would not waste the time or the effort on one of those useless beasts!" Zarkas had answered with a sneer. "We hunt only dangerous game. For it to be dangerous, it has to be intelligent."

"I do not agree with that. When a creature's actions are motivated by pure unthinking rage, then it is more unpredictable and therefore more dangerous."

"So then, you believe those dumb beasts to be dangerous?"

"Yes!"

"And you would not mind hanging a zin-za's head upon your wall?"

"A head would be too big to haul all the way back to Bryntha, but I would proudly hang its horn over my fireplace."

"Well I would certainly be too embarrassed to do something like that!"

"I think you are scared!" Groad had said in a serious tone whilst hiding a smile.

"You know what they will say back in Bryntha?" Zarkas had replied, ignoring Groad's remark. "Zarkas is getting too old for hunting *real* game. So now he amuses himself by slaying the poor, dumb defenseless zin-zas. Next he will be nailing insects to his wall."

"You are definitely scared!"

Zarkas had glared at Groad. "Very well, young Groad! We will go and get you a zin-za's horn, but on one condition only!"

"Which is?"

"You must never tell anyone that I helped you to get it."

"Am I allowed to tell them what happened if you should get killed?" Groad had asked barely able to conceal his mirth.

"By the elder gods!" Zarkas had exclaimed chuckling. "*That* would be tragic. Gu Shora, Baltrath's finest warrior, slain by a zin-za. I will be bashing on *Dakur's* golden gates for all eternity!"

Through the ages and through circumstance, the Kithians had developed into a nation of thanatophiliacs, worshipers of Death and the dead. It was more than just a belief in ancestral spirits. Dakur, in all his forms, represents only that which is good and positive. Death to Kith's enemies means victory. Death to a Kithian, especially in battle, is the glorious uniting with the all-powerful Dakur himself.

Grimwald forest consists mainly of high trees that are widely spaced. This made it possible for fast and easy traveling on horseback. It is probably also the reason why the zin-zas took up residence in this particular woodland. They are able to move their enormous bulks around without much encumberment.

Groad had been first to see the zin-za. It was male and was obviously hungry because it was awake and sniffing the air. Pulling back on his reins, he had given a silent prayer to Dakur, not only thanking him that they were downwind, but also for the fact that zin-zas always hunted alone.

"Do you see him?" Groad had whispered.

"Yes!" Zarkas had said in a brazen tone. "Now let us put a quick end to this foolish and unnecessary excursion so that we may renew our quest to hunting something more worthwhile and challenging." Dismounting he had removed the crossbow strung across his back and marched off between the trees. Without looking back he had shouted, "Come on, young Groad, or it will all be over by the time you get here!"

Groad had quickly jumped down off the horse, and stringing an arrow into his bow, followed after Zarkas. His blood had turned cold at the sight he had seen before him.

Zarkas had reached the edge of a clearing, in the centre of which, its back towards them, towered the enormous zin-za. It had obviously picked up Zarkas' scent as it was now sniffing the air in a state of frenzy.

Zarkas stepped forward into the clearing, and raising his arms shouted, "Ho, stupid! Here I am!"

"Have you taken leave of your senses?" shouted Groad taking refuge behind a large tree.

Zarkas spun around. "What are you doing all the way back there? Do not tell me the beast frightens you?"

"Be careful! The zin-za has seen us!"

"*Us*? I doubt even with such a large eye he could see you cowering so far back there in the shadows!" smirked Zarkas turning to face the zin-za. "Come, you vile, ugly brute! If you want me, you are going to have to come and get me!"

The zin-za stood there blinking and frowning. Its head leaned to one side as it studied the small noisy creature. It could not understand why its next meal was just standing there yapping instead of trying to flee. Then with a snarl that revealed a set of jagged yellow teeth it began to advance on Zarkas.

"That is it!" shouted Zarkas bringing the crossbow in to his shoulder. "Just keep glaring at me with that big, soft eye, because behind that eye is your small, soft brain."

Zarkas was one of the finest archers on the face of Baltrath. His skill with both crossbow and longbow were legendary. He could remove the tailfeathers from a small bird at fifty paces.

The zin-za was a mere twenty paces and closing.

"Now, Zarkas, now!" shouted Groad, his heart racing loudly in his ears.

"Not till I see the white of his eye!"

"I can already see the white of his eye from back here."

Zarkas smiled. He was going to savour this moment for a very long time. Friend or not, he would enjoy embarrassing Groad on many occasions, repeating the story of how he had killed this asinine animal, whilst Groad was busy voiding his bladder behind a tree. This would also be a lesson to Groad that he should never again question the judgment of the great and learned Shora.

Zarkas' aim was true, but nature has a marvelous way in its multitudinous designs. Should it give a creature but a single eye, it will no doubt grant it the instinctive knowledge to safeguard that valuable solitary organ of sight at all costs. It will also, most likely, confer the beast with a means to protect it as well.

The reflex action was so fast that Groad had hardly seen the actual movement. The zin-za bent its head forward and the once deadly bolt ricocheted harmlessly off the hard fibrous substance of the horn. In the same movement the beast had closed the gap between itself and the weapons master.

Zarkas' brain still had not comprehended the gravity of the situation when the zin-za's left paw closed tightly around his torso and lifted him off the ground.

He was helpless. His arms were pinned at his sides and he felt himself losing consciousness as the brute squeezed the very air out of his lungs.

The spikes on Zarkas' armour bit into the tough flesh of the creatures paws, but the pain was nothing compared to the pangs which it felt deep inside its belly.

Groad's fear was quickly replaced with unthinking rage. He rushed from his place of concealment towards the zin-za. He pulled back on his bow almost to the point of breaking before letting the arrow fly straight at the creature's chest.

The shaft struck the left breast, but did not penetrate deep enough through the tough hide and thick hair that covered most of the beast's trunk.

Still holding onto Zarkas with one paw, the zin-za brushed the shaft off its chest as one would do to an annoying insect. Content with its catch for the day, it turned and lumbered off between the trees with its prize.

Groad chased after it, sending shaft after shaft into the creature's hind.

The result was always the same; they had no more influence than the irritating bite of some small insect.

Groad cursed, wishing the zin-za would turn around once more so that he too may try a shot at the beast's eye.

The zin-za entered another clearing. Groad saw that the opposite side of the clearing did not contain more trees, but a wide ravine.

He hoped that this would force the creature back towards him, but with uncanny ease the beast leapt across the gorge, landing solidly on a wide ledge. Without hesitation and still clutching tightly to its prey, the zin-za trudged off along the ledge, moving parallel with the ravine, its back still towards Groad.

Groad surveyed the length of the ravine. It was too wide and too deep. There was no way he could cross it in time to save his friend.

In the distance the gorge curved inward. If he could reach there in time, and if the zin-za remained on the ledge, he would be able to get a clear shot at its eye as it entered the bend.

Groad's lungs burned from the crisp air as he sprinted across the clearing. He would have to enter the forest again to reach the bend in the ravine.

In between the trees he would have no visual contact of the zin-za. He would just have to hope and pray that he had guessed the beast's route correctly.

It seemed to Groad as though it had taken him an eternity to reach the bend in the ravine. He had fallen along the way, losing his quiver and arrows amongst the long grass. There had been no time to search for them. Holding on tightly to the bow and arrow in his hand, he had continued the race.

Standing on the edge of the chasm, his view blocked in both directions by thick foliage, he could not tell if the zin-za had already passed or if it was yet to come around the curve on the opposite cliff-face. Now he could only wait anxiously, hoping for the beast to appear.

He studied the ledge on the far side of the gorge. It was narrower at that point than where the creature had leapt across. This would probably slow the zin-za down, making the shot less difficult. It also meant that if he managed to fatally wound the beast, it would most likely tumble into the ravine, taking Zarkas with it.

These thoughts were still rushing through Groad's head when the zin-za began to round the bend. Groad went down on one knee, resting one end of the bow on the ground. He had always found this position most suitable for a difficult shot that needed steadiness. Taking a deep breath, he pulled back hard on the bowstring.

A trickle of blood ran down out of Zarkas' nose and formed a pool in the corner of his mouth. His eyes flickered open.

Even across the distance, Groad could see the intense anguish that filled those bloodshot orbs.

A wave of nausea passed over Groad, and in that same instant it became clear to him what had to be done. Adjusting his aim, he slowly exhaled until there was no more air left in his lungs. Then with one last prayer he released the arrow.

* * *

To read more you can find the book now available in trade paperback and ebook versions at:

amazon.com
amazon.co.uk
smashwords.com

About the author:

Gary Kuyper began his professional literary career writing self-help and general interest articles for Daan Retief Publishers who produced a monthly book for their woman's club called Woman's Forum. These articles would sometimes require research and had titles as diverse as The Human Brain and Body Painting!

Being a professional photographer on a part-time basis Gary has also managed to have his articles on photography (With accompanying photographs) published in books and magazines.

Over the past four years he has constantly managed to be one of the top finalists in the Nova Short Story Competition (A competition for budding writers of science fiction and/or fantasy).
Last year (2009) Gary had the pleasure of seeing The Devil's Little Tadpoles grace the pages of the local SF & Fantasy Fanzine Probe.

He is an avid film buff and amateur film maker. A few years ago he managed to take first prize in the SA Ten Best Film Makers Competition with a short film entitled The Crimson Cobra.

He is a qualified prosthetics make-up artist and has used this talent on both amateur and professional productions. He has also appeared on television in a youth program especially made for enlightening people in the art of special effects make-up.

In 2008 he entered the SF / Fantasy Mini Radio Play Competition and took first prize with his The Adventures of Captain Max Power of the Intergalactic Police - an obvious homage to the early Flash Gordon radio series'.

All his literary and photojournalistic accomplishments have been done on a part-time basis due to the fact that his full time career is lecturing mathematics as well as engineering science at a Technical College. Although this is a most fulfilling profession, it has long been Gary's ideal to become a full-time writer.

Gary is currently working on an anthology of short stories as well as Book 2 of *The Chronicles of Baltrath.*

* * *

Biography of Lazlo Ferran

Lazlo Ferran has lived and worked in London since 1985 and grew up in the home counties of England. His varied past has included a career in Graphics, a three-year stint as a full-time busker, followed by a long and successful career in internet design leading to the post of IT Manager at a prestigious London institute. He has traveled widely, experiencing cultures in most European countries, South America and Central Asia amongst others.

2560383R00110

Printed in Great Britain
by Amazon.co.uk, Ltd.,
Marston Gate.